SEASONED GREETINGS

a novel

by

John E. Hakala

5-1-2012

FOR CAROL !

John E. Hakala

COPYRIGHT

ISBN-13
978-0-615-54077-1

Cressida
P.O. Box 2042
Simi Valley, CA 93062

Cover graphic by Kirk Skadden

DEDICATION

This book is dedicated to my extraordinary wife, Iris, for her unwavering faith in me and the novel's message. Her loving encouragement to complete it overcame my doubts, too numerous delays and interruptions.

I also wish to acknowledge the many valuable suggestions freely offered by Kent Johnson and Jim Dyer. Both men have awesome story element insight drawn from their vast experience in the motion picture and television industry.

"Suppose you preferred a certain brand of marmalade, for example, not because of its taste, not because of advertising or a celebrity's endorsement or price or any other factor people customarily use to select one brand over another. Would that be an interesting situation?"

- 1 -

Atlantic City
Friday

Mr. T. Thornton Walsh stood his ground at the less-crowded end of the craps table in the noisy Firebird Casino. The forward slouch of his thick shoulders betrayed his fatigue as he absently drew a thumbnail back and forth across the chips in his rack. A woman with a bluish blonde bouffant at the opposite end of the table held the dice in a hand she vigorously pumped in the air.

"Gimme an eight!" a full-bellied man in a bright yellow tee next to her demanded. A stretched, faded green stencil of a *John Deere* tractor on the front of his shirt seemed to plow an invisible field as he breathed.

"You want an *eight*?" the woman screeched. "Here's an eight!"

She lurched forward and flung the cubes across the emerald green felt, the sudden movement dislodging her plastic-framed eyeglasses. She caught them

1

awkwardly, juggled them a moment, then stuck them back on her sun-weathered face.

Walsh frowned. He moved his gaze from the woman and watched the dice bounce to a stop below him.

"Six," the lanky stickman called out in a hoarse voice. "Six, easy." He corralled the cubes into the crook of a short willow stick, then deftly snaked them between several stacks of chips positioned around large yellow numbers on the table. He brought them to rest in front of the woman.

She reached down and rolled them over one at a time to expose four white dimples on each, then stacked them one atop the other and plucked them from the felt.

"For godsake, Mildred," the tractor man said, "don't fondle 'em. Just throw the friggin' eight!"

"Patience, Huber. I gotta charm it out."

She pumped her arm in the air several times then hurled the dice across the table, striking Walsh's three green twenty-five-dollar chips on the pass line. The dice caromed off and settled at the base of the hard foam bumper behind them.

"Ten!" the stickman shouted. "Ten, easy."

The dealer set two black hundred-dollar chips on the table in front of Walsh, paying him for a hundred dollar place bet on the ten. Walsh slipped the chips into his rack.

"Four!" the stickman called out after the dice came to rest again. "Four easy. Four."

Walsh tossed a black chip onto the table. "Buy the four," he told the dealer.

2

"Throw me a red one," the dealer said. "For the juice."

Walsh dropped the five dollar chip onto the table, then scanned the value of his other chips spread across the yellow numbers. One thousand eighty. So far, so good. The blue-haired woman made him two hundred and the next roll would bring more -- as long as it wasn't a seven.

"Seven out," the stickman called when the dice stopped, "eight was. Take the line. Pay the don'ts."

Walsh groaned with the rest of the players as the dealers hurriedly raked the players' chips from the table and stacked them in neat towers below their twitching fingers.

"New shooter," the stickman said. He rapped the stick on the table below the man in the *John Deere* tractor shirt. "Shoot 'em, sir?" the stickman asked.

The man waved a callused hand, giving up his turn with the dice. "Not me. My wife just cost me twenty bucks. I'm through." He took the woman's arm and led her from the table.

Walsh watched them for a moment as they sauntered in the direction of the cashier's cage. "Twenty bucks?" Walsh groused under his breath. "Your bitch cost me over a grand."

He sighed as he fingered his way through the rack of black chips five at a time, then added the green ones four at a time. He didn't bother with the red or white dollar chips. Twenty-two hundred and change. He glanced at the four vanilla-colored disks on the felt in front of the impassive table boss seated on a stool

3

across from the stickman. Walsh's ten-thousand-dollar markers were still there, waiting to be redeemed.

Erwin, the pit boss, glided up. "How's it going tonight?"

Walsh eyed the tall man in a dark tailored suit. "Your gatekeeper's letting in too many hicks," he said.

"Seven. Winner. Pay the line," the stickman ordered.

Walsh glanced down at the table as the dealers paid the line bets. He didn't have one. He snatched two green chips from his tray and set them on the pass line.

"Is your room alright?" Erwin asked.

"Always is."

"Three. Craps. Three," the stickman announced.

The dealer snatched Walsh's fifty-dollar bet from the table.

Walsh grimaced and tossed a black chip onto the felt. It spun around twice before landing in the space the two green ones occupied before.

"Glad to hear it," Erwin said. "Want to see a show?"

"Who's here?"

"Some magician, I think. I'll find out."

"Naw, thanks, anyway. I'm kinda beat. Think I'll just turn in tonight."

"How long will you be with us this trip?"

"Day after tomorrow ... Sunday ... God willing." Walsh waved a hand over the dwindling supply of chips in his rack.

"You'll turn it around," Erwin said.

Walsh frowned. "Sure. Right after I part the Red Sea—again."

4

Walsh scanned the players at the opposite end of the table. They controlled the dice but none had the telltale signs of a winner. No heavy necklaces of gold draped around tanned necks. No blinding diamond rings adorning smooth fingers. No one with a Texas drawl. Just rookies and hicks.

"Carl asked if you would stop by to say 'hi' when you're done," Erwin said.

Walsh turned back to the pit boss. "What the hell's Massini want?"

Erwin laughed. "You know Carl. He likes to keep in touch with our best players when they're in town. Probably wants to pick your brain about the stock market and buy you a drink. Should I tell him you'll stop by?"

"Twelve. Craps," the stickman said, shaking his head.

"Shit!" Walsh said. "Where do you find these shooters?"

He slammed two more black chips on the pass line, replacing the last one. The dice moved to a young woman at the far corner of the table. She was magazine-cover pretty, with long, black hair that spilled across her shoulders and cascaded down her back. A tough, blond V-body type stood next to her. He seemed disinterested in the men at the table who stared reverently at the girl's ample breasts when she leaned over the rail to pick up the dice and throw them.

"I'll bet he paid plenty for those tits," Erwin gruffly whispered, nodding at the bodybuilder.

"Five. Mark five," the stickman said.

Walsh straightened and grabbed five black chips and two green ones. "Five-fifty across," he instructed the dealer as he dropped the chips onto the table. "Buy the four and ten." He stacked three more black chips behind his two-hundred-dollar line bet, taking the odds. "Listen. I'd love to chat, Erwin," Walsh said, turning back to the pit boss, "but someone finally got a point."

Erwin gave a polite smile. "Of course. And Mr. Massini? Will you be stopping by for that drink?"

"Not tonight. Maybe tomorrow."

"I'll let him know to expect you then. Good luck." Erwin turned away.

Walsh clenched his fists. "Why do you guys always say that? You know I hate that 'good luck' shit! If I ever had any coming my way tonight, you just queered it, Erwin. Don't *ever* say that to me again!"

"Uh, sorry, Mr. Walsh. Didn't mean anything--"

"You guys already got forty thousand of my markers tonight. At least give me a fighting chance to make something with it!"

"I am sorry, Mr. Walsh. Here, let me get you something." He clapped his hands twice above his head and nodded to a nearby cocktail waitress. The girl scurried to the table. "Get Mr. Walsh whatever he wants. Anything."

The waitress took an order for a double shot of Chivas Regal, neat, and two Monte Cristo No. 2 torpedo cigars, then hurried off.

"Ten. Ten, ten, ten. Hard ten," the stickman announced when the dice stopped. "There's nobody on the hard ten. Who wants the hard ten?"

Walsh stared across the table at the girl. Asian, but not Japanese. Somewhere around Malaysia. Very fit. Very pretty. He nodded. *Very* pretty. But can she make a five?

She rolled six more numbers and Walsh pressed each with their payoff. On her seventh toss the dice added up to five. Walsh immediately tallied his chips. Thirteen hundred on place bets and close to two thousand in his rack. He threw four black chips onto the table in front of the stickman.

"All the hard ways," he said.

"All the hard ways," the dealer instructed the stickman. "A hundred each."

The stickman shuffled the chips around to cover the four, six, eight and ten hard-way bets in the spaces on the felt below him.

The girl glanced across the table at Walsh and smiled with wide, bright brown eyes.

Impulsively, Walsh tossed another black chip in front of the stickman. "For the shooter. All the hard ways. A quarter each." He smiled back at the girl.

She picked the dice from the table without looking at them, her gaze still fixed on Walsh, then she slowly rubbed the cubes across the exposed half of her left breast. Walsh watched, mesmerized as she cocked her arm and threw the dice.

"Four. Hard!" the stickman shouted. "Two deuces."

A roar of applause exploded from the players.

The dealer slid seven hundred in chips in front of Walsh for the hard four win and added two hundred more for the place bet. The dealer at the other end of the table paid the girl a hundred seventy-five dollars for the bet Walsh made for her. When she smiled a coy 'thank you,' an electrifying rush overwhelmed him. He'd felt it before.

Walsh quickly called to the table boss. "Tony. Give me another ten."

Tony swiveled around to Erwin who stood at a tall table in the center of the craps pit. The table held a phone and a computer. "Erwin," Tony said. He nodded toward Walsh. "He wants another ten thousand."

Erwin eyed Walsh with indifference and picked up the phone. He hung up a few seconds later. "Give it to him."

Tony added another vanilla-colored disk to the others, then counted out ten thousand dollars in chips. He slid the stacks to the dealer who pushed them across the table to Walsh. Walsh scooped them up and set them in his rack. Erwin slipped a casino check onto a small, clear plastic clipboard and brought it around to Walsh.

"Mr. Massini wanted me to wish you good … ah … fortune," Erwin said. "He has also asked that you see him this evening—not tomorrow."

Walsh squinted at Erwin, then took the clipboard and scribbled his signature on the marker check. "Okay, okay. I'll see him. And tell him not to worry about his precious money. One other thing, I want my limit doubled on the numbers."

Erwin glanced around the table, then back at Walsh. "You want to go to four thousand on each number?"

"That's right."

Erwin gestured to the table boss, holding up four fingers. "No problem, Mr. Walsh."

"You want to know why, Erwin?"

Erwin raised his brows but said nothing.

"I'll tell you why." Walsh pulled the cigar from his mouth and blew a cloud of gray smoke into Erwin's face. "Because I know something you don't." He pointed his cigar at the shooter. "You see that girl down there? The one with the dice and expensive tits you were drooling over?"

Erwin didn't look. He was fanning the smoke away.

"She's the Messiah, Erwin. She's the one I've been waiting for the last three hours, the one who's going to let me beat you boys. The Messiah! Now go away and stop bothering me."

Erwin floated away, leaving Mr. T. Thornton Walsh in the care of the black-haired Messiah with the store-bought breasts.

- 2 -

Boston Police Department

Sergeant Traci Ross quietly drummed her fingers on the arm of the wooden chair as Lieutenant Hale studied the four rape reports on his desk.

"I don't see more than one perpetrator here," the young lieutenant finally said. "All the victims describe the same assailant." He looked up. "That's the way the dicks see it too."

"Well, I think the detectives got it wrong and I'd like to do some follow-ups."

Hale leaned back and clasped his hands behind his head of short, wiry black hair. "Your enthusiasm is commendable, Sergeant, but follow-ups are their job. Besides, deployment's down and I can't spare you."

"The interviews shouldn't take long, sir. There are only four and I could do them between calls."

The holstered 9mm Smith & Wesson pistol on her belt was stabbing into her leg. She slid it back a few inches.

Hale glanced down at the reports. "I don't know. I think it'd just be a waste of time. They all say the same thing. Average height, average weight, slightly balding. I don't see where you come up with more than one perp. Are you basing that on some kind of woman's intuition thing, or do you have something more concrete?"

"Intuition? Hardly. But maybe it takes a woman to see the holes in their investigations."

"Holes? What holes?"

"Just between you and me, Lieutenant, I don't think those detectives could find shopping carts in an A & P parking lot. Did you look at the times? They're way too close to be the work of one guy."

Hale rechecked the time of each attack. Two overlapped by ten minutes.

He waved a hand dismissively over the papers. "You know victims, Traci. They're always getting the facts wrong. They get all heated up and their minds turn to mush--and we're talking bag ladies here. All of these victims are bag ladies, you know."

Traci nodded.

Hale continued. "How lucid could the mind of a bag lady be under the best of circumstances, especially after being raped? If they really were raped."

"We'll never know unless I do the follow-ups. If you read the narratives you could see the detectives just blew 'em off. There's hardly any story at all. Besides, it's my beat and I'm the one who's accountable ... not the detectives."

Hale slowly shook his head. "I don't know."

"This isn't the work of a serial rapist, Lieutenant. There's no pattern, nothing similar about the women.

11

Except for being homeless, there's no apparent connection between any of them—at least as far as *those* reports go."

Hale leaned back in his chair and combed his hair with the fingers of one hand. "How long have you been out of patrol, Traci?"

"What's that got to do with anything?"

"About five years, isn't that about right? Five out of the seven you've been on the job … including the academy?"

"More or less."

He moved a manila folder to the center of his desk and opened it. Traci recognized her personnel file.

"Let's see." He scanned the entries. "Nice. Finished at the top of your academy class, then the mandatory year in patrol and transferred to Community Relations. Spent nearly five years there."

"They put me there. It wasn't my choice." She shifted in her chair.

Hale went on, "Then got promoted to Sergeant." He closed the file and looked up at her. "Why are you here?"

She pointed to his desk. "Because …"

"No, no." He waved his hand in a stopping motion. "Not that. I don't mean why are you in this office. I mean why are you a cop?"

"Well, I--"

"And please spare me the crap I hear from candidates when I sit on entry level interview boards. If you needed a job to pay your bookie that's okay, so just say so. If the mall was closed and you had nothing better to do the day the test was given, that's okay, too. I'm just looking for an honest answer."

"There's more to getting hired than taking a test, Lieutenant."

"I know, I know. And don't get me wrong, because I'm thrilled to have you here. I'm just curious." He leaned forward. "You may have noticed most of our female officers look like linebackers for the Rams. You, on the other hand, look like you'd be more at home sippin' mint juleps on the fantail of some oil baron's yacht."

"Is that a compliment, sir? Or would you like to reword what you just said?"

"I—"

"Because it sounded a bit sexist to me."

His face reddened. "Sorry." He reopened her personnel file and turned a few more pages. "Ah. Right." He tapped the page. "Then after your promotion you got shipped down here."

"I didn't get *shipped*. I put in for this precinct. It was *my* choice to come here, Lieutenant. "

"God knows why. Most of my people are clamoring to get out, me included."

"What can I say? I happen to like it here."

"You see, that's what I don't understand. You leave a cushy job in Community Relations—I know you turned down an offer to work in the commissioner's office—and you come here. Then still more puzzling, you go out of your way to do a detective's job—and investigate what? Not burglaries. Not murders, but rapes. So that makes me curious and I have to wonder if there's something personal I'm missing."

"I see."

"So, what is it? What am I missing?"

"It's … ah … it's personal, sir."

He stared at her for several seconds, then nodded. "Okay. I won't intrude. We *are* happy to have you here, so I'll let it go at that."

"Thank you."

A moment of awkward silence followed.

Traci leaned forward. "Sir, can I do the follow-ups?"

He rolled his eyes. "You've been out of patrol for five years, Traci, and things have changed. Everything moves faster now. Crime is up, caseloads are up, citizen complaints are up. About the only thing that isn't up is our deployment." He tapped the reports on his desk. "Maybe these aren't the best examples of good police work but I know the detectives who took 'em. They've been doing their job a long time and they wouldn't kiss off a rape unless they had some sense about it."

"We're talking about *four*, Lieutenant, not one."

"Yeah, well--"

"Maybe they've been at it *too* long," she said. "I don't know those detectives but in my opinion the victims should have been interviewed by a woman, not two burly men."

Hale laughed. "Now, *that's* a sexist comment if I ever heard one."

She shook her head. "No it isn't. Rape victims won't open up to a man. They need to feel the interviewer has some kind of empathy with them and a man won't show it."

"Hah! Do you know where you are, Sergeant? This precinct is in the city's armpit and these victims are nothing but tiny hairs in that armpit. They don't care about your empathy. All they care about is surviving one day to the next. We don't have socialites down here."

"They're still women."

He shrugged. "Anatomically, maybe, but they're a helluva lot tougher than you can imagine. By the time they've hit Skid Row, they're desensitized to everything but hunger. Believe me, getting raped is *not* going to ruin their day."

"So we just shine 'em on? Is that what you're saying?"

"I'm not saying that at all."

"Well, that's what those reports say. All they say is someone went out and filled in the blanks on a piece of paper. End of story."

"You've got a thing against detectives, don't you?"

"I've got a thing against sloppy work."

He was quiet for a moment, then, "Okay, okay. You think you can do better? Go ahead." He passed the reports back to her. "Ask a few questions but you'll see."

"Maybe. It's all in eight, Lieutenant."

"Right." He nodded. "All in eight."

- 3 -

Atlantic City
Firebird Casino

Walsh stepped off the elevator on the third floor and wound his way to the regal office of the Firebird Casino Credit Manager. His Rolex Submariner and his headache told him it was after 3 A.M. but Carl Massini would be up and waiting for him.

"Thornton," Massini said as Walsh stepped into the opulent office. "How wonderful to see you again." The slender man shook Walsh's hand forcefully then slapped him hard on the shoulder. "Really good to see you."

"Yeah. Good to see you too, Carl. What's up?"

Massini smiled as he led Walsh to a gold-veined mirrored wet bar. "You know? That's what I've always liked about you."

"What's that?"

"You're direct. No chit-chat. Just get to the point."

"Yeah, well it's late and I'm tired and not in a very chit-chat kind of mood."

"Of course you aren't. But let's have a drink and relax a minute."

He poured an inch of Remy Martin Luis XIII cognac into a large Venetian snifter for his guest, then poured decaffeinated coffee for himself.

Walsh rubbed a hand over his face. It felt puffier than usual. He loosened his tie and brushed back the remnants of his thinning black hair. Massini looked the same as always. Tall, tanned, dressed neat as a pin. An accountant, not a thug. That's who ran the casinos now. Not like the old days, Walsh thought.

"Did anyone ever tell you you look like Roy Scheider?" Walsh said. "I think the tinted glasses make you look like him."

"I've heard that before. Yes."

"You know I'm good for the eighty thou," Walsh said, accepting the cognac.

"Of course I do but let's not talk about money right now."

Massini gestured to an overstuffed tan-and-white-striped sofa near his desk. They sunk into the luxurious fabric.

"Your room is satisfactory?"

"You always take good care of me, Carl."

"I want you to be happy." He patted Walsh paternally on one knee.

Walsh moved it away. "I'll get you the eighty thousand," he said.

Massini smiled. "And how's your brother?"

"Oscar's okay. He's in Oregon." Walsh took a swallow of the cognac.

"Really? Oregon is such a beautiful state. A long way from Atlantic City. What's he doing there?"

"Something with a logging company. Choker Setter, I think he called it. I don't know what it is. He stomps around in the woods. What do I know about logging?"

"I know what you mean. You want some firewood, you go to the A & P and buy it."

"Exactly."

The men nodded.

"Carl, we go way back. How many years have I been coming here? Twelve? Fifteen?"

"At least."

"And I've been in a spot before. Right?"

Massini nodded. "More than once."

"Right. And how many times have I beat you out of your money?"

"Never."

Walsh leaned back into the sofa, crossed his short legs and took another sip of cognac. "You'll get your eighty thousand," he said.

"Alright." Massini set his cup down. "If you insist upon talking business." He leaned forward and retrieved a manila folder from the desk. "It isn't me, Thornton. I know you're good for it but we've got stockholders now. They don't know you like I do. I can be patient. They can't."

"Don't give me that." Walsh uncrossed his legs. "Don't give me that stockholder crap. I've always made good on my markers. You'll get it."

"When?"

"Six months. Like always."

18

Massini opened the folder and slowly turned through the pages of columned numbers.

"The last time you were down ... looks like about a year ago. It was forty-four thousand and you took eight months, plus a visit from Solly."

"Yeah. And that was chicken shit sending Solly. What the hell was he gonna do? Hang me upside-down by my ankles out the window? Break my arms? What was the point of that?"

"I had nothing to do with sending Solly. Somebody else made that decision."

"Somebody else, huh. Shit! You guys know where I live, where I work. You even know my brother for chrissake. Where was I going to go for a crummy forty-four thou?"

"Like I said, I had nothing to do with Solly. He takes orders from someone else. I told them to give you more time ... that you were good for it. Hell, you're one of our best players."

"You mean one of your best losers."

"You had a run of bad luck tonight, that's all."

Walsh ran a hand through his hair then slapped the arm of the sofa. "It was that cocksucker, Erwin. He's the one that queered it. You should have seen that girl down there, Carl. She was beautiful and her hand was hot as a furnace. I could smell the roll coming ... *feel* it. It was one of those moments that come ... I don't know ... come along .... It was rare and I knew she was gonna go the distance but that fucker Erwin said 'good luck' and the girl took a shit the second I loaded up on her. Threw the freakin' seven like it was some cosmic design that I should be wiped out." He shook

19

his head. "I've never been wrong about it before. I've always known." He looked at Massini. "You know that feeling I get in my gut, Carl. It's never been wrong and she'd have done it if that prick Erwin had kept his mouth shut. He's the one that owes you the eighty, not me."

Massini set the folder back on the desk. "Forget about Erwin," he said, "and forget about the girl. Let's talk about when you're going to settle up."

"Sure. Six months. Just like I said. No. Make it nine, just to be safe. Nine months, tops."

"I can give you six days."

Walsh jerked forward. "Six days? Are you crazy? What are you talking about, six days! I can't get my hands on eighty thousand dollars in six days!"

"I was told to give you two."

"Two? Who told you?"

"It doesn't matter."

"You bet it matters! Who's the asshole that told you to give me two? I want to know!"

Massini hesitated a moment, then said, "Okay. You'd figure it out, anyway. It was Phil."

Walsh's eyes widened. He slumped back into the sofa. "Sonuvabitch. *Sonuvabitch*! Phil? Why's he involved?" Walsh gulped at the cognac. "Did he send Solly?"

"I don't know. He's still the general manager, you know."

"Phil would do this to me? I can't believe it."

"Six days," Massini repeated.

"Hell, you might as well call Solly in and have him shoot me right here. I'm telling you I can't do it in six

20

days." Walsh shook a fist in the air. "That fucker Erwin!" He slammed the fist down hard on the sofa's arm.

"Will you forget about Erwin? Erwin's not your problem right now."

"You tell me, Carl. How am I supposed to come up with eighty thousand dollars in six days? What am I …." Walsh stopped and eyed Massini. "Did you know Phil was gonna squeeze me like this?"

Carl said nothing.

"Shit! You *did* know, didn't you? And you kept giving me markers all along, and all along you knew Phil was going to hammer me." He threw his arms up. "You're *all* a bunch of assholes!"

"Yelling at me isn't going to help, Thornton. I'm on your side. Phil wanted it in two days. I got you six." Massini leaned back and frowned indignantly. "And you call me an asshole."

"So, who kept approving the markers? You or Phil?"

"I did."

Walsh shook his head. "If you were as much my pal as you say you are, why didn't you cut me at thirty? Or forty? Why did you let me go to eighty? You saw I was losing my ass down there." He waved a hand at the bank of six closed-circuit television monitors in the wall across from Massini's desk. "Why didn't you cut me sooner?"

"If it was up to me, I would have cut you at twenty. But it wasn't."

"Phil was behind this?"

Massini said nothing.

"Why?" Walsh rocked forward. "What does he want from me?"

Neither spoke.

Massini eased back on the sofa. "How's the stock market?" he finally said. "Looks like it's been going pretty good lately."

Walsh wasn't listening.

"You're still with that firm… What's it called?"

"Huh? What?"

"The name of the firm you're with. What's it called?"

"Herschel and Wicks. What's going on here, Carl? You're supposed to be my friend, right? My good buddy, right? Just what the hell is this all about?"

Massini nodded thoughtfully. "Herschel and Wicks. They're a big outfit. I see their ads on TV all the time. They were the first to recommend Cisco Systems, weren't they?"

"Cisco was *my* recommendation."

"That's right. I remember when you told Phil and me about it. Too bad we didn't buy any."

"Could've made a freakin' fortune," Walsh said.

"That was an unfortunate error on our part. But your batting average wasn't too good at the time, was it?"

"Cisco worked out just fine. Would've more than made up for the others."

"You're probably right but you can see why we were a little gun shy."

"Well, you gotta take the bitter with the sour."

Massini chuckled. "So, how are things going with you and Herschel and Wicks up there in the Big Apple? Are you going to get your old job back?"

"I don't know why you're so interested in my job right now. I've still got one, if that's what you're worried about."

"Phil and I were truly upset for you when we heard they kicked you down to Junior Analyst. Probably no windows in the office of a junior analyst."

"I'll survive. Couldn't see out those scummy windows anyway. It was no loss to me."

"Probably not," Massini said. "No windows and no fancy title. They probably just leave you pretty much alone, right?"

"I have my moments."

"I'm sure you do. But they probably aren't looking over your shoulder either. Right? I mean, you're not responsible for the Cisco's and IBM's and Microsoft's anymore, so they probably leave you alone. Would that be an accurate statement?"

"Cats and dogs, Carl. That's what they gave me after the merger." He swallowed the last of the cognac. "Brought in their own bun-boys and gave me cats and dogs and has-beens. Like they're trying to make me now."

"You were the king of the hill once, weren't you, Thornton? The king of the freakin' hill before the merger."

Walsh sighed. "The king of the hill."

"And what did they do to you?"

"What? Sorry. What did you say?"

23

"They threw you away like yesterday's paper," Massini said. "Kicked you down to junior analyst. Took away your windows and your staff and turned you into a grunt."

Walsh slowly nodded. "That they did. That they did."

"I'll bet the view was pretty good … way up on top of that hill."

Walsh allowed a thin smile. "You'd never believe *how* good, Carl."

Massini leaned toward Walsh. "Do you want it back?"

"What?" Walsh's thoughts lingered on the top of the hill.

"I said, do you want it back? Your place on the top of the hill. Do you want it back?"

"Does a bear shit in the woods? Of course I want it back. But it'll never happen."

"You don't need the hill at Herschel and Wicks, Thornton."

Walsh screwed his bloodshot eyes into Massini's small, clear ones.

"There are lots of hills," Massini said. "Herschel and Wicks doesn't own them all."

"Are you telling me to change firms?"

"No—"

"If that's what you're saying, Carl, I've got a flash for you. Wall Street's got a one-page phone book and all the numbers are the same. I can't change firms."

"I'm not saying you *should* change firms."

"Then what?"

Massini reached for Walsh's empty glass. "Let me freshen that for you."

"No thanks. Just get to the point, will you? I've got hammers pounding in my head and I can hardly keep my eyes open."

"In a minute. First tell me about what you do. Just exactly what does an analyst do, anyway?"

"Jesus Christ, Carl. This is going to have to wait." Walsh pushed himself out of the sofa and rose. "I'm not in the mood for an economics lesson. My brain is fried and I've got to get some sleep."

Massini's eyes narrowed. "Sit down, Thornton."

"I told you, Carl. I'm good for the eighty gee's. Forget the six days, though. Tell Phil something. Tell him we talked and you're comfortable with nine months. Okay?"

Massini said nothing.

"Okay. Six months. I'll have it for him in six months. Jesus, Carl, I'm cooked right now. I've got to find my room and unplug my brain. Okay? Six months. Tops."

"Sit down, Thornton!"

Walsh swayed where he stood, his gaze darted back and forth between the door and Massini. "Shit." He threw his hands up. "Alright. I gotta drain my lizard first."

He staggered away to the bathroom while Massini replenished the snifter with cognac. Two minutes later, Walsh returned and sat hard on the sofa. He took a swallow of the mind-numbing liquor.

"Okay," Walsh said. "You want to know what I do? I analyze publicly- traded companies. If I find one that looks like it's worth a shit, I recommend it to the firm. If they go along, they recommend it to their customers. That's it."

"And how do you determine if it's 'worth a shit,' as you put it?"

"Oh, brother. You want everything? Okay. I go over their financials, talk to their management, take a trip through their plant—if they've got one—check their competitors. Stuff like that."

"And the price goes up?"

"Goes up?"

"The stock's price. It goes up after you recommend it?"

"Always."

Massini smiled. "And who knows if you're going to recommend a stock?"

"There's a panel, a review board. I make a recommendation to the board and they either approve it or they don't." Walsh swirled down the last of the cognac.

"And how long after their approval does the public find out about it?"

"Not long. Days usually. A teletype is sent to all of our offices with the recommendation and the brokers call their customers and push the stock."

Massini nodded thoughtfully. "And the price always goes up."

"Of course." Walsh frowned at the obvious conclusion. "Whether it *stays* up or not, that's another question but it goes up initially from all the buying."

Massini uncrossed his long legs and leaned forward. "So, if someone knew about your recommendation, knew before you made it, bought a bunch of the stock before your firm sent that teletype, they could--"

"Forget it, Carl. It would never happen."

"Because?"

"Because it's a very closely guarded secret, that's why. You'd never find out before everyone else. It just wouldn't happen. The SEC has rules about that. People have gone to prison over that. *I'd* go to prison. It just wouldn't happen."

"How would they know?" Massini asked. "How would the SEC find out?"

"Hell, Carl, they've got people on their staff whose only reason for getting up in the morning is to find some insider-trading activity, then haul 'em into court and throw their ass in jail. They know what to look for. I'm telling you it can't be done."

"What, exactly, *do* they look for?"

Walsh massaged the bridge of his nose then closed his eyes. The hammering throbs of pain inside his skull had grown more intense. "You got any aspirin?" he asked, his eyes still closed. "I've got a killer headache." He set the empty snifter on the arm of the sofa and rubbed at his temples while Massini filled a glass with ice and water and brought him two Tylenol tablets.

Walsh tossed them down.

"You were about to tell me what the SEC looks for," Massini said.

Walsh took a gulp of water then rolled the cold glass across his temples and forehead. "How many shares are we talking about?" He closed his eyes again. "A thousand? Ten thousand? How many?"

"That would depend; enough to net at least five million on an investment of no more than ten percent of that."

"Ten to one, huh?" Walsh forced his eyes open. "With a trade spike that size you've got red flags flying all over the Washington Monument." He set the glass on the carpet. "The SEC would be on you like flies on a fresh turd."

Massini leaned back and re-crossed his legs. "Okay, Thornton. I can see we aren't getting anywhere here, so I'll get to the quick and tell you what Phil wants to do for you."

"*For* me? That's a laugh. You mean *to* me."

"Will you be quiet a second?"

Walsh closed his mouth.

"Despite your opinion of him as an asshole, he likes you. And whether you believe it or not, he was truly disappointed when you were demoted. Thought they gave you a raw deal. And now … now he wants to help."

"Yeah, right. Good ol' Phil wants to help by putting me in hock to my eyebrows. What a pal."

"Will you hear me out? I think you'll come to a different conclusion by the time I'm done."

Walsh rolled his eyes. "I'm listening."

"Phil is a very sick man, Thornton. Prostate cancer. He let it go too long and it's gobbling him up. You remember how he was. Full of piss and vinegar. Never a care in the world. Always good for a laugh."

"That's Phil. Even if the laugh was usually at someone else's expense."

"Yes, well … he's different now. You wouldn't recognize him he's withering so fast. He'd like to have some fun before he goes, Thornton, but his wife cleaned him out in that messy divorce." Massini frowned and waved a hand at Walsh. "I don't have to tell *you* how messy a divorce can be, right?"

Walsh grimaced.

"Anyway, Phil needs money. *You* need money. Hell, we *all* need money."

"I didn't need it before Phil fucked me tonight."

"Now just who fucked who? I watched you play." He nodded at the TV monitors. Each bore views of gaming on selected craps and blackjack tables in the casino below. "I didn't see anyone with a gun to your head, forcing you to ask for one marker after another. No. Nobody fucked you, Thornton. You did it to yourself."

Walsh groaned.

"Now let's be adult about this," Massini continued. "It can all be worked out to everyone's satisfaction. You'll get your hill back—not Herschel and Wicks' hill but a hill nonetheless—and Phil will get his chance to go out with a smile. Are you ready to listen?"

Walsh slowly turned his head. "I can hardly wait," he muttered.

"That's better. Here's the deal. Phil is prepared to put up five hundred thousand for a quick turnaround net of five million. When it's done, you keep a million."

"A million? That's my hill?"

"That's a helluva hill in my book."

"And Phil gets the rest?"

29

"He'll get the lion's share, of course, less a small, shall we say, management fee."

"I figured you'd be in there somewhere."

Massini shrugged.

"Four million, huh. That's a hell of a retirement party for Phil."

"He'll make do. All you have to do is give me a call before you make your next recommendation and we'll take care of the rest."

Walsh looked at Massini with eyes that begged to slam shut. The scheme was not unlike an idea he toyed with a hundred times before.

"I thought Phil was broke," Walsh said. "Where's he coming up with half a million?"

"That's not your concern."

Walsh laughed. "The casino, right?"

Massini said nothing.

"He wants to front the deal with the casino's money?" Walsh laughed again. "What about all those freakin' stockholders you were so concerned about?"

"It has to be a quick turnaround," Massini repeated. "A few days."

"What happened there, Carl? Did Phil's brain fart? Wherever did he come up with such a ridiculous idea? The *casino's* money? Jesus."

Massini said nothing.

Walsh stood, then paced between the desk and sofa as Massini opened the manila folder and withdrew the eight, ten-thousand-dollar casino marker checks. He held them up for Walsh to see.

"Phil can make these disappear, Thornton. It's all up to you. He's offering you a choice. For the next six days, *your* reason for getting up in the morning can be to find a way to keep those flies from finding that turd—or you can come up with the eighty thousand. It's real simple. One or the other. Make the phone call or pay the casino their money. Either way, you've got six days."

Walsh sighed. "Some choice. I either get Solly or prison."

"You don't have to decide right now." Massini stood and set the folder on the desk. "Go to bed. Get some rest. Call me when you get up." He patted Walsh on the shoulder. "I know you'll do the right thing."

- 4 -

Atlantic City
Saturday, late morning

Walsh pressed the phone harder against his ear. "Oscar? Speak up! I'm in a train station and it's noisy!"

He glared at three frantic adults who were attempting, without much success, to coral a group of sixth graders who were running and playing near the bank of phones.

"This is Sheriff Marsden!" the man on the other end of the line shouted.

"Who?!" Walsh shouted back.

"Sheriff Marsden!"

"I'm calling for Oscar Walsh! Did I dial the wrong number?"

"Who's calling?" Sheriff Marsden asked.

"This is his brother! Thornton Walsh!"

The boarding announcement for a departing train sounded. An instant later the children let out a thunderous roar. The throng ran to the gate and mobbed the attendant.

"This is his brother," Walsh repeated in a normal voice tone. "Sorry to yell but it was hard to talk with all the noise."

"Don't give it another thought, Mr. Walsh," the sheriff said. "Oscar's right here."

Marsden passed the phone.

"Teetee?" Oscar said.

"What's going on there, Oscar? Are you alright?"

"Nothin's goin' on, Teetee. Are you in Roseburg?"

"Why did the sheriff answer the phone?"

"I was takin' a leak."

"What I mean is, why is he there?"

"He came over to talk but I think we're done. Do you want to talk to him?"

"Yes. Put him back on the line."

"Yes sir?" the sheriff said.

"Is my brother in trouble again?"

Marsden chuckled. "It ain't no big thing, Mr. Walsh. Just a little somethin' down at the Safeway earlier."

"What 'little something?'"

"Aw, it ain't much. But got to do my follow-up here with Oscar and get it straightened out."

"If it isn't a big deal, do you mind telling me what it is?"

"Sure, I can do that. You know, it's kinda hot here but it's nice an' cool in the Safeway ... 'specially right there by the open freezer where they keep the ice cream an' TV dinners an' all."

"Yes?"

"Well, Oscar here kinda likes to hang around that freezer on these nice, hot days an' sorta stare at the ladies. Know what I mean?"

"No."

"Well …. You a married man, Mr. Walsh?"

"Divorced."

"Okay. Then you know about how hot and cold and … well … how it can do certain things to a certain part of a woman's body. Right?"

"What are you talking about, Sheriff? Hot and cold. What's that got to do with Oscar?"

"Well, huh." The sheriff paused. "Their nipples, Mr. Walsh. You know how a woman's nipples just sorta pop out when they get cold after being out in the hot of the day?"

"Oh. Okay. Yeah. I know."

"Well, Oscar here's been makin' kinda a pest a hisself down there at the Safeway an' Albert, he's the manager there, you know. Well, Albert wanted me to talk to Oscar and sorta keep him away."

"I see."

"You know, it really ain't nothin', Mr. Walsh, but the ladies get kinda jittery when he's there, gawkin' at 'em an' all and it's just bad for business. Know what I mean?"

Walsh sighed. "Yes. Yes, I do." He sighed again. "Has anyone pressed charges?"

"No, not yet, and we want to keep it that-a-way."

"What's going to happen to Oscar now?"

"Nothin' much. We're just gonna have a little talk about the Safeway thing and that's it."

"Alright, Sheriff." Walsh frowned. "I'm going to give you my number. Will you please call me if something like this comes up again?"

"Of course, Mr. Walsh. I think I still have it somewhere but I don't want you to start worryin' much 'cause things is gonna work out here with me an' Oscar. Right, Oscar? Right. Oscar says it's gonna work out okay."

"That's good."

"But you know, Mr. Walsh, Oscar's been kinda rambunctious the last few weeks and we sure don't want anything else ta happen."

"No, we don't. Can I talk to my brother?"

"Sure."

Marsden passed the phone.

"When are you coming to see me?" Oscar asked.

"For chrissake, Oscar. You're thirty-four years old. What the hell are you doing staring at women's breasts in a grocery store? Huh? What are you doing?"

"Don't be mad, Teetee. I didn't bother no one. I didn't touch 'em or nothin'. Just looked."

"For God's sake, Oscar. I can't believe it! You're damn lucky the sheriff doesn't throw you in jail for something like that. Are you taking your medicine?"

"Yeah. I'm takin' it."

"Regular?"

"Almost. Sometimes I forget, though."

"You've got to take it every day, Oscar."

"I know."

"Alice has been wiring money to your bank every month. Have you been getting it?"

"Sure. And I only spend half … like you told me."

"Then you don't have any excuse for not taking your medication, do you?"

"No, I don't. I'm sorry, Teetee. I just forget sometimes."

"You can't forget, Oscar. You have to take it every day. It's important."

"Every day. I know."

"Why'd you do that, Oscar? At the Safeway. What were you thinking?"

Oscar laughed. "Just having fun."

Walsh groaned. "What am I going to do with you, Oscar?"

"I miss you, Teetee."

"I miss you, too, Oscar, but listen to me. Don't do any more of those dumb stunts. Okay? Just go to work, take your medicine, and go to bed. Okay? Nothing stupid."

"Okay, Teetee. Gee, you sure sound mad."

"I'm *not* mad! I just don't want you getting into any more trouble. Now don't do anything dumb, because I'm going to call you in a few days and check."

"Okay, Teetee. Don't worry. I won't. When are you coming out to see me?"

"Soon, Oscar, but not now. I'm in Jersey and I've got to get back to New York. We'll get together soon, though. Okay?"

"O-o-o ka-a-ay."

"I promise, Oscar. We *will* get together soon. Just as soon as I can. Now take care of yourself and I'll call you in a few days."

"Teetee?"

"Yes, Oscar?"

"I love you, Teetee."

Walsh sighed. "I love you too, Oscar."

- 5 -

Boston

"God … you're … an … ani … mal," Shirley got out between Bert's rhythmic thrusts.

He withdrew, gently rolled her onto her stomach and remounted her.

"O-o-o-oh. I like it that way," she cooed. "Do me hard, Bertie. Do me hard and deep."

A few more strokes and Bert was done. He lay quietly on top of her for another minute, then rolled off her back and onto the cardboard covering their small squat on the sidewalk.

Shirley turned over and ran a rag over her vagina, cleaning Bert's semen from her crotch, then pulled their soiled wool blanket over their still bodies. "God, Bertie, you sure know how to satisfy a woman."

He grunted.

"Don't know what's gotten into you lately," she said, "but I like it."

He said nothing as she ran her fingers over his head and kissed him lightly on his shoulder.

"I think I found where your hair went," she said, messing what was left of a once-thick carpet of black hair on his scalp.

"Where?"

"Here." She touched his shoulder. "And here." She stroked his wide chest.

Bert shrugged. "It didn't move, Shirl."

"I know, Bertie." She giggled. "It just seems more. I think it's gettin' thicker."

She drew wide circles with a finger in the mat of hair on his chest.

"What do you want from me, Shirl? It just grew there, okay?"

"Don't be angry." She patted his shoulder. "I just never noticed how much there was before."

"Lots of men have hair on their chest and arms."

"I know. Seems a lot more, that's all."

Bert pushed the blanket aside and pulled on his trousers and loafers.

"You aren't mad at me, are ya, Bertie?"

"'Course not. I'm goin' out."

"Where?"

"Korman's."

"All that lovin' make ya hungry?"

Bert brushed a kiss across her lips. "I'll be right back, Shirl."

"I'll be here."

He checked the change in his pocket, gathered several empty soda bottles and crushed drink cans into a paper sack, then opened the flap of the sagging cardboard furniture box and crawled into the cool night air.

Small fires, tended by groups of huddled, silent men, flickered in muted orange tones along the sidewalk to his right and left. Bert said nothing to the men as he stepped around their shelters of cardboard and tarpaulin and they said nothing to him.

He moved quietly along the littered street and the silent men watched him obliquely, making certain he neither disturbed their inventory of rummagings nor encroached upon their space on the sidewalk. Bert sighed. They were islands unto themselves, hollow souls wishing only for privacy and distance from one another.

He turned left at the corner and continued another half-block to Korman's Market. Quan was inside, hunched behind the counter and reading a newspaper. He glanced up as Bert went in, then returned his attention to the paper. When Bert finished setting the pop bottles and cans from his sack near the register, Quan straightened and rang up their redemption value. He gave Bert the cash.

"We all out a Premium," Quan said. "Just have kibble."

"Will you check the back?" Bert asked. "I don't want the kibble."

"Already did. We all out. Sold last can twenty minute ago."

"Damn. Mind if I take a look myself?"

"You look all you want on shelf. No look in back."

Quan returned to the newspaper as Bert walked around to the pet food section among the narrow rows of shelving. The kibble was there and lots of it. He

39

pushed the small green and yellow sacks around to check for an errant tin of Pride Premium.

"Who else has it?" Bert asked when he returned to the front of the small store.

"Don't know," Quan said, not looking up. "Come back tomorrow in afternoon. Truck come then. We have more tomorrow."

"Tomorrow? I don't want to wait 'til tomorrow."

"Truck come tomorrow," Quan said, still reading.

Bert stuffed the bottle and can money into his pocket and left. Arrow Neighborhood Market was two blocks away. He hurried over to it.

Three men in soiled baggy clothing and the old clerk were inside when Bert entered.

"Where do you get off charging two dollars?" the shortest of the men demanded. "All the other stuff is seventy cents."

"Take it or leave it," the clerk said. He reached a hand under the sales counter.

"Two dollars ain't shit to you," the taller man said, "but it's a fortune to us!"

"I don't set the prices," the clerk said. "I just sell it. Either buy something or get out."

The men grumbled among themselves as they counted the coins shared between them. Bert ignored them, found a tin of Pride Premium and brought it to the counter.

"Well, well. Look what we got here," the short man said. "Mr. Rockefeller. Step aside, boys. Let him through."

"Pudge," Bert said to the short man as he set the tin on the counter.

40

"You gonna pay two bucks?" Pudge asked.

"If that's what it is."

"Shit!" Pudge snorted. "I ain't gonna pay no two bucks for a can a dog food. No fuckin' way!"

Bert ignored Pudge and handed the clerk two dollars in coin.

"I ain't gonna pay it and that's all there is to it!" Pudge lurched forward and grabbed the tin from the counter.

"Hey!" the clerk yelled. "Give that back!"

Pudge bolted out the door to the sidewalk as the clerk pulled a shotgun from under the counter. He cocked the hammers and ran outside. Bert followed. Pudge was thirty yards down the block, running headlong into the darkness. The distance between them quickly widened.

"You're never coming back here, again!" the clerk yelled out after him. "Never!"

Pudge ran to the end of the block then disappeared around the corner.

"Goddamn winos," the clerk cursed to no one as he hurried back into the store.

The other two men sauntered past him on their way out.

"You tell your friend he's not allowed in here ever again," the clerk said.

The men said nothing as they left.

"I'll just get another can," Bert said to the clerk.

"Sure. That'll be two dollars."

"I just paid you two."

"That's right and Pudge took it. I know all you guys were in on it. You want another can, it'll be two dollars."

Bert grabbed the man by the neck and jerked him forward. "Listen here, pal," he said, an inch from the man's face. "I wasn't with those guys. Pudge took *your* can, not mine." He shook the man for effect. "You got that?"

The man's leathery face turned crimson and his eyes bulged.

"Gimme that." Bert pulled the shotgun from the man's grip. "You're not gonna use that on me." He flipped the ejector with his free hand and the gun broke at the breech. The two shells fell to the floor. He tossed the empty gun behind the counter. "You're coming with me."

He dragged the clerk to the pet food shelf.

"*This* is my can," Bert said, picking up a tin of Pride Premium. "I paid for it and now I'm taking it."

"Okay, okay," the clerk said. "Take it."

Bert released his grip and the man fell to his knees. He was still on the floor when Bert walked out and started back to Shirley's squat on the sidewalk.

- 6 -

New York City
Monday

Walsh threw his pencil hard against the far wall of his office. "This is impossible," he growled. "Nothing but crap!"

He rifled through the pile of financial reports strewn across his desk one more time, then sighed and slumped back in his chair. He punched a button on the phone's speed-dialer. "Mr. Stevens? Walsh, here. Do you have a minute?"

"That's about all I've got," Stevens said.

"Well, sir, I've been looking through my series and ... uh ... I'd really like to get my teeth into something great, but ... uh ... quite frankly, there isn't a star in the stack."

"Did you look at Carter Steel?"

"Carter? I looked at Carter, sure. But there's nothing exciting about Carter."

"You're wrong there, my boy."

Walsh clenched his teeth.

43

"Steel is exciting," Stevens continued, "and Carter makes steel. Ergot, Carter is exciting. You see the connection?"

Walsh rolled his eyes. "Uh ... yes, sir. Of course. But Carter aside, I don't have anything with any pizzazz."

"Pizzazz?"

"Nothing I can get my teeth into, sir. Nothing I can rally behind, and I was wondering if—"

"My boy, you're not going to waste my time with another conversation about something we've discussed too many times already, are you?"

"No, sir. Of course not. I was only wondering if I could ... uh ... get together with Schroeder and maybe shuffle some of his load over to my desk. That's all I was going to say."

"Schroeder's doing just fine. He's keeping up—and doing a damn fine job of it, I might add. You don't have to worry yourself about Schroeder."

"It's not that I'm *worried* about him. I was just thinking we might be able to shuffle things around a bit so I could get something fresh. I really need something fresh." Walsh glanced over the cluttered reports on his desk and frowned.

"No," Stevens said. "I don't want to disturb Schroeder right now. I like what he's doing for us, so let's not shake his tree."

"Shake his tree?"

"But now that you've brought him up, I certainly wouldn't be averse to you and Schroeder sitting down over a drink sometime and letting him give you a few pointers on how he goes about his work. I wouldn't be averse to that at all. In fact, I'd encourage it."

"Yeah, well, I'll pencil that in somewhere between a snack and a head call."

"Now don't go getting testy with *me*!" Stevens barked. "I'm not going to tolerate any of that kind of talk!"

"It wasn't meant to be testy, sir."

"Well, I don't know what else you'd call it but I'm not going to dignify it with any further discussion. You just make your calls, do your job, and stay away from Schroeder's files. Is that understood?"

"Yes, sir."

"Good. Now, I'll expect to hear something positive about Carter Steel from you in the meeting on Wednesday. Are we clear on this?"

"Quite clear."

"The Carter's are longtime friends of mine and I'll be damned if I'm going to let your sniveling stop us from doing right by their stock. Got it?"

"Yes, sir. I've got it."

"Good. Now, no more talk about shuffling portfolios around. Don't waste any more of my time about that."

Stevens hung up.

"Asshole!" Walsh shouted at the handset before slamming it onto the hook. "What a dickhead!"

He pulled a panatela from his desk and lit it, inhaling the first draw of rich smoke deep into his lungs. He took two more quick drags then turned to the papers on his desk. A couple more calls and he'd go home. Exactly *who* he called really didn't matter much.

He set the list of fourteen companies in his series in front of him, closed his eyes and blindly jabbed a finger at the page. The name below his finger was Bigelow Tire. He stabbed the paper again and this time his finger pointed to Pride Pet Foods. How either managed to stay in business was nothing short of amazing, he thought. He dialed up Bigelow Tire.

"Malcolm?"

"Yes?" the president of the tire company answered.

"Malcolm. How are you, sir? This is Thornton Walsh ... over here at Herschel and Wicks."

"Oh, yes, Mr. Walsh. I'm fine. How are you?"

"Good, sir. I was calling to see how your quarter's shaping up."

"I'm glad you called," he said. "Things have gotten pretty exciting over here at Bigelow."

"Really? That's good to hear."

Walsh fished a new pencil from his desk and poised it over a tablet.

"Yes, sir, Mr. Walsh. Damn exciting."

"Tell me about it."

"Well, the biggest news is we're about to get that breakthrough on the airless."

Walsh dropped the pencil.

"We're so close," Malcolm continued, "I can smell it. And you know what that's going to do to our bottom line, right?"

"Right." Walsh groaned. "Almost got that airless, huh?" His gaze wandered around the office. Only a tall, dust-covered plastic palm in the corner. Even the view through a scum-encrusted window would have been a welcome distraction.

"Now, I know what you're probably thinking, Mr. Walsh. You're thinking 'here he goes again. Talking about that airless. Same old tune, same old verse.' Right?"

"Well— "

"I know, I know. We've talked about the airless … I don't know how many times but it's different now. We've just about got it put to bed."

"That's good to hear. When can I come down to take a look?"

"How's June sound?"

"June? That's nine months away."

"Right. June or July. Right around there and we'll have something that'll really knock the socks off your clients at Herschel and Wicks. June or July."

"I'm sure they'll be thrilled. How about your current quarter, though? How's that shaping up?"

"Just a little more red ink. The R & D on the airless is still affecting our earnings but it's money well spent. You're going to agree with us on that when you come down here next summer."

"Malcolm."

"Yes?"

"Malcolm, can you possibly tell me why Firestone and Goodyear and Michelin and everybody else who tried to make an airless threw in the towel but you're still forging ahead with it? I don't mean to be rude, sir, but when their marketing people said it wasn't worth it, why are *you* still pursuing it?"

"I know a-l-l-l about what their marketing people said but they're wrong. Dead wrong. And we're going to prove it. Just hang with us a little while longer and

47

you're going to be a hero over there at Herschel. Just a little while longer."

"I'm sure you know what you're doing, Malcolm, but your stock is in the toilet." He punched up the current quote on Bigelow Tire. "A buck twenty-five, Malcolm."

"I know."

"That's a long way from thirty-eight."

"I know but—"

"Quite frankly, Malcolm, I'm the only analyst following Bigelow anymore, and I don't know how much longer I can keep your 'hold' rating."

"I know."

"Actually, Bigelow doesn't even warrant a rating at a buck twenty-five."

"I know that, Mr. Walsh, and don't think I don't appreciate what you've been doing for us."

"Without something solid, Malcolm, I'm going to have no choice but to drop Bigelow."

Malcolm was silent.

"Did you hear me, Malcolm?"

"Yes. I heard you."

"Can you give me something? Anything? Anything at all I can tell our clients?"

"Well, let's see.... These are very preliminary, mind you, but looks like sales will be off only sixteen percent this quarter. And ... we'll only lose three cents per share versus the four-cent loss the same quarter last year. That's not too bad."

Walsh did the math in his head. "That'll be the tenth quarter in a row with negative earnings and declining sales. Does that sound about right, Malcolm?"

"Sounds about right but I'm telling you the airless is going to turn the ship around for us at Bigelow Tire. Turn it around and head upstream."

"How about if I put you in touch with our mergers and acquisition people, Malcolm? What would you say to that?"

"Sell *out*? Is that what you're suggesting, Mr. Walsh? You want me to sell out?"

"It's only a suggestion, Malcolm. Bigelow isn't a ship anymore. It's a barge and it's taking on water fast. If you're putting everything into the airless, you'll sink it."

"You know, Mr. Walsh? I don't like your tone. I've been nothing less than candid and cordial with you and what do you do? You insult me, that's what."

"I'm simply trying to give you a reality check, sir. The airless is going to capsize what's left of your company. I'm just trying to be helpful."

"That kind of help we don't need here at Bigelow. Not at all. We've had some problems, true enough, but we're working them through. Now, if selling out is all you've got to talk about, this conversation is finished."

"Just think about it, Malcolm. That's all I'm asking you to do."

"I already have. Good day, sir."

Malcolm hung up.

Walsh shook his head. "What is *with* these people?" he asked the empty room. "Fuck 'em." He drew a red line through Bigelow Tire and made a note in the margin to recommend removal of their stock from Herschel's 'hold' list during Wednesday's meeting.

Pride Pet Foods would be a far friendlier call. He dialed the number.

"Good afternoon," he greeted the president's secretary. "This is Thornton Walsh. May I speak with Mr. Ledford?"

"Let me see if he's in, Mr. Walsh. Who did you say you're with?"

"Herschel and Wicks. New York."

"Thank you. One moment, please."

She put him on hold and Walsh searched his mind for a fresh joke to tell the man.

"I'm sorry, Mr. Walsh," the girl said, returning to the line. "He's unavailable."

"What? Did you tell him it was me? Thornton Walsh?"

"Yes, sir."

"I don't think so. I don't think he knows it's me. Tell him again."

"I did tell him, sir."

"Just tell him again. Okay?"

"I will, sir, but I did tell him. Hold, please."

Walsh lightly drummed his fingers on his desk while listening to a recorded pitch about Pride's latest line of products and an 800 number to call for sales locations.

"Mr. Walsh?" the secretary said.

"Yes?"

"I told Mr. Ledford you were calling. He's still unavailable."

Walsh slumped back. "I see. Okay. Thank you very much."

He hung up and grabbed the three-month-old Pride financials. He turned to the middle and checked the numbers. Earnings, down. Sales, down. Market share almost non-existent. He flipped to the last page and read every stilted word of the accountant's qualifying statement. His bottom line opinion: bankruptcy was a near certainty. He turned to the front of the report and the usual photo of company president James Cleatis Ledford, dressed in a dark blue suit, white shirt, and red, white and blue striped tie. A million-dollar smile and deep tan completed the image of an eminently successful leader of an eminently successful company.

"What a joke," Walsh said to the empty room. "Another fool at the helm of another barge."

He drew a red line through Pride Pet Foods and started to write in the margin but stopped. No problem red-lining Bigelow. Their numbers were in the tank. But Pride was another story. He couldn't sell Stevens on dropping them just because their president refused to talk to him. Stevens knew they were tight and if he thought Ledford was clamming up, he'd perceive that as a weakness in Walsh. No telling *what* Stevens might do, then. He might cut his series. Hell, he might even cut him!

His watch said 3:45. If he left right away, he could make the drive to Ledford's plant before five o'clock. No way Ledford would turn him away if he showed at his door. He grabbed the Pride Pet Foods report and put it in his briefcase, then stuffed the rest of the papers from his desk into a drawer and left.

At five minutes 'til five, Walsh drove up to the gated entrance to the Pride Pet Foods access road and stopped. A rotund uniformed security guard stepped from a newly constructed shack and approached him. He gripped a clipboard in one hand.

"How long has all this been here?" Walsh asked as he gestured at the shack and tall, chain-link security fence topped with spiraling coils of razor wire.

"Four months," the chubby guard said with a stone face. "Who are you here to see?"

"Cleat ... uh ... James Ledford."

"Your name, sir?"

"Thornton Walsh."

The guard checked a paper on the clipboard. "It wasn't called in," he said, not looking up. "Do you have an appointment?"

"I don't need one. We're old friends."

"I'll have to check," the guard said. "Please wait over there." He motioned to a wide turnout ten yards back.

Walsh moved his car into the area, then scanned the narrow road ahead and parking lot in the distance. Five o'clock and still full of cars. For a company on the verge of bankruptcy, business seemed to be booming.

A long, black limousine cruised past him. The rear window was halfway down and Walsh only caught a glimpse of the man in the back seat but there was no mistaking the heavy jowls and huge pocked nose of the man's unmistakable face. The limo slowed at the gate, then sped away when the guard raised the control arm and waved it through.

A minute later, the guard came out of the shack and marched up to Walsh. "Mr. Ledford can't see you today. His secretary asked that you call for an appointment."

"What? You've got to be kidding."

"No, sir."

"You go back in there and tell him I drove all the way up from New York and I'm not leaving until I talk to him."

"My instructions were quite definite, sir."

"I don't give a shit about what Ledford's secretary told you!"

The guard took a step back.

"I'm telling you to call her back and tell her just what I said!"

The guard moved his hand to the baton on his belt.

"Go on," Walsh said. "Call her!"

"Alright, sir."

The pudgy man took a few steps backward while carefully eyeing Walsh, then turned around and went into the shack. A minute later, he returned. "Mr. Ledford would like to speak to you, sir."

"I knew you'd get it straight." Walsh started his car. "I know the way."

"He's on the phone," the guard said.

"What?"

"Right over there, sir." He gestured at the guard shack.

"This is horse shit," Walsh grumbled. He followed the guard into the shack and picked up the dangling receiver. "Cleat? What the hell's going on?"

"I'm sorry you drove all the way out here, Thorny. This has just been one of those days."

"Well, I can understand that but why didn't you take my call earlier?"

"You called? When did you call?"

"Over an hour ago. Your secretary said you were unavailable, of all things."

"Hell, Thorny, I was never told."

"Whatever. Anyway, I'm here, now. Let's sit down for a minute."

A pause. "I'm afraid that won't be possible right now," Ledford said. "But let's do that soon. Okay?"

"Cleat. It's me. Thornton. *Thorny*. What can possibly be so important? I drove all the way up here from the city."

"Yes. I know. You should have called first. I would have told you this was not a good time."

"I *did* call! That twit secretary you've got wouldn't put me through."

"Well, I'll have to speak to her about that. But this really isn't a good time. I'll give you a call."

"You'll give me a call." Walsh shook his head.

"That's right. And we'll get together."

"I'm all the way out here but you'll give me a call."

"I don't have time for this, Thorny. I'll call you." He hung up.

Walsh stood motionless, the phone at his ear, the insistent dial tone buzzing.

"Will there be anything else?" the guard asked.

"What?"

"Is there anything else?"

Walsh slowly set the handset onto its cradle. He looked out at the full parking lot and the four salmon-colored buildings of Pride Pet Foods. Forklifts laden with full pallets of product scurried from one building to the next while men and women in white coveralls hurried about. He checked his watch again. Five-fifteen.

"Is everybody working overtime today?" Walsh asked.

"No, sir. It's the second shift."

"*Second* shift? How long has there been a second shift?"

"About three months. Is there anything else?" The guard shifted back and forth on his feet.

Walsh ignored it. "How many people work here?"

"At this plant?"

"What? There's more than one?"

"Two … and another under construction."

"*Two* plants?" Walsh's eyes widened. "Is the other one just as busy as this one?"

"Busier. Got three shifts at the Placer plant and it's bigger than this one by twenty acres."

Walsh shook his head. "Is that right."

"What's that?"

"No. Nothing."

"Sir, I really need to get back to work. So, if there isn't anything else … "

"That's all. Thank you very much."

Walsh left the shack and sauntered to his car. He sat quietly for a moment then dialed his secretary from his cell phone. "Alice."

"Yes, sir?"

"What's the close on Pride Pet Foods?"

She punched up the quote. "One and three-quarters at two."

"And the volume?"

"Nineteen thousand, three hundred."

"Pretty thin. I know it's late, Alice, but please Call Dun & Bradstreet for me and get the vendor list for

Pride Pet Foods. Have them fax it. Will you take care of that for me?"

"Yes, sir."

"Thank you. As soon as you get it, fax the list to me at my apartment. Okay?"

"Sure, Mr. Walsh."

"A couple more things. Call our contacts in advertising at the three major networks and see if Pride has any TV ads scheduled. If they do, get the run dates and times."

"Run dates and times," she repeated. "I'll take care of it, sir. Do you want that faxed to you as well?"

"No, that won't be necessary. Also get the name of the agency handling the Pride advertising account and the name of the exec in charge. Leave his name and number on my desk for me with the other stuff."

"Very good, sir."

"Thanks, Alice. You're a sweetheart. One last thing. Call Pride's headquarters. They're probably closed now but you'll get a recorded message referencing an 800 number for their product sales locations. Call the number and get the addresses of about a dozen locations near my apartment. Okay?"

"A dozen locations near your apartment. I'll get it."

"Good. Then fax the list to me and that'll be it."

"I'll take care of it, Mr. Walsh. Do you mind my asking what's going on?"

"I'd tell you, Alice, but I really don't know myself. I'll tell you this much, though, I just saw John Westfield ride into Pride Pet Foods like he owned the place."

"*The* John Westfield? Omni Foods CEO?"

"None other."

"Nasty guy. What would—"

"Exactly. What would a titan like Westfield be doing at a piece of crap dump like Pride?"

"Maybe they're friends," she said.

"Yeah, right," Walsh sneered. "Friends."

"Are you coming back to the office?"

"Not tonight. And I'll probably be late getting in tomorrow. I want to check on a few things. I'll see you sometime around mid-morning."

"Very well, sir. Good night."

- 7 -

Baltimore

"He won't eat, doctor." Pam Tucker stroked a hand over her dog's short white and black coat. "Poor Ralphie."

The veterinarian looked thoughtfully at the quaking American Bulldog on the metal table as he poked his fingers into the animal's sides and abdomen. "I don't feel anything, Mrs. Tucker," he said. "The X-rays didn't show any abnormality and neither did the blood work."

"Well, he's just not the same, doctor. He won't eat, he snaps at the children, paces around the house. I don't know what …" She looked down at the dozens of white and black hairs on the table. "And his fur's falling out."

"Nothing to be alarmed about there, Mrs. Tucker. A dog's coat thins and grows all the time." The vet stopped probing the dog and looked at the young woman. "We can pretty much rule out any organic causation, so there has to be something else. Has anything changed at home? Any houseguests? A new pet? Anything different recently?"

"No. Nothing. Everything's the same."

"And how long has this been going on? Two days, did you say?"

"That's right. Started a couple of days after we picked him up from my mom's."

"And how long ago was that, again ... that you picked him up?"

"Saturday. Three days ago." She stroked the fur along the bottom of Ralph's neck. "Poor Ralphie," she cooed. "Haven't eaten in two days? You must be *starving*."

"Probably very hungry," the vet said, "but not starving. And I think I know why."

"Really?"

"How long was Ralph at your mother's?"

"Ten days. We took a vacation. I wasn't going to put Ralph in a kennel." She shook her head. "No, sir." She nuzzled her face on the top of the dog's head. "Not my Ralphie."

The doctor chuckled. "That's what I thought. He's upset."

"Upset?" She looked up at the vet. "About what?"

"How long have you had Ralph?"

"Four years."

"And have you ever gone away like that before? Left him?"

"Never."

"Exactly. That's why he's acting like this, Mrs. Tucker. He's angry at you and your family for leaving him. Ralph has feelings just like you and me. He's upset with you for going away."

"Really?"

"Absolutely. He felt abandoned and now he's getting back at you."

"You're sure that's all it is?"

"Positive. It's a fairly well-known phenomenon. We call it Separation Anxiety."

"Separation Anxiety? I never would have thought ..."

"I wouldn't be too hard on myself if I were you." He patted Ralph lightly. "He'll get over it. Ralph will be just fine but I want to give him something just the same."

"You don't know what a relief that is," Pam said. "I thought he picked up a bug or something at Mom's."

"No. He's fine. Does he drink plenty of water?"

"He sure does. Harold calls him a bilge pump."

"That's good. Just make sure he gets plenty of water. He'll eat when he gets hungry enough."

The dog jerked when the vet stabbed it with a hypodermic needle.

"What's that you're giving him?"

"B-12," he said. "It'll pep him up a bit." He withdrew the needle.

Pam cupped the dog's ears in her hands and stared into his eyes. "Did the doctor hurt you, Ralphie? Did he make an ouchie? O-o-o-oh. Poor baby." She looked up at the vet. "What should I do, doctor? Is there something I should give him or something special I should do?"

"Just keep doing what you have been. Keep giving him lots of love. As soon as he realizes things are back to normal, he'll snap out of it." He patted the animal's head. "But, if you don't see a change in a few days, bring him back in and we'll have another look. He should be fine, though." The doctor patted the dog again then scribbled something on a page in Ralph's treatment folder.

"Thank you, doctor. He'll get plenty of love, alright. I'll guarantee you that. And Ralphie thanks you, too."

The vet closed the folder and handed it to her. "Give this to my receptionist on your way out, if you will. She'll prepare your bill."

Harold climbed out of the Jeep Cherokee when his wife came outside with Ralph. He went around to the back and opened the vehicle's rear hatch. "What's the verdict?" he asked.

"Ralph's upset."

Harold turned around and stuck his hands on his hips. "He's what?"

"He's angry at me for leaving him when we went on vacation. I told you we should have taken him."

"They don't let dogs on cruise ships."

"Then we should have gone somewhere else."

He threw up his hands. "Give me a break, Pam."

"Next year we're taking him. I don't care what you say. I'll stay home if I have to but I'm not leaving Ralphie alone."

"He wasn't alone. He was at your mother's for crying out loud."

"It's not the same."

"So that's what's wrong with him? He's pissed 'cause we left him with your mother?"

"That's right."

"You've got to be kidding."

"I am not. Ralph has feelings too, you know. Just like you and me."

"Who'd you see in there? A veterinarian or psychiatrist?"

"Very funny, Harold."

"What about the fur? Did you ask him about all the fur he's shedding?"

"He said it's normal. Come, Ralphie," she said. "Up, up." Pam encouraged Ralph into the rear of the Jeep then she went around to the front and got into the passenger seat. "Are you coming?"

"Damn dog is getting hair all over my car." Harold spread a bed sheet under the pacing animal, then closed the hatch and climbed in behind the wheel. "So, how much was Ralph's visit today with Dr. Freud?"

"Real funny, Harold. You just come up with one knee-slapper after another."

"Okay, Pam." Harold switched on the engine and began to drive out of the parking lot. "How much did Dr. *Lewis* charge for his diagnosis of abandonment?"

"Two seventy-five."

"*Two seventy-five*?!" Harold slammed on the brake. "He charged two hundred seventy-five dollars to tell you Ralph is upset?!" He banged his fist on the wheel.

"Lower your voice, Harold."

He glanced in the rearview mirror when Ralph barked. "Did he even do any tests? Just what the hell did he do for two hundred seventy-five dollars?"

"Lower your voice, Harold. You're making Ralph nervous." She turned in her seat to check the dog then turned back around. "Of course he did tests. He took X-rays, did blood tests. He did a lot."

"You were in there twenty-three minutes, Pam. That's over ten dollars a minute!"

"And worth every penny of it."

"Damn near twelve dollars a minute!"

"Still cheap."

"That dog's gonna put me in the poor house." Harold resumed driving.

"You love Ralphie. I don't know why you're complaining so much. Call Mom and put her on the speaker. She wanted to know."

He placed the call.

"Mom. We just left Dr. Lewis and he said Ralph didn't catch anything. He's just upset."

"That's good news, dear. What's he upset about?"

"Because we took a cruise," Harold said, "and he couldn't come."

Pam shot an angry look at her husband. "That's not it at all, Mom. Don't listen to Harold. *He's* upset because of Dr. Lewis' bill."

"How much was the bill, dear?"

"It wasn't—"

"Two hundred and seventy-five dollars!" Harold said.

"Oh, my. Well, Dr. Lewis is the best."

"That's what I tried to tell Harold. Anyway … Mom, Dr. Lewis wanted to know if anything happened recently. Of course we were away but did anything happen at your house? He asked about house guests and new pets."

"No, dear. There was just your father and me. No one else stayed with us."

"Hmmm. Did he get along with Snuggles okay? Was there any problem there?"

"Not at all, Pammy. They played together fine. Well, they squabbled a bit the first day but after that they got along fine. I was surprised, to tell you the truth. For a Pekinese, I thought Snuggles would be after Ralph for sure but she wasn't. They seemed to have a good time together."

"Okay, Mom. Just wanted to check."

"Are you supposed to do anything?"

"Nothing. Dr. Lewis said Ralph would snap out of it when he saw things were normal again."

"That's good. Your father and I were worried something might be wrong with Ralph."

"No. He took blood and did X-rays. Ralph's just angry but he'll get over it. I'm going to give him lots of love." She turned around and gave Ralph an assuring nod.

"Are you going home now?"

"Yes. Oh, by the way, what did you feed Ralph?"

"The same thing we give Snuggles. Ralph seemed to really like it."

"What was it?"

"Pride Premium. Not the kibble. The can."

"We're *not* buying Pride Premium!" Harold shouted.

"Why not," Pam said, "if that's what Ralphie likes?"

"Pride's the most expensive brand, that's why! That damn dog will put me in the poor house!"

"There he goes, again. Mom, don't listen to—. Harold, there's an A & P. Stop and run in and get some food for Ralph."

"I'm not going—"

"Mom. I'm hanging up now. I'll call you later."

"Alright, dear."

They clicked off.

"You're going right by it, Harold. I told you to stop at the A & P and you're going right by it."

"We've got a whole sack of Alpo at home. I'm not spending any more money on dog food until that's gone."

"Fine! You either stop right now or I'm driving back here after we get Ralph home. Either way, Ralphie is going to have Pride Premium for dinner tonight."

"Have it your way." He drove home.

- 8 -

Boston

Traci gave a firm poke to Mary's blanket-covered shoulder. The woman's eyes were closed, her forehead knotted and swollen.

"Mary?" Traci said.

"Huh?"

"I'm Sergeant Ross. Boston Police Department."

"Wha-a-a-t? I'm sleepin'!"

"Are you Mary Funace?"

"What about it?"

"I want to talk to you, Mary … about the attack a couple of days ago."

The woman rolled from her side and onto her back. Her eyelids blinked open, framing bloodshot pits in an oval spider-veined face. "What attack?"

"Two days ago. I have a crime report that says you were raped." Traci held the report in front of the woman.

She wearily raised a hand to shade her eyes from the bright sun and squinted. "Hell, yes, I was raped. Don't know nothin' 'bout no attack." She struggled to sit up. Traci helped her. "Did ya get the asshole?"

"Not yet, Mary. That's why I'm here."

"Shit." Mary groped the sidewalk under the blanket with bony fingers and found the bottle of Thunderbird. She unscrewed the cap and took two quick swallows.

"I need to ask you a few questions," Traci said. "It'll help with our investigation."

"Already told the two guys at the hospital. There ain't nothin' else to tell."

"Those men were the detectives, Mary. I know you gave them a statement and I've read it. I just want to review a couple of things, then I'll leave you alone."

Mary took two more quick swallows from the bottle then screwed the lid on tight. "Got a cigarette?"

"Sorry. I don't smoke." Traci wished she did—anything to mask the acrid stench of cheap wine and wet vomit on the old woman's blouse and blanket.

"Shit." Mary edged back and leaned against the hot bricks of the building. She pulled the blanket to her neck.

"Let's start with the attacker," Traci said. "What can you tell me about him? About how old was he?"

"Don't know how old he was. Come up behind and clobbered me. Knocked me down. Look." She lifted the bottom of the blanket, revealing deep lacerations on her left knee. The right knee was bruised and swollen. Puss oozed from several sores near the cuts where their scabs were scraped away. "Threw me down on the sidewalk then put it to me. Didn't see how old he was."

"Take a guess, Mary. It's important."

"Shit. Okay. Over twenty and under eighty."

"How do you know?"

"I don't know! You said take a guess an' I guessed!"

"I meant, how do you know he was over twenty and under eighty?"

Mary rubbed at her eyes. "I don't. You said guess. That's what I did."

Traci came down to one knee, closer to the woman. "Could you narrow it down a bit? Sixty years is a big range."

"No, I can't. He was a man. That's all."

Traci made a note on the crime report. "About how much did he weigh?"

"Are you sure you don't have a cigarette? I could really use a butt."

"No, ma'am. I don't have any. Could you give me an estimate as to how much he weighed? Approximately."

"He was on top of me, for chrissake. He was pumpin' me and pumpin' hard, too."

"Well, from being on top of you, could you get a sense of how much he might have weighed?"

"No, I can't! I'll ask next time, okay? I didn't weigh him. Maybe he was two hundred. Maybe one seventy-five. I don't know. All I could think about was that big boner goin' in an' outta me. That's all I was thinkin' about. I wasn't thinkin' about his weight."

"I understand. I know it was a traumatic experience for you. Did he say anything to you? Can you tell me anything about his voice?"

"What?"

"Did he say anything?"

The woman shook her matted cords of hair and frowned. "You mean did he whisper sweet nothin's in my ear while he was pourin' the pork to me? Did we discuss wedding plans? Shit like that?"

"Anything."

"Get real, Officer."

"Sergeant."

"Get real, Sergeant."

"He didn't say anything?"

"Nothin' I remember."

Traci jotted another note on the report. "How about jewelry?" she asked. "Did the man wear any rings or a necklace? A wrist watch?"

"A ring. Yeah. Maybe. Maybe he had a ring."

"Did you see what kind it was? Was it a wedding ring? A college ring? What?"

"I don't know. He hit me in the face." She ran a hand over her puffy face and eyes. "I might of seen it. Wasn't paying no never-mind."

"Which hand do you think it was on? Right or left?"

Mary pressed harder against the building then rubbed her back against the rough bricks in a tight circular motion. "Which hand? Maybe right. I don't know."

Traci made another note. "What race was he? Caucasian? Black? Asian? What?"

"White guy. A fuzzy white guy." She unscrewed the wine bottle and took another swallow.

"What do you mean 'fuzzy?'"

"Fuzzy. Furry. He had a lotta hair."

"Where? On his head?"

"On his body. Lots of hair. Thought a big dog was fuckin' me. Saint Bernard or somethin'."

"Did you see what color it was?"

"Nope, I didn't. It was dark. Jesus, I could use a cigarette." She looked around the sidewalk as she screwed the cap back on the bottle. "Hey! Dashboard!" She yelled to a man on her left, fifteen feet away. He was curled in a fetal position on the sidewalk. "Gimme a smoke! You owe me a smoke, you ugly S.O.B." She gave a short laugh. The man did not stir. She turned back to Traci. "He's got 'em. I know he's got 'em."

"We're almost done, Mary. You're doing great. You're being very helpful."

"Swell." She ran a hand over her sticky mat of hair and brushed it from her eyes.

"What can you tell me about his clothes?"

"Yeah. He had clothes."

"I meant what was he wearing? What *kind* of clothes?"

"Regular clothes. Coat. Pants. Prob'ly had shoes. Didn't see no shoes, though. Guess he had shoes but no shirt." She looked over at the man on the sidewalk. No movement.

"Do you remember the color of his pants or coat?"

"It was dark! I told you that! It was dark and, no, I don't know 'bout the colors. His clothes was old, that's all I know."

"Street clothes? Bowery clothes?"

"Bum's clothes."

Traci made another note. "Have you lived down here long, Mary?"

The woman stopped moving and the slits of her eyes narrowed in on Traci's. "An eternity," she said.

"I don't suppose you've seen the man before."

"Now, if I seen him before, don't you think I woulda told 'em at the hospital?"

"I had to ask, Mary."

"Well, it's a dumb question."

"Can you think of anything else? Anything that might help us catch the man who raped you?"

"Am I gonna get pregnant?" She rubbed her bloated stomach. "Did that asshole make me pregnant?"

"I don't know. The report indicates you were given a vaginal flush at the hospital but I don't know if you'll get pregnant."

Mary began to cry in soft sobs. She raised her crusty hands to her face and rubbed her eyes with the heels of her hands. "I can't get pregnant. I can't."

Traci patted the woman on her shoulder. "Can I do something for you, Mary? There's a counseling center a few blocks from here. It's free. Can I take you there?"

The woman's fleshy body shook as she sobbed harder.

Traci gave another pat then pulled a police department business card from her uniform shirt pocket. "Here's my card, Mary. My number's on it. Call me if I can do anything for you or if you can think of anything else. Okay?" She pushed the card between the woman's dirty fingers. "Call me anytime. If I'm not there, leave a message. Okay?"

Mary stopped shaking and dropped her hands. The card dropped to the blanket. "I ain't gonna call nobody." Her voice was low and firm. "You ain't gonna find him 'cause you ain't gonna look."

"Yes I am, Mary. That's why I'm here."

Mary again screwed her eyes into Traci's. "No you ain't, so stop the bullshit. When I first come to the Row ... 'bout ... God I don't know how long ago ... when I come here that first night was real cold an' me an' a fella were sharin' a bottle an' standin' in that alley there." She nodded to her right. "And a little guy, little Filipino guy an' a Spic started gettin' into it by that dumpster." She nodded again. "No more 'an eight feet from me. Then," her body gave a quick, violent shiver, "then the little guy takes a 'sparagus knife an' shoves it into the Spic's throat ... You ever seen a 'sparagus knife, Sergeant?"

"No."

"Well, it's got a long blade at the end of a rod an' wood handle an' the point ain't a point but cut across the end ... at an angle. Angled an' sharp to stab through the dirt an' slice off the 'sparagus spear below."

"Oh."

"That little Flip shoved it into the Spic's throat and out the back a his neck. Clean through. An' all the Spic could do was twitch an' wiggle against the dumpster 'cause the little guy was holdin' him real tight an' not lettin' him drop. You hear what I'm sayin' ?"

"I do."

"Then, after a while, the Spic stops wigglin' and the Flip picks him up and tosses him into the dumpster. Just like that." She made a heaving motion with her arms. "Then he turns an' looks at me an' my man an' stares ... holdin' that 'sparagus knife an' starin' at us.

Maybe a minute he stares, then he just turns away and walks outta the alley an' I thought, my God in heaven, I just seen a man get killed! Eight feet away! A man died eight feet away an' I thought this is unbelievable an' it would be in the papers as headlines the next day." She sighed. "An' the next day I found the papers an' nothin'. An' I looked the day after that an' the day after that an' nothin'. No news 'bout the Spic with the hole through his throat an' out the back. No news 'bout a dead bum in an alley dumpster. Lotsa news 'bout Donald Trump, though. Lotsa news 'bout Katherine Devonshire's daughter and her comin' out party. Lots a news 'bout the stock market but nothin', *not one damn word* 'bout the dead Spic in the dumpster on the Row. Not ... one ... damn ... word!"

"Mary, I can't—"

"No, Sergeant. Don't 'spect no call from me." She turned away. "Just leave me alone. Go away an' leave me be."

"I'm sorry, Mary. I'll go but I *will* look for the man who attacked you. I promise that to you."

"Whatever."

73

- 9 -

Tuesday

"Carl? Walsh here."

"Thornton," Massini said. "What happened? You were supposed to get back to me but you checked out without saying a word."

"Yeah, well--"

"Why didn't you call?"

"I've been busy."

"Busy? That's good."

"Right. So, I'm calling now to tell you I've got the eighty thousand. When do you want it?"

"You got the money? Where'd you get your hands on eighty thousand dollars so fast?"

"What do you care?"

"Well ... I don't, really. I just never thought.... But, hey, that's good. I'll let Phil know."

"Do that. And tell him I'll be taking my business to the Taj Mahal in the future, too."

"Now, Thornton. You know the Taj won't take care of you like we do at the Firebird."

74

"God, Carl. I sure hope not."

"So, you've got the eighty thousand," Massini said.

"You sound surprised."

"Well, yes ... uh ... quite frankly, I am."

"It wasn't too hard. To tell you the truth, Carl, I owe you a big debt of gratitude."

"How's that?"

"I got to thinking about what you and Phil wanted me to do and I thought, what the hell, why not? But then I thought why not do it just for myself?"

"You found a way?"

"Smooth as your tight ass, Carl."

"You got a stock?"

"Not *just* a stock. A gold mine."

"Well, I'm happy for you, Thornton. You wouldn't care to share the name with me, would you?"

"Not a chance."

"I understand." He paused, then, "That good, huh?"

"Better than good. Better than Cisco Systems ever dreamed of being a great company."

"What can I say, Thornton? I'm happy for you, of course. You deserve it."

"Aw, gosh, Carl. You make me melt when you get all syrupy like that."

"Really. It couldn't happen to a nicer guy. I hope you make a ton."

"Oh, I'll make a ton, alright."

"That's great."

"Cut the crap, Carl. I know you're pissed. You and Phil set me up and somehow it isn't quite turning out like you wanted. So just tell me how you want the eighty gee's. I'll send a check or have my bank wire it. It's up to you."

"Uh … let me get back to you on that, Thornton. Will you be around?"

"I'll be right here but make it fast. I've got a lot to do to get the deal together and I'm running out of time."

"It'll just be a few."

They hung up.

Walsh grinned widely as he leaned back in his chair and pulled a fresh panatela from his desk. He drew the narrow cigar back and forth under his nose a few times to savor the aroma before moistening and lighting it.

"Hook, line, and soon the sinker," he said aloud. He took the first drag on the cigar without inhaling then blew a small ring of smoke into the air above his desk. It billowed wider and wider as it rose then drifted off and fell away. The only questions were how long would it take and who would call. His money was on Phil and it wouldn't take long.

Four minutes later, the phone rang.

"Thorny, Thorny, Thorny," Phil gushed. "What's all this talk about the Taj?"

"Well, now my day's complete," Walsh said.

"You think The Donald is going to care two cents about you? You think he's going to give you a beautiful suite at the last minute like we do here at the Firebird? And the girls? You think he's going to give you the pick of the line? This is your *home*, Thorny. We're *family*."

"Family, Phil? You must be talking about the Addams family. You can't be talking about any family I've ever known."

"Well—"

"But maybe that's how it works in *your* family. Tell me, Phil. You gather your kids together, then sit around and put the screws to each other to see who screams first? Is that how it is in *your* family?"

"You're absolutely right, Thorny. It was wrong of me to do that to you. I was thinking only of myself and that was the wrong thing to do."

"You're goddamn right it was wrong, Phil. You and Carl fucked me at the tables and then you tried to stick it to me again."

"You're right, you're right. We did all that. I admit it. I feel terrible about it and I'm going to make it up to you."

"How's that, Phil? You going to spring for a free breakfast in your coffee shop? Or did you figure out some other way to get me into hock to you boys? Just what did you have in mind, Phil? How're you going to screw me, now?"

"You're upset. I can tell. And you've got every reason to be. The fact is, I like you Thorny and—"

"Yeah, and I— "

"Hear me out, Thorny. Just hear me out, if you will. Please?"

"Alright, I'll listen but make it snappy. The market's closing in a few hours and I've got to make some calls and get some trades in."

"I will, Thorny. I won't take long ... I *can't* take long." He paused. "It's the big C, Thorny. It's eating me up and I don't think right. I'm desperate and the cancer makes me do desperate things. Things like I tried to do

77

to you. It's turned me into a monster. You know I wouldn't have done that if I was well."

Walsh said nothing. A vision of Phil's baby-face and his famous *woe-is-me* look flashed by. His lower lip would be quaking.

"You do know that. Don't you?" Phil said.

"I don't know shit, Phil. I thought I did. I thought I added up to more than a zero in your book but you do stupid things like sending Solly after me a while back and now you do this. You give me one marker after the next when you know I'm on a losing streak and insult me even more by trying to get me to do something that'll put my ass in prison. I don't know shit about what's going through your alleged brain. After what we've been through, I don't know how you could do this to me." Walsh took a long drag on his cigar and slowly blew the smoke out. "So, the answer to your question is 'no.' I don't know you wouldn't try to screw me—cancer or no cancer."

"I can see how you might look at it like that, Thorny. You've made your point and I'm going to make it up to you. So forget about the money. Forget about the eighty thousand. Here, listen."

The phone clanked down and then came the sound of paper tearing.

"Did you hear that?" Phil said, coming back on the line. "I just tore up your markers. They're history. All eight of 'em. I'm throwing 'em away. I don't want your money. I did a terrible thing to you and I don't want the money."

"You don't want it? Just like that, you don't want it?"

"That's right. You keep it. Keep the eighty thousand and be happy. Okay?"

Bingo! The sinker.

"Gee, Phil. I don't know what to say."

"Don't say anything. I want to do this for you. Make it up to you, like I said. Alright?"

"What about your stockholders?"

"I run things here, Thorny. I'll take care of them."

"Well, I—"

"We're friends?" Phil asked.

"How couldn't we be with a gesture like that?"

"And you'll forget all that talk about going to the Taj, right?"

"Who needs the Taj Mahal when I've got pals like you and Carl looking after me?"

"There you go."

"Okay, Phil. It's all forgotten."

"Good. It's this cancer thing, Thorny. It's been a terrible burden. The doctors ... they don't know what to do and I've seen the best, the very best. But their answers are all the same ... and they're not good. It's taking its toll on me. It's *killing* me."

"I heard, Phil. Carl told me your prostate was shot and I was sorry to hear about that. Can I make some calls for you? There might be someone up here who can help."

"No. I appreciate that. I really do. It's just too late."

"How much time do they give you?"

"Six months, maybe nine. A year at the outside."

"That's rough."

"Sure, it's rough. Damn rough. It took a while but I've finally accepted it, come to terms with my early mortality. But you know what the worst part is?"

"Your kids?"

"Kids? Oh, yeah, sure, the kids, yeah. No. They're taking it okay but worse than that, what's really worse than that is all I can do is sit here and count the hours until I'm dead. That's the worst of it. The waiting."

Walsh smiled and took another drag on his cigar. "Gee, Phil, why are you sitting around? Why aren't you getting out and enjoying yourself?"

"I'd love nothing more, Thorny. Do you remember that week we spent in Barcelona after getting discharged? Before coming back stateside?"

"Who could forget? We had one helluva fabulous good time, didn't we? And even lived to tell about it."

Both laughed.

"I was going through some boxes in the garage the other day, Thorny, and came across some of those pictures we took twenty-five years ago and, God, did those memories fly right in."

"Yeah. That was a helluva kick. Except the part when I got arrested."

They laughed again.

"I want to do it again," Phil said. "I need to go back again and have some fun ... before my ticket gets punched. Before it's too late."

"You should, Phil. You owe it to yourself to do that."

"I know I do but I can't."

"Why not? Your kids are grown. You're not married anymore. What's keeping you?"

"One word. Money."

Walsh smiled and took another long drag on the cigar. "Hell, Phil. I'll advance you some money. How much do you need? Five thousand? Ten thousand? Just tell me how much and it's yours."

Phil laughed loudly. "You're priceless, Thorny, really priceless."

"More?" Walsh asked. "How about twenty? You should be able to have a pretty good time in Barcelona on twenty thousand."

"I appreciate your offer, Thorny, I really do but twenty thousand wouldn't even see me through the week. I'll need a lot more than that. A helluva lot more."

"Okay, Phil. What is it? You want the eighty thousand? Is that what you're after?"

"No. Forget the eighty thousand. I told you that's behind us."

"Well, what, then?"

"I'm almost embarrassed to ask. If I was well we wouldn't even be having this conversation but I'm not well. I'm dying, Thorny, and I'm broke and I'll go crazy if I just sit around and do nothing. You can understand that."

"Sure."

"I have to get away. I have to have some fun. Go back to Barcelona and have some fun … like we did in the old days after we got out of the navy. I *have* to do it."

"Of course, you have to. So, what can I do to help?"

"I'm going to need a lot of money, Thorny, and Carl told me you've got a deal coming up. The deal he talked to you about last week."

"True."

"I want in. It's a dying man's wish. You can't deny a dying man's wish."

"Ask me something else, Phil. Ask me to do anything else and it's yours. Let me make some calls for you. Maybe there's a doctor up here or a machine or something. They're coming out with new stuff to treat cancer every day. Maybe there's something new here your doctors haven't heard about. Let me—"

"Thornton!"

"What?"

"Have you heard anything I've been telling you?"

"Of course."

"Then stop with the doctor shit. You're starting to piss me off. There aren't any machines and I don't want you to make any calls. Am I getting through to you, sailor?"

"Loud and clear."

"Good. Now I'll put it as simple as I can. I want in on your deal. The same deal Carl talked to you about Friday night."

"I'm sorry, Phil. I just can't."

"You owe me, Goddammit!"

"I *owe* you? How's that? I owe you because you forgave the eighty thousand debt you and Carl screwed me into? I owe you because we're old navy pals who had a few laughs in Spain after the war? What, Phil? Tell me why I owe you."

"You ungrateful prick! You know Goddamn well why you owe me!"

"Roberta and I are divorced, Phil. You can't hurt me with any of that now."

"I kept my mouth shut a lot of years for you, Thorny, and that's worth something."

"Something, sure. But not this deal. Not this."

"God damn you! I'm trying to be nice and what do I get? I tear up your markers and pour my heart out to you and what do you do? You stomp all over it. You ungrateful cocksucker!"

Walsh leaned forward in his chair. "Okay, okay. Don't have a coronary, too, for chrissake. I'll cut you in but on my terms, not yours."

"And *wha*t, exactly, are *your* terms?"

"Carl said you can get your hands on five hundred thousand. Wire it up here and I'll cut you a check for three million by Tuesday of next week."

"You've got to be joking. I'm not letting half a million out of my sight for a heartbeat, and I'm certainly not settling for three million. I want five million. You tell me the stock and I'll take it from there."

"No deal."

"And why's that?"

"'Cause you'll screw it up and we'll all end up as cellmates in Sing Sing, that's why."

"You don't have to worry about my end. I'll make sure your name never comes up."

Walsh laughed. "Sure you won't."

"You'll have to trust me on that."

"I don't trust my mother and I absolutely don't trust you. I control the deal or there isn't any deal."

Silence.

"The deal's sound?" Phil asked finally.

"As the dollar used to be."

More silence.

"Alright," Phil said. "But I get four million."

"I'm not going to negotiate on that," Walsh said. "You get three million and that's final."

"You prick! Alright. Three million but you goddamn-well better come through."

"It's money in the bank. In fact, you can make out the deposit slip the same time you're arranging the wire."

"No wire."

"You don't seem to understand, Phil. I need your money right now. Today! It has to be wired or it won't get here in time."

"You'll have it. Solly will bring it."

"Solly? Why Solly?"

"You don't trust me. I don't trust you."

"Okay, whatever. Just have him here before 3:30 or the deal's off."

"He'll be there."

"Three-thirty. Not a minute later," Walsh repeated.

"I *said* he'll be there. And he'll be watching you, too, so don't screw up."

Phil slammed down the phone.

- 10 -

Walsh thrust a hand up and waved. "Ben. Over here."

Ben Weinstein threaded between the small tables in the crowded Chock Full o' Nuts coffee shop. Though thirty-three, an unfailing grin, deep dimples and an out of control cowlick gave him the appearance of a man many years younger, all of which earned him the affectionate moniker of 'Lollipop' by his colleagues at Mouldine, Lloyd & Silver, a brokerage firm a block down Wall Street from Herschel & Wicks. "Hey, kiddo," Ben said. He pulled a chair out and sat across from Walsh. The grin widened over his tanned face. "How're they hangin'?"

"Good. Real good." Walsh extended a hand and Ben shook it vigorously. "Thanks for coming," Walsh said.

"No problem but why'd you pick this place? Nobody from the Street comes here. I can't even get a sandwich."

"Forget about your career for a minute." Walsh glanced around the room. "I wanted our little meeting to be private, away from Street people."

"Sure. Okay. Should watch my weight, anyway. What's up?"

"I need a large, Benny."

"Sure. Name it."

"I just got this big client and I need your help on a trade. I can't do it at Herschel and I'm asking you to run it through your house. Will you do it?"

He shrugged. "Don't see why not. What's the deal?"

Walsh inhaled deeply then let it out with a rush. "The stock's thin, only trades about twenty-five thousand shares a day and my client wants ten times that amount. I called Chemical Bank, their transfer agent, and they tell me you've got that much in one of your institutional accounts."

"Okay. What's the company?"

Walsh glanced around the room again, then leaned half-way across the table. "Pride Pet Foods," he whispered.

Ben laughed. "Pride? That piece-a-shit? This is a joke, right?" He rocked back and clapped his hands. "That's rich." He laughed some more.

Walsh scowled and waved a hand for Ben to lower his voice. "No joke," he said.

Ben stopped. The sparkle left his brown eyes and he straightened. "You're serious? You've got some nut who wants to pick up two hundred and fifty thousand shares of Pride Pet Foods?"

"Dammit, Benny! Keep your voice down." Walsh set his forearms on the table and leaned in at the man. "Will you do it?"

Ben cocked his head to one side. "What's going on, Thorny? Is there something happening with Pride I don't know about?"

"Nothing."

"Then why the hell would your client want a big block of their stock?"

"Beats me," Walsh said. "Maybe he wants a tax loss. I didn't ask."

"You didn't *ask?*"

"Look, Benny, I'm not going to question the intentions of someone who comes to me with a trade that size. Would you?"

Ben flicked a hand out. "I see your point."

"So, will you do it?"

"Well, sure. Let me think a minute." He drummed his manicured fingernails on the table. "Yeah." He stopped drumming. "They'll probably give it up. Sure. They'd probably *love* to give it up. Teamsters, I think. Pipe Fitters union pension fund, if I remember correctly. I think they've got more, though. If they've got more, do you want more?"

"No. Thanks, anyway. I'm working on a dollar amount."

"Okay. I understand. I don't even follow Pride anymore. Where's it at?"

"Twenty minutes ago, it was one and three-quarters at two."

Ben laughed. "Good. I'll kick it to you at one and seven-eighths and you can stick it to your client at two. The Pipe Fitters'll think I'm a hero."

Walsh shrugged. "Whatever."

"We'll split the eighth," Ben said, "fifty-fifty." He tilted his head up and smiled. "That's a little over thirty grand."

Walsh sat back. "You keep it," he said

"What?" Ben's eyes widened. "You'd give up fifteen thou for the trade? Who's the client? Some broad you're trying to schtup?"

Walsh frowned. "It's not some broad. I can't tell you who it is."

"I don't understand. Why give up the split?"

"I have my reasons. Okay? Let it go at that."

"For thirty grand, it's gone."

"You've got to do the trade off the tape, though," Walsh said. "I want it done quietly. It has to be a stealth trade."

"Sure. No problem. I can do that."

"Another thing. I want you to put the shares in a nominal account. No name. Leave it in your house account."

Ben slumped in his chair. "*That's* a problem. What am I supposed to tell Richards when he sees two hundred and fifty thousand shares of Pride Pet Foods, of all things, floating around in the house account? He'll think I've gone soft in the head."

"Tell him there's a player to be named later. You can do that."

"For IBM, I could do that. For General Motors, I could do that. Pride's a different story. It's crap. He'd never go for it." Ben shook his head. "What about the money? He'll match the trade with the wire and the cat'll be out of the bag."

"There won't be a wire. It's a cash deal."

"You mean a check."

"No, cash."

Ben's eyes widened. "Your client's going to bring me half a million in *cash*?"

"The coin of the realm, Benny. U. S. currency."

"Jesus, Thorny. This is getting weird." He chewed at his lower lip. "You're going to get me in trouble. Give me a couple of days to think about it."

"Today, Benny. I need it done today."

"Today? No. Not possible. Forget it. Even if I did want to do it, which I'm inclined not to now, I'd need time to set it up. Get approval. You know the drill. No. Forget it. I can't do it today."

Walsh glanced at his watch. "It's two-thirty. You've got an hour and a half to put it together."

Ben leaned in. "I guess you didn't hear me, Thorny. I said forget it for today."

Walsh rapped the table once with his knuckles. "This is important to me, Ben. I know you can do this for me. I *need* you to do this for me."

"I'd love to help you out, Thorny. You know I would but I smell trouble on this."

"Not even for thirty thousand?"

"Hell, that's not hardly enough if it costs me my license."

"Shit, Ben, I got you your damn job. You owe me big time."

"You made a phone call is all. *I'm* the one who got me my job."

"The call got you in the door. That's worth a lot in itself. You owe me for that, at least."

Ben shook his head. "How many times are you going to bring that up? How many times have I thanked you already? Jesus, I don't believe you're still tossing that in my face."

Walsh grimaced, then nodded. "Okay. Forget it. You're right. I'm sorry."

"I'd like to forget it, if you'd only let me."

"Okay, okay." Walsh fell quiet.

Ben frowned and looked away as he drummed his fingers again.

"How's Ann?" Walsh asked.

"The wife's good," he said without looking at Walsh.

"Great. That's great. She still active in the gardening club?"

"Still got her hands in dirt." He kept drumming.

"Hey, I'm sorry about bringing that up about your job."

"Forget it."

"Of course you're the one who got it. What's the big deal about a phone call, anyway. Right?"

"You're too much, Thorny. Too much."

Walsh ignored the comment. "And Sarah and little Ben? How're they doing?"

Ben's face brightened. He looked up. "Super. Really super. Sarah started pre-school last month and Ben's in Indian Guides. He loves it. We do a lot of stuff together. It's a great organization."

"I've heard that and I'm glad you're spending time with your son."

"You bet."

Walsh paused, then said, "You sure you won't do the deal? Help me out on the trade?"

"I'd love to, Thorny, I really would but I can't. You know Richards. He'd shit bricks if I did an end-around on him. Platinum bricks."

Walsh took a gulp of coffee and held the cup in his hands. He turned it slowly from side to side and stared at it as though it were a rare fossil. Then he looked up and locked his gaze onto Ben's. "Let me ask you something."

"Sure. What?"

"I can't figure it out and it's been keeping me awake nights."

"What?"

"Is it the 'B' part or the 'D' part that does it for you?"

Ben stopped drumming. "Huh?"

"You heard me. Is it the bondage or the domination that gets you off?"

"I, ah—"

"What are their names again? The twins?" Walsh rolled his eyes up as though trying to remember. "Oh, yeah. Mistress Sheila and Mistress Shilah. Real beautes, I'm told."

Ben shifted in his chair. "How do you know about the twins?"

"I know."

"I don't see the twins anymore."

"Cut the crap."

Ben turned away.

"I need a refill," Walsh said, standing. "What can I get for you?"

Ben said nothing.

"Regular?"

Ben sighed.

"I'll get you regular."

Walsh strode to the sales counter. He returned with two cups of coffee with cream and sat.

"Tell me something," Walsh said. "How do you think little Ben would feel if he knew his daddy was into whips and chains? Might be something for show and tell at his school, don't you think? Or maybe share with the other kids at Indian Guides?"

Ben jerked forward, jarring the table and splashing hot coffee from his cup. "Listen here, Walsh. You say one fucking word to him—just *one*—and I'll kill you!"

Walsh thrust his hands up. "Don't worry about me, Benny. I wouldn't breathe it to a soul."

"You goddamn-well better not!"

Walsh dropped his hands and began to swab the coffee from the table with a fistful of paper napkins. "No, not me," he said. "I wouldn't *dream* of telling little Ben his daddy's into leather action. But…" he stopped cleaning and looked Ben in the eye "… then again, I don't have any control over Schroeder and there's just no telling what *that* jerk-off might say."

Ben slumped back and said nothing.

"Isn't Schroeder's wife in the same gardening club with Ann?" Walsh said.

Ben stared vacantly through the busy coffee shop.

Walsh looked at his watch. "Well, this has been nice, Benny, but I've got to find someone who'll do the deal for me and time is getting short." He pushed his chair back and stood. "Say 'hi' to Ann and your kids for me." He turned to leave.

Ben caught the sleeve of Walsh's suit jacket and tugged. "Sit down, Thorny."

- 11 -

Boston

"Mind if I sit with you a few minutes?" Traci asked.

Carla looked up from her tray of food. A shallow, three-inch-long laceration stretched from the corner of her swollen left eye to her ear. It was healing poorly. "I got a feeling I ain't got much of a choice," she said. "Go ahead." She nodded at the empty chair across from her and resumed eating.

Traci sat and watched the middle-aged Jamaican woman push the remnant of a baking powder biscuit around the edge of her plate, sopping up puddles of jelled brown gravy.

"I'm Sergeant Ross," Traci said. "Boston Police Department."

Carla glanced over her uniform. "Didn't think you was with the MTA."

"I won't take much of your time, Carla. I just want to ask you a couple of questions about the rape."

"Well, you're in luck. Secretary cleared my calendar for the mornin'."

Traci smiled, then unfolded the crime report and set it on the table in front of her.

"How are you doing, Carla? The experience must have been a horrible ordeal. Are you okay?"

She nodded though her black greasy dreadlocks did not budge. "Yeah. I'm okay. It ain't somethin' I'd care to go through again but I'm doin' alright."

"Do you need some counseling? Can I arrange something like that for you?"

"If you really want to help, you can leave me be. Okay?"

"I will, Carla. I've only got a few questions then I'll go."

"Good." Carla forked the gravy-laden roll into her mouth.

"It says here it happened at 2:47 in the morning. Are you sure of that?"

"Sure, I'm sure. What? You think I made it up?" She rubbed gravy from black hairs around her wide mouth with a crumpled napkin then shoved the napkin under the cuff of her blouse.

"No, not at all. I was only wondering how you could be so certain of the time. We almost never get reports with specific times like that and I was wondering how you could be so sure it was 2:47 and not, say, 2:45 or 2:50. Know what I mean?"

"I know what you mean. It was the sprinklers. That's how I know."

"Sprinklers?"

"Yeah, sprinklers."

"I don't—"

"Look, Sergeant." Carla stopped eating. Her wide-set brown eyes were glazed but alert. "I don't know how long you been a cop or where you done your job as a cop but obviously you ain't been a cop around here." She waved a hand at the room of derelicts gathered in the St. Vincent de Paul soup kitchen.

"That's true," Traci said. "I transferred here a month ago."

"Figured. Look, most of us ain't got no place an' we crash anywhere it ain't cold. Might be under a toll way, might be in a dumpster, might be in the alcove of a store. I got my squat at the door of the army surplus but the man don't like that and he put up a sprinkler to go on an' off. Try to keep me an' my kind away. That's how I know."

"He waters the sidewalk?"

"And the alcove."

"At two forty-seven in the morning?"

"An' five-thirty."

"That's terrible," Traci said.

Carla shook her head. "No, it ain't. It's good. Washes out the piss. Keeps my squat clean. Most times, like in the summer, I don't move much. The sprinkler feels real good in the summer, or like now, in the fall, if it's hot. Don't like it in the winter, though, when snow's on the ground. Don't like it then, at all."

"So, the time *is* accurate." Traci glanced at the report.

"Yeah. They'd just come on an' it was cool an' I was movin' my bedroll outta the way when the bastard jumped me. Got me all wet … him wet, too. Four minutes later, he was off. Sprinkler only runs four minutes. That's how I know how long he was doin' me."

Traci jotted a note on the report. "Did you get a look at him? It says here he was average height and weight."

"Is that what that says?" Carla snatched the report from the table. "I never told nobody that." She eyed the report then tossed it back to Traci. "Shit. Who put that in there?"

"Didn't the detectives talk to you?"

"Hell yes, they talked to me. 'Bout two minutes worth. Seemed like a big bother to 'em. I just shined 'em."

"What do you mean?"

"They says, was he an average man? I says no, he weren't no average man. They says, was there anything different 'bout him? I says yeah, there's lots different. Stuff like that."

Traci scanned the report. "I don't see…. Did they ask you what was different? Anything about that?"

"Shit, no. They was in a hurry. Didn't wanna waste their time with a bag lady like me. I just shined 'em. He ain't gonna get caught no-how, anyway."

"Why do you say that?"

"'Cause I know he ain't. No cop's gonna waste their time trying to catch a man what jumps a bag lady. That's how I know." She started to pick up her tray.

"*I'm* going to try," Traci said. "That's why I'm here. I'm going to do everything I can, Carla, but I'll need your help for a few more minutes."

The woman shrugged, then slumped back against her chair and sighed. "Okay. Like I said. Got no 'pointments this mornin'."

"Have you seen this man before?"

"Couple a times. Lonely man. Sticks to hisself. Ugly, lonely man. Ain't no woman wanna tumble with him, if you know what I'm sayin'."

Traci nodded. "Sure. Do you know his name?"

She shook her head no. "Anyways if I did it wouldn't be his real one. Nobody uses their real ones down here."

"Sure. Then let's start with his age. How old do you think he was?"

"Thirty. Give or take."

"Give or take what?"

"A year or two. No more than that."

"How about his race?"

"Beaner."

Traci frowned.

"Sorry. *La-tin-o*."

"How tall was he?"

"'Bout five-five. Maybe five-six. Short man. Stinky and short. His dick weren't short, though." Her thick brows wrinkled as she nodded. "That sucker was *big*."

"How about his weight. What do you think he weighed?"

"'Round a hundred twenty-five. Maybe less. Not heavy. He ain't been down on his luck for long."

"How do you know?"

"Stomach was flat. Ain't been down here long enough to bloat up on starch from the kitchens or parasites from the dumpsters. 'Less he's got worms."

She cocked her head to one side, thinking. "Might have worms."

"Did he wear any jewelry?"

She touched the laceration near her eye. "Must've had somethin' to make this. Didn't see what it was, though."

Traci leaned in for a closer look at the cut along the woman's large head. "You've got to keep that clean," she said. "Would you like me to take you back to the hospital and have them clean that up for you, Carla?"

"Naw. I'll live. Thanks."

"Are you sure? It wouldn't take long."

Her eyes bulged and glared at Traci. "I *said* I'm *fine!*"

"Okay. Sorry."

"Don't have to be sorry. Don't want to go back there, that's all."

"Okay. Uh … anything else you can remember about him physically?"

"If you're gonna keep talkin', I'm gonna get me some more coffee." She pushed her chair back. "Want anything?"

"Sure, but let me get it."

Carla smiled. "That'd be nice. And I'll have a sweet roll, too."

"I'll be right back."

Traci brought the roll and two coffees—one black and the other with cream and sugar—to the table and sat. She kept the black one. "Did you remember anything else about the way he looked?"

"Couple a things. He was losin' a lotta hair for bein' so young. Thought that was kinda odd for a beaner … uh, Latino. And his voice was real deep. Like a radio announcer's got. You know the kind?" She began to open packets of sugar.

"You may want to taste that, first," Traci said.

Carla took a sip. "Almost right." She smiled.

"What did he say to you? Do you remember his words?"

"Like they was tattooed under my eyelids. To remind me every time I blinked."

"Yes?"

"He says, 'this ain't personal.' Can you believe it?" She leaned forward. "If fuckin' ain't personal, I don't know what is. An' he said it so eerie ... with that low, deep voice, like paparazzi."

"Pavarotti."

"Who?"

"You mean the tenor. Pavarotti."

"Yeah. Like him." She poured four packets of sugar into her coffee and stirred it in with a finger.

"Did he say anything else?"

"Nope. Just got his rocks and left." She slurped a gulp of coffee through a gap in her front teeth where two were missing.

"You said you saw him before. Do you remember where that was?"

"Yeah, I seen him but it was a while ago an' I don't 'member where. Don't know where he hangs now."

"Okay. Anything else you do remember?"

"Nope. Can't think of nothin'." She slurped again at the coffee.

"How long have you been here, Carla? How long have you been homeless?"

The woman threw her head back and gave a low, throaty laugh. "Homeless? Who?" She poked a long finger at her chest. "Me?"

Traci glanced around the large, busy dining room then brought her eyes back to Carla's. "Did I say something funny?" she asked.

Carla offered a wide, toothless smile. "Lady, you got lots to learn. I ain't homeless." She made a sweeping motion with her hand at a neighboring table of men and women who were quietly eating. "Hey, Shirley." She spoke to a short Caucasian woman of about fifty at the next table. "You homeless, Shirley?" The woman looked up at Carla, grunted something unintelligible, then turned back to her food. Carla eyed Traci. "Me an' them ain't homeless, lady. We's *houseless* but we ain't homeless. The Row's our home." Carla swiped a lock of greasy hair from her face and leaned forward. "Lemme axe you somethin', lady. Did you see a fence around the Row when you come down here today? Big fence with a gate maybe?"

Traci wrinkled her brow. "No ... uh ... no there's no fence. Why do you ask?"

"Just checkin'. Wondered if maybe someone put up a fence so we couldn't walk out if we wanted."

"I don't understand."

Carla took another slurp of coffee. "Did ya happen to notice those pigeons on the sidewalk outside? Did ya see them scrawny, scruffy pigeons there, peckin' away at God knows what?"

"Yes, I saw them. They looked awful."

"Ah," Carla said, nodding.

"What are you saying, Carla? A fence? Pigeons? I don't understand."

"What I'm saying, Sergeant, is them pigeons can fly away anytime they want, fly anywhere their tiny heart's desire but they don't. They stay right here on the Row. Just like me." She waved a hand around the room. "Just like all of us. You understand? You get what I'm telling ya?"

"I'm beginning to."

"We *gots* a home, Sergeant. The Row's our home. We *ain't* homeless."

Traci nodded. "I see what you're saying. I didn't know. Thank you for telling me."

"You're welcome." The woman sat back and wiped coffee from her lips.

Traci pushed her chair back and gave the woman her card. "I'm going to do everything I can to find the man who attacked you, Carla. Will you call me if you think of anything else or if you see him again?"

Carla studied the card and sighed. "What the hell. Why not?"

Traci rose and started to leave, then stopped. "I almost forgot. You said he was short and stinky. Stinky how?"

"His breath," she said. "Stunk real bad. Smelled like a dog's breath."

- 12 -

"Mr. Walsh?" Alice said over the intercom. "There's someone here to see you."

Walsh checked his watch. Three-ten. "Who is it, Alice?"

"He won't give his name. He said he has a three-thirty but I don't see a three-thirty in your book."

"Is he a big, dumb-looking guy?"

"*Huge*, dumb-looking guy," she whispered back.

"You can send him in, Alice."

Ten seconds later, Solly squeezed through the doorway and lumbered into the office. He was a living steamer trunk with thick arms and legs and a red crew cut above a fat, oval face. His enormous frame dwarfed the aluminum-sided suitcase he carried. He heaved it onto Walsh's desk without regard for the neat arrangement of papers and other items already on it.

"Count it," Solly said.

"Nice earrings," Walsh said as he unsnapped the two clasps and raised the lid. "I'll have to ask your boyfriend where he got 'em."

Solly scowled.

Walsh looked inside the open suitcase. Stacks of neatly bundled hundred-dollar bills filled it completely. "It'll take me a week to count this," Walsh said. He poked a hand around the money. "Looks like it's all here."

"Sign this," Solly said. He held up a slip of paper.

Walsh took it and gave it a quick look. "Phil wants a receipt? I don't think that's a very bright idea."

"Nobody cares what you think. Sign it."

Walsh scribbled his name at the bottom of the paper and gave it back.

"Phil said to give you this," Solly said. He passed a sealed envelope. Walsh opened it. The eight, torn, ten-thousand-dollar casino marker checks were inside.

"Tell Phil thanks," Walsh said. He stuffed the envelope into his back pocket then moved around to the front of the desk. "Well, I know you're probably in a hurry to get back to Atlantic City, so I won't keep you. Have a nice trip."

"I ain't goin' nowhere, funny boy. I stay with the money."

"Suit yourself but you're not staying in my office and you're not staying in this building. We have appearances to keep." Walsh waved with the back of his hand. "Run along outside, now. Pretend you're a refrigerator or something."

Solly grunted and turned to leave. "Uh, almost forgot," he said. "This is from Phil, too." He shot an enormous fist through the air. It hammered Walsh's nose. Walsh screamed and staggered back, banging his hip against the desk. He grabbed his face. Blood squirted between his fingers and quickly ran onto the front of his starched white shirt.

"What was that for?" Walsh yelled at the beast.

"A reminder, funny boy. Don't even think about doin' somethin' cute."

The door opened and Alice peered in. She gasped.

"Your boss needs a couple a tampons for his nose," Solly said as he lumbered past her on his way out.

"Mr. Walsh!" She ran over to him. "What happened?"

"Get some ice in a towel, will you?"

"Did that man— "

"Now? Please?"

Walsh moved behind his desk as Alice hurried away. He slowly sunk into the chair and tilted his head back. Jeez, that guy could hit! Was that a fist or a bowling ball? He tried to move his nose from side to side but needles of excruciating pain lanced his brain. Probably broken, he thought. He punched his speed-dialer.

"Benny."

"Who's this?"

"It's me. Walsh." He winced.

"You sound different," Ben said. "Didn't recognize your voice."

"Forget about that. Did you get it?"

"Still working on it."

"What do you mean you're still working on it?" He checked his watch. "The market's closing in twenty-eight minutes. You've got to get it done. Now!"

"Jesus, Thorny. I'm trying my best. I can't get a hold of the Union's treasurer. I've left messages all over the place, put in pages to him, sent texts and everything. He hasn't called back and he's the only one who can bless the trade. I can't do it without his okay."

"Goddammit, Benny. Do it! With or without him. Just do it! Tell him about it later if you have to. Just do the freakin' trade. Now!" He slammed the phone down as Alice whirled back into the office with the ice and towel.

"You ought to lie down," she said.

"I'll be fine." Walsh flushed as he gingerly set the ice pack around his nose.

"Is it broken?" she asked.

"Probably."

"I'll call your doctor and make him take you right away."

Alice dashed off. Two minutes later, the phone rang.

Ben whispered. "It's done."

"Good work."

"Yeah, great. I sure the shit hope you know what you're doing. The SEC is bad enough. I don't want the teamsters after me, too."

"Relax, Benny. You said yourself Pride's a piece of shit. Just tell the teamsters you saw a chance to get them out and took it. They'll thank you for it. It's all under control. Relax."

"I sure hope you're right."

"I am. Now, send over one of your clerks to pick up the money. Make sure he's big enough to carry it."

"That's too much cash. I'll have Brink's come over."

"Not necessary. Just send a clerk."

106

"Damn, Thorny. You're talking half a million. I'm not going to trust that much cash to a clerk for chrissake."

"Stop worrying. He won't run off with it. There's somebody who'll make sure of that."

"What're you talking about?"

"Never mind. Just send your clerk."

"Alright. How long do I have to hide the stock?"

"No more than a week."

"A week? I can't do that. Not a week."

"For a thirty-thousand-dollar commission you'll find a way."

"Christ, Thorny. You're gonna get my ass in a sling for sure."

"One more thing. Call Chemical Bank. Tell them to hold off on journaling over the certificate for a few days. I'll call you with a name when it's time."

He hung up.

- 13 -

Wednesday

Walsh breezed into his office. "Good morning, Alice."

She looked up from her desk and cupped a hand to her cheek. "Oh, my. Was it broken?"

"'Fraid so." He gingerly touched the metal splint and white bandages covering his swollen nose. "Do I look horrible?"

"No, sir. I wouldn't say horrible but with two black eyes and that white bandage, you do look rather Halloweenish."

"That's okay with me. Nothing's going to bother me today."

"I do admire your attitude, sir. Does it hurt?"

"Not too much. Thanks for asking. Tylenol with codeine helps. Anything I should know?"

She stood and handed him a thick, manila folder. "I put the files together for your meeting with Mr. Stevens and the board this morning, and there're a few messages. Only one sounded important. They're on your desk."

"Efficient as always. Thanks, Alice. Now, if you'll just find some coffee I'll be ready for anything."

"Coming up, sir."

She hurried away as Walsh stepped into his private office and sat behind the desk. He quickly thumbed through the small stack of messages, tossing two from his ex-wife into the trash. He turned to one from Ben Weinstein marked 'urgent.' He punched the speed-dialer.

"Just got in, Benny. What's going on?"

"He's all over me, Thorny. I've gotta get rid of that stock!"

"Hold on a second. You're talking so fast I can't understand you."

"My boss, Thorny! Richards! When he came in this morning and saw the trade all hell broke loose. I gotta bust the trade."

"What?"

"I gotta put that two hundred fifty thousand shares of Pride back into the Pipefitters Union pension fund account."

"What are you talking about?"

"You remember I told you I couldn't get a hold of their treasurer yesterday?"

"Yeah, yeah."

"Richards was playing' *golf* with him, for chrissake! That's why I couldn't get him. Of all the freakin' luck."

"I don't understand how that changes anything."

"He *knows*, Thorny. You dumb shit! Richards knows I couldn't possibly have gotten the okay to make the trade because he was with the treasurer all afternoon. I'm fucked!"

"Hold on, Benny. Settle down. Let's think about this a minute."

"We don't have time to think. I've got to do something *now*. This minute! Don't you understand? I don't have discretion over that account. I can't just make a trade whenever I feel like it. I've got to get approval first. Have you ever been down to their union hall?"

"Well, no..."

"I have and I've seen those guys that hang out down there. They're gorillas, Walsh, and they're not polite. They'll bust *me* if I don't bust the trade. Richards is gonna be coming out of his office any second and he's gonna have my balls for breakfast. He's gonna want to know why I did the trade without authorization and where the money came from to buy it. Jesus, Thorny. Five hundred thousand dollars *cash*? Who does business like that? Nobody legitimate, that's for shit-sure. Richards knows that. You know that. I know that. I'm fucked, Thorny. You're gonna take a big fall on this, too."

"Okay, okay. Hold on. How about this? How about calling the treasurer right now and telling him you did the trade with his best interests in mind and get him to go along with it? Can you do that?"

"How the hell do you expect me to do that? What could I possibly tell him? He'll think I'm some kind of maverick and have my ass fired. No. I gotta bust the trade, if Richards hasn't done it already."

Walsh punched up the quote on Pride. "There's no change on the price. It's still one and three-quarters at two. The last trade was at three-quarters."

"So what? Goddammit, Thorny! I *knew* this was gonna be trouble."

"Calm down, will you? I'm thinking." He punched the keys on his Quotron for the volume and size. "Only thirty-five hundred shares have traded. Richards hasn't done anything yet. Nobody's caught wind of it, yet. The size is a hundred by five hundred."

"I see him, Thorny. Richards is coming out of his office right now! What do I do? What do I tell him?"

"Get up. Right now, Benny. Get up from your desk and take the treasurer's number with you. Go down to the lobby but take the stairs. Got it?"

"Yeah. Lobby. Then what?"

"Use a pay phone. Do *not* use your cell. Call the treasurer and tell him you sold his quarter-million shares yesterday at one and seven-eighths."

"Are you nuts? That's the most ridiculous—"

"Do it! Do it, Benny. Now! Take the stairs. Go!"

Walsh hung up, then quickly dialed Herschel and Wicks' trading desk. He barked an order to the trader, hung up and lit a fresh panatela as Alice delivered his cup of coffee.

"Problem?" she asked.

"Nope. Everything's everything." He took a sip of the coffee, then began to review his notes for the meeting. Ten minutes later, Alice told him Ben was waiting on line two.

"Walsh," Ben said, "you're a damn genius!"

"Everything's okay?"

"Are you kiddin'? Richards wants to give me a bonus. Can you believe it? It's almost embarrassing."

Walsh smiled. "That's nice, Benny. And the teamsters are okay with what you did?"

"Okay? Hell, when the treasurer saw the price had dropped a half a point and I'd saved them a hundred and twenty-five thousand dollars, I thought the guy was going to crawl through the phone and kiss me. Jesus, Walsh, how did you ever think of that? Dumping a block on the market to kill the bid. That was sheer genius!"

"Stop slobbering, Benny. I told you everything was under control."

"Almost. We're not out of the woods yet. You gotta give me a name for the trade. Richards wants it out of the house account. I told him the transfer was in the works this morning, so give me a name."

"You're a royal pain in the ass, Benny. Alright. Call Chemical and give them 'Oscar Walsh.'"

"Oscar Walsh. Okay. Address?"

"Roseburg Oregon somewhere. I'll have Alice get back to you on that."

"Okay, that'll be enough for now."

"Gotta go, Benny. I've got a meeting in five minutes. Give the twins a kiss for me."

- 14 -

Walsh straightened in his chair when Schroeder stepped out of the boardroom. Two years earlier, Schroeder played quarterback for the New England Patriots. Now, he humped stocks for Herschel and Wicks at four hundred thousand a year. Stevens favored big, formidable-appearing men and Schroeder filled that bill nicely. Walsh resented such men for an advantage earned only by a quirk of nature.

"What the hell happened to you?" Schroeder asked. "She cross her legs?"

Walsh smiled and lightly tapped around the bandages on his nose. "Had no idea your wife was so strong."

"Real funny, Walsh. Seriously. What happened?"

"Nothing really. Had a polyp removed."

Schroeder leaned in and squinted at Walsh's face. "Looks like it hurts. Does it hurt?"

"No. Thanks. I'm fine."

Schroeder straightened. "That's good. Anyway, sorry I ran over a bit but they're all warmed up. You should have an easy time of it."

"A bit?" Walsh checked his watch. "Thirty minutes over to be exact."

"Couldn't be helped. They were begging for more. Went along with every one of my recommendations. Like putty in my hands."

"No doubt about it, when you're good you're good." Walsh rose and shook his colleague's hand. "Of course, it helps if you've got something worth talking about."

"I know. I saw they gave you a lot of schlock after the merger and I'll take that up with Stevens, if you'd like. We're from the same alma mater, you know. Maybe we can move some of what we've got around. Kinda spread the wealth."

"Don't bother. I already tried and the idea wasn't well-received."

Schroeder shrugged. "Suit yourself. Let me know if you change your mind."

"They're ready for you, Mr. Walsh," the secretary said.

"Good luck," Schroeder offered.

"Thanks."

Walsh tucked his files under his arm and entered the boardroom.

"Come right in, my boy," Stevens said, smiling widely and motioning for him to sit on the opposite side of the polished oval table.

Walsh sat where he was told.

Stevens peered over the top of his wire-rimmed glasses. "What happened to your nose, lad? A gift from another satisfied client?"

Two men seated next to Stevens arched their brows.

"Just a polyp, sir. Had it removed last night."

"My aunt had that done once," Stevens said. "She didn't look like that when hers was removed."

"What can I say, sir. Gotta take the butchers the firm's medical plan allows."

"Yes, well…. Let's get started. You know Bradley, vice president of sales." Stevens motioned a thick hand at the impeccably dressed tall man with a crew cut on his left.

"Yes, sir."

Stevens nodded at the squat, older man on his right. "And Carmichael, Operations V.P."

"Good morning, sir," Walsh said. "How's Mrs. Carmichael?"

"Very good, thank you."

"Please let her know my thoughts are with her for a speedy recovery."

Carmichael nodded. "I'll do that, Thornton. She'll appreciate your concern."

"Uh-huh," Stevens said. "Now then, what have you got for us?"

"I'll run through it alphabetically," Walsh said, "if that's alright."

"That'll be fine, son."

"The first one is Bigelow Tire and it's running on a flat, pardon the pun. All the air there ever was in their future is being bled out for research on an airless tire. They can't seem to let go of it."

Carmichael glanced at Stevens, then back at Walsh. "What's an airless tire?"

"Malcolm Ripps, their president, only described it to me once a couple of years ago but I recall it involved placing corrugated strips of rubber spaced at intervals inside the tire where the air goes. The strips are supposed to give the tire all the characteristics of conventional tires, like ride and wear, but the tire won't go flat if it's cut or punctured."

"Sounds like a clever idea to me," Carmichael said.

"Conceptually, sir, yes, but not in practice. Several of the majors worked on an airless for a while, then gave it up. Their marketing people said the demand wouldn't be there because of the cost. Malcolm's still plugging away at it, though, and bleeding the company dry to support the R & D."

"What about their core business?" Carmichael asked. "Is that still solid?"

"Only so-so and that's what's been keeping them afloat so far. Any further downturn in sales will sink 'em fast."

"What are you proposing?" Bradley asked. A mouth-breather, his mouth hung open after the question.

"I offered to put the firm's M & A people in touch with Malcolm but he wouldn't hear of it. Right now we're carrying a 'hold' on their stock but I think it's time to cut them loose. The firm's credibility is at stake if we retain any rating at all on Bigelow in the face of Malcolm's refusal to listen to reason."

Carmichael scanned a sheet of paper on the table in front of him then looked up. "How are their overall sales and earnings?"

116

"That's another problem. Malcolm's preliminaries for the quarter are a loss of three cents on a sales drop of sixteen percent. That'll be their tenth consecutive quarterly decline."

"Seems pretty clear to me," Bradley said. "Any more discussion?"

"Not from me," Carmichael said.

"Alright, son," Stevens said. "We'll drop the rating." He pushed his glasses back up his bulbous nose and made a notation on Walsh's series list. "Let's hear about Carter Steel." He sat back and smiled. "What have you got for us on Carter?"

Walsh shifted in his chair. "Well, as you know Carter is one of those old-line foundries that developed a strong niche in the specialty cold-rolled steel market. Their sales and earnings have been growing every quarter at about eight percent sequentially for the last seven years."

Stevens' smile broadened.

Walsh considered telling Stevens his hairpiece was off-center but decided against it. "Unlike the Japanese," he said instead, "Carter hasn't frittered their money away on equipment upgrades and that's helped keep them in the black."

Bradley looked at the other men, then back at Walsh. "Sounds a bit dangerous," he said.

"Of course, sir."

"How long have they been using their current plant and equipment?" Carmichael asked. "That stuff must be about twenty years old by now."

"Twenty-eight years to be exact," Walsh said.

"Twenty-eight years? What are their plans for upgrading, Thornton? If you know."

"They don't have any, Mr. Carmichael, at least not in the foreseeable future."

Stevens shifted to one side of his chair. His smile disappeared. "I don't see that as a concern," he said, "not for the present, anyway. Foundry equipment has a very long service life and I'm sure Carter will replace it when they feel it's necessary."

"Just how long is the service life, Thornton?" Carmichael asked.

"About twenty or so years," Walsh said.

"Twenty years?" He glanced at Stevens, then back to the papers on the table in front of him. "I see we've got an accumulate rating on Carter. Where's the stock now?"

Stevens punched up the quote. "Twenty-one at a-half."

"And the P-E?"

"Sells at thirty-six times earnings," Walsh said.

"Thirty-six?" Carmichael leaned forward. "That's ludicrous. Shouldn't be any higher than eighteen, maybe twenty at the very most but certainly not thirty-six."

Bradley brought a hand to his cheek and stroked it lightly with his fingers. "Why are we recommending accumulate to our clients," he asked, "when their equipment is nearly thirty percent beyond its expected service life and their stock is trading at thirty-six times earnings? What price target are you projecting for their shares?"

Walsh felt the blood in his face rapidly flowing to the surface. Stevens looked at him with raised brows, his eyes widening.

"I'm looking for twenty-eight on the stock near term," Walsh said.

Carmichael eased back in his chair and folded his arms. "I'd certainly be interested in hearing why."

"A couple of reasons, sir. First of all, interest rates are low and housing starts are skyrocketing. I know Carter doesn't have much in the way of sales in the housing market right now but their small size is an advantage since they can adapt to change very quickly. Secondly, I'm also hearing a lot of talk about a possible labor strike. Carter has an advantage there, too, since the United Steel Workers will likely go after one of the majors, like Bethlehem or U. S. Steel, to get the greatest impact from a strike. Also, as you probably know, a good percentage of new-home construction now is being done with steel beams and two-by-fours instead of wood. If a strike materializes, and I think it will, Carter can be cranking out steel beams and studs in a matter of days."

Stevens stopped fidgeting and beamed. "Very good, lad," he said.

Carmichael shook his head. "I'm not so sure," he said. "Sounds like a lot of ifs to me."

"Let's just see how it all unfolds," Stevens said quickly. "It looks like Walsh has his fingers on all the pieces. Let's give it a chance."

"What'd you say we're carrying on Carter?" Bradley asked, looking down and poking at his set of papers.

"Accumulate, sir."

Stevens nodded at Walsh. "I believe your analysis warrants something a bit spicier than that, son. How about raising it to a buy? What would you say to that?"

"I'd say you'd be putting my ass in a sling."

Stevens jerked forward. "Of all the impertinence! You don't have the courage to stand by your projections? Are you here to waste our time? Is that what you're doing?"

"No, sir."

Carmichael and Bradley stared at Stevens.

Stevens shot out an arm and waved a finger at Walsh. "I've about reached the end of my rope with you," he said, "*and* your testy attitude! If you don't have the balls to stand behind what you've just been telling us, I'll find someone who will."

Bradley's jaw dropped. He turned to Stevens. "I don't think he was—"

"I'll handle this, Brad. Walsh belongs to me and I'll deal with him as I see fit."

"Okay," Walsh said, glaring back at Stevens. "You want me to recommend a buy? Fine. How about a super buy? Can I make a new category and do that? How about extraordinary buy? Or maybe—"

"Alright, alright," Bradley broke in. He motioned with long arms in front of him, palms down. "Let's all calm down. Obviously Thornton isn't comfortable with a buy rating at the moment, so let's just leave it where it is." He turned to Carmichael. The man nodded. Bradley looked at Stevens. "How about it? Are you okay with that?"

Stevens rapped the table once with his fist. "No! I'm *not* okay with that. Walsh comes in here and gives

120

us a glowing account of the prospects for Carter, then wants our clients to merely nibble away at it. I think the man ought to put his money where his mouth is and make a commitment. I think he ought to raise his rating and make the stock a buy or find some other line of work. *That's* what I think."

Bradley turned in his chair and cocked his head at Stevens. "Just how big *is* your position in Carter?" he asked. "Or is there something else we don't know about to make you push so hard for the buy rating?"

"Certainly not!" Stevens said.

"Then, what is it? I don't understand what's going on here. Carter's trading with a P-E of thirty-six, their equipment has to be falling apart by now," he waved a hand at Walsh, "and your man is only looking for another six points or so in the stock, *if* everything goes right. And that sounds like a real big question mark to me. So, what is it?"

Stevens dropped his gaze to the papers on the table in front of him.

"Is there something we're missing, Thornton?" Bradley asked.

Stevens glared over the top of his glasses at Walsh.

Walsh's mouth started to open. He knew about the hundred thousand shares held in Stevens' wife's trust account under her maiden name: a fact Stevens failed to divulge prior to or since the firm's merger and a fact the SEC wouldn't care about—unless the position was not disclosed to the public. And it wasn't. The words formed in his mouth but he shut it before they could escape.

"Alright, then," Bradley said. "Leave it at accumulate and let's move on." He checked the sheet on Walsh's series. "Looks like Castle Pharmaceutical."

Without further comment from Stevens, Walsh settled back and reviewed Castle and the next ten companies on his list.

"The last one I have to talk about is Pride Pet Foods," Walsh said. "It's not only the last, it's the very best. We currently have a hold rating for the stock but I want to raise it immediately to a strong buy. My reasons are—"

Stevens laughed. "Where have you been, son?"

"Pardon, me?"

"I said, where the hell have you been this morning?"

"This morning? Mostly waiting for you in the outer office. Is there a problem?"

"Not for me. I'm not the one who blew out ten thousand shares of Pride an hour ago at *half* their current value."

"What are you talking about?"

"Pride, you moron. There's a trading halt. They're privatizing. It's been all over the tape this morning." He gestured indifference with a flick of his hand. "But, you're only the analyst. No reason for *you* to stay on top of a development like that."

Walsh's jaw dropped. "Privatizing?"

"That's right, my boy. They're buying their stock back at four dollars a share. That sell you made this morning cost you twenty thousand dollars."

Walsh jumped up. "*Four dollars?*"

"Here, I'll read it to you," Stevens said, chuckling. He punched up the news release on the Quotron. "'James C. Ledford, President, today announced the tender for all outstanding shares of Pride Pet Foods. Mr. Ledford cited a restructuring and consolidation of their pet food lines and a downsizing of operations as reasons for the repurchase at this time.' Blah, blah, blah." Stevens looked over the top of his glasses at Walsh. "The only thing I can't figure out is where he got all the cash for the buy-back. Even at four dollars a share it has to cost them plenty."

"Bullshit!" Walsh yelled. "They aren't downsizing, they're *expanding*, for chrissake! They've *tripled* their operation, they aren't cutting it! That stock's worth at least ten, maybe twenty and Cleat's buying it for *four*?! That asshole! No wonder he wouldn't talk to me."

Carmichael looked at the other men, then back at Walsh. "Twenty dollars?" he said. "How do you know it's worth twenty?"

"That prick! I'm as good as dead," Walsh said. His knees weakened and he fell back onto his chair. His mind numbed.

"Mr. Walsh?" Carmichael said

Nothing.

"Mr. Walsh!"

"Huh?"

"You said it's worth ten, maybe twenty."

"Every penny of it."

"How do you know?"

"I've checked. Ten dollars? Twenty? What difference does it make? Cleat's got the tender in at four."

123

"The man's right," Bradley said, flicking a hand up. "They're de-listing from the exchange. I don't know how many of our clients have any of that crap but they either sell at four or use the certificates for wallpaper."

"Maybe not," Carmichael said. "If Thornton says Pride could be worth twenty maybe we should consider putting a syndicate together and making an offer of our own? I'd like to hear why Thornton thinks it could be worth twenty."

"Fair enough," Bradley said. "How about it, Mr. Walsh?"

Walsh gave a heavy sigh. "It doesn't matter how I know or what I know. Ledford and his directors have a controlling stake in the company. There aren't enough shares in public hands to get a controlling interest. If Ledford wants to take his company private, he's got the cards to do it."

Stevens rapped the table with his hand. "That's it, then," he said. He checked his watch. "And it looks like it's about time for lunch." He rose. "You can go now, Walsh. Or maybe you'd rather sit a bit and lick your wounds?"

Carmichael and Bradley shook their heads, then got up and started for the door.

"Tough luck, Thornton," Bradley said as he passed him. "You'll get the twenty thousand back on something else."

"Yeah. Real tough," Carmichael said, patting him on the shoulder. "I'll tell Mrs. Carmichael what you said. She'll appreciate your thoughtfulness."

Walsh slumped further into the chair and stared at the ceiling as Stevens shut the lights off and the men left the boardroom. A vision of Solly gleefully twisting off his arms and legs one by one played in his head. Benny would be calling too. By now, the Teamsters would have heard about the buyout at four and Benny's head would probably roll for the five hundred thousand dollars the Pipefitters union pension fund didn't make.

His brain throbbed. The pulse of blood through his temples felt like rapid blows from a croquet mallet. He drew his legs onto the chair, then curled his arms around his knees and shut his eyes. An hour passed before he moved from the cold, dark room.

- 15 -

Traci peered through the open doorway to Lieutenant Hale's office. "You wanted to see me, sir?"

He waved her in. "Have a seat, Sergeant."

She sat in a bare oak chair across from Hale's cluttered desk, then pulled three bobby pins from the mound of her hair and fluffed the long brunette strands over her shoulders. "It's going to be a hot one today," she said. "I wish those weathermen would get it right."

"That's for sure." Hale leaned back. "You'd think with satellites and millions worth of equipment they could get it straight. Heavy rain? Give me a break. Must be over a hundred out there."

"Every bit of that. An old man with arthritis could do better."

Hale grinned. "I know just the guy."

They laughed.

"Did you bring me in for a weather report, Lieutenant, or was there something else?"

He plucked a file from his desk. "Read your follow-ups on the bag lady rapes. Captain did, too."

"Oh?"

"Good piece of detective work, Sergeant, mighty good piece of work."

She smiled. "I'm glad you're pleased."

"So much so, the captain wants to loan you to detectives for a while—until we get some arrests. What do you say?"

Traci beamed. "I'd say that'd be great. But I thought deployment was down in patrol."

"Not a problem. The captain's making a swap and I'm getting one of their dicks." He waved the file in the air. "One of the men who took these reports. We're calling it cross-training. The detective's probably calling it something else."

"You sure you want to do this? I don't want to step on anyone's toes."

"I wouldn't worry too much about that. The transfers are only temporary and they'll do you both good."

"Fine with me. When do I start?"

"Right away." He passed the file to her. "The first four reports are in there, plus three more. They came in last night. I'd like you to re-interview the victims on the three new ones and see if we're getting a pattern somewhere or if we've just got a bunch of sex fiends on the loose."

"I'll get right on it." She opened the file and glanced over the three new rape reports.

"Seems we're not the only city that's been experiencing an outbreak of rapes in Skid Row areas," Hale said.

She looked up. "Really?"

He pointed at the file. "Some teletypes from New York, Connecticut and Maryland are in there, too. They make pretty interesting reading. Go over them later and you'll see."

She nodded and fingered the folder.

"Don't know what to make of it," Hale said. "To tell you the truth, it's a real head-scratcher. Anyway, NYPD is hosting a symposium on the situation starting tomorrow and detectives from several other departments will be there to share information." He leaned forward. "We'd like you to attend, Sergeant, unless you have something more pressing."

"Go to New York?"

"On our dime, of course."

"Sure. I'll go but why me?"

Hale laughed. "You're our resident expert on the bag-lady rapists. The only one who took an interest."

"Oh. Well, I appreciate your confidence, Lieutenant."

"Think nothing of it." He leaned back, again. "Besides, you're single and none of the other detectives wanted to make the trip."

A frown replaced her smile. "So, that's it? I drew the short straw?"

"I wouldn't call it that. You'll have a good time and it's only three days."

"Three days? I thought you said it was tomorrow."

"I said it *started* tomorrow."

"My vacation starts on Saturday."

"Shouldn't be a problem. It wraps up on Saturday. You should be back in town in plenty of time for your date." He winked.

"I don't have a date, Lieutenant, but I do have plans to fly down to Miami to visit my dad this weekend. Guess I could still do it if my flight can be rescheduled. I don't want to get stuck with a penalty, though."

"Not a problem. Call me later with your flight number and I'll have our travel bureau take care of it."

"Fair enough." She nodded. "Count me in."

"Excellent."

"When do you want the re-interviews done? Now or when I get back?"

"Now. Work overtime if you have to. Your air tickets and hotel vouchers are in that file but you'll have to stop by Fiscal Operations to pick up a credit card and a check for your cash expenses."

"Okay. Anything else?"

He started to speak but stopped as he darted a look past her. "Hey!" He shouted to the last of three uniformed officers who ran past his open door. "What's going on out there?"

The officer jerked to a stop and stuck his head into Hale's office. "Got a combative male … in the drunk tank, sir," he panted out. "Jailer hit the panic button." The officer ran off.

Hale quickly stood. "What the hell's going on? That's the fourth one this week. Let's have a look."

Traci followed Hale down the narrow hallway to the jail. Six officers were piled on top of a prisoner while three more held seven other prisoners at bay in the large holding cell. The man on the bottom flailed a free arm and leg.

"Get the cord cuffs," the officer immediately above the man shouted. "Somebody get that leg."

Moments later, the man's arms and legs were bound and the officers crawled off. Snot and blood drooled from the prisoner's nose. His bulging eyes glared and his muscles jerked uselessly against the nylon cord cuff restraints.

"Strip him and throw him in the pads," Hale ordered as he stepped around to the jailer. The man was seated on the floor, massaging his neck. "Let me take a look," Hale said.

The jailer moved his hand away, revealing two rows of teeth marks where the prisoner bit him. The skin was broken inside three of the marks.

Hale helped the jailer to his feet. "What happened?" he asked.

"Don't know," the shaken jailer said. "I was hosing down the tank when the dirt-bag started screaming and jumped me. I can't figure it out. He was one of my best prisoners. Never heard a peep out of the guy." He rubbed his neck again.

"We'll get that bite taken care of right away," Hale said. "Guttierez, take him to the hospital for an M.T."

"Thanks, Lieutenant," the jailer said. "Sorry about all this."

"Forget it." He turned to Traci. "C'mon, Sergeant. Let's take a look at our prisoner."

Hale and Traci strode thirty feet further down the hall to the padded cell and peered through the door's small window. The prisoner screamed in ear-piercing shrieks as two officers removed the last of his clothing. Traci turned away.

When he was naked, they re-cuffed his hands and legs and went out. Hale stepped into the four-by-four-foot cell. Traci held the door ajar and waited outside while Hale studied the bearded, balding man lying hogtied on the floor.

"Damn," Hale said, "looks like his arm's broken." The man screamed louder when Hale gently rolled him onto his side. Hale grimaced at what he saw. The jagged tip of the prisoner's ulna protruded an inch though his bloodied skin. "Better get a couple of officers to transport this guy to the hospital, Traci. Have them take him to a different one."

She hurried off to find the officers who stripped the prisoner. She knew they knew the arm was broken. Leaving a combative prisoner in a little pain was common jailhouse justice. She found the two in the parking lot as they were getting into their patrol car. After a reprimand for not reporting the injury, she sent them back to the pads.

She joined Lieutenant Hale in the Watch Commander's office. He was reading the prisoner's rap sheet.

"That guy's a real psycho," Hale said. "Eight 415 arrests in the last nine months. Three more for aggravated assault. Nothing in the last three months, though." He turned to Traci. "What do you make of it?"

"What's he in for now?"

"Six forty-seven F."

"Drunk in public," she said absently. "How long's he been here?"

Hale checked the arrest report. "Four days."

"Where was he popped?"

"Eighteenth and Turk."

131

"That's my beat. I wonder … Can you throw a towel over him? I'd like to take a look."

Traci returned to the padded cell and told the officers to wait while Hale looked for a towel. A minute later he stepped into the cell. The man was still on his side and moaning but no longer combative. Hale laid several cleaning rags over the prisoner's buttocks and groin, then gave a quick rap on the door. Traci went in.

"Could be," she said after looking at the flabby man on the floor. She stepped over him and checked his chest. As with his back and arms, it was thick with hair. His head was balding. Thin purple lines spidered across the skin of his stomach. "Okay. I'm done."

"He's all yours," Hale told the waiting officers when Traci left the cell. "Take him for the M.T., then bring him back and rebook him for Battery on a Police Officer." He turned to Traci. "See something?"

"Maybe. I'll take a copy of his mug shot and see if any of my victims recognize him."

"Think he might be your perp?"

"Might be one of them."

"Let me know."

- 16 -

"I'm ready for the firing squad," Walsh said as he shuffled through the door and into his offices.

"Didn't go well?" Alice asked.

"The meeting went fine, if that's what you meant. That wasn't any problem at all. There's another matter that didn't quite work out."

"Anything I can help you with?"

"Not this time. Thanks anyway. Messages?"

Alice laughed. "Only about twelve from Ben Weinstein. He sounded irritated. Shall I dial his number for you?"

Walsh sighed. "You might as well but hold my calls, Alice. I need to get some work done."

She dialed as Walsh sauntered into his private office and shut the door behind him. The blinking light on his phone beckoned.

"Benny, I just got back. Been in a meeting all morning. What's up?"

"What's *up?*!" Ben screamed. "You ask me what's *up*? Pride's up, you asshole! You screwed my client out of half a million dollars!"

"Calm down, Benny. I swear to God I had no idea they were going to do that. I swear to God."

"You lying sack of shit! You knew all along. You couldn't wait. Had to do the trade yesterday. A stealth trade, you said. Threatened me. You prick!"

"Swear to God, Benny. I had no idea. None."

"Do you know what you've done to me? Do you know what I've been going through the last two hours?"

"I'm telling you, I didn't have a clue. I was as shocked as anyone."

"You're the fuckin' analyst for chrissake! Don't tell me you didn't have a clue. You knew Ledford was privatizing and you raped my client for half a mil and he's not going to stand for it!"

"Ben, I don't know what to tell you. I *didn't* know and screaming at me isn't going to change that. I lost money, too."

"Well, I'm not losing any money, that's for damn sure, and my client's not losing any either."

"What are you saying?"

"I'm gonna blow out that trade, that's what! I'm gonna tell Richards to unwind it. You're not gonna get away with this, Walsh. No way!"

"Wait a minute, Ben. You can't do that. That trade's a done deal."

"No, it isn't. Not when you pull this shit. No way it's a done deal."

"Richards won't go along with it," Walsh said. "He can't. Not without my approval and I'm not giving it!"

"He'll do it if I tell him how it went down."

Walsh slumped into his chair. "Jesus, Benny, you're driving me crazy. Calm down, will you? Let's talk about this. Let's just compose ourselves and discuss this."

"You're nuts! I listened to you before. All under control, you said, and now I've got the fuckin' Teamsters coming down on my ass! I'm not listening to you anymore, Walsh. I knew this was gonna be trouble but this is way more than trouble. Way, *way* more!"

"Have you talked to Richards?"

"No, but that's exactly what I intend to do as soon as he gets in. I'm going in there and tell him to blow it out."

"Alright, alright. Slow down a minute, Benny. Just slow down and listen to me for a second."

"You're not talking me out of this, Walsh. I'm not listening to you this time."

"Will you just hold on a second and relax?! I'm not going to try to talk you out of anything. You do what you gotta do."

"You're goddamn right."

"You can kill the trade if that's what you think you have to do, but I'm going to ask you for one small favor."

"Favor? Ha! I gotta hear this."

"You do what you think is right. Just don't do it now. Okay? Wait 'til tomorrow. You can bust it then. What do you say?"

"Tomorrow? What difference can that possibly make?"

"Exactly. Just give me twenty-four hours and you can do whatever you want. How about it?"

"What kind of trick are you gonna pull now, Walsh?"

"No tricks. I just need some time to get with my client and smooth things out. Okay? I need to think of something to tell him. That's all. No tricks."

"Forget it, Thorny. You tell him anything you want. That's got nothing to do with me. My career's on the line here. I'm gonna tell Richards to kill the trade and you can tell your client whatever, whenever."

"Just twenty-four hours, Benny. That's all I'm asking."

"No way!"

"Please?"

"Fuck you, Walsh. If you want to blab it up about the twins, I'll have to deal with that, but I'm through with you. You got me into some serious trouble and I gotta put a stop to it right now."

"Benny. Listen to me. Do you really think I'd rat you out like that? Is that what you think?"

"Sure sounded convincing to me."

"Come on, Benny. We're pals, for crying out loud. I would never do anything like that to you."

Ben was silent.

"When's Richards due in?" Walsh asked.

"About an hour."

"Alright. Let me work on this a couple of minutes and I'll call you back. Okay?"

Ben said nothing.

"Just give me the hour, Goddammit! Promise me you won't do anything 'til then. Okay?"

Silence.

"Please?"

"Shit. Alright. One hour. But, that's it!"

They hung up and Walsh quickly dialed another number.

"Phil. Walsh here."

"What's happening, Thorny? Everything going okay?"

"Yeah. Fine. Everything's fine. Just one thing."

"What's that?"

"I'm not going to do the deal. Have Solly come by my office tomorrow and I'll give him your money. The deal's off."

"Is that so."

"Yeah. I've given it some more thought and I'm backing out. Sorry, Phil. I can't do it."

"Really. Well, let me tell you something, Thorny. You'll do it, alright. How you do it is of no concern to me but it'll be done."

"I don't think you've got the picture, Phil. When I tell you it can't be done, it can't be done. I thought I had something going but I got thrown a curve and it's not going to pan out." He loosened the knot on his tie. "Believe me, Phil, no one's more upset about this than me. I spent a lot of energy on this deal but it just fell apart. Shit happens. Know what I mean? I've still got your five hundred, though, so send Solly over tomorrow to pick it up."

Phil was silent.

Walsh wiped rivulets of sweat from his forehead. "I'll tell you what, Phil. I feel terrible about all this and I'll give you the eighty thousand for the markers and throw in another twenty for the inconvenience. How's that for a good faith offer? An even hundred thousand. It's the best I can do."

Silence.

"Are you there? Hello …?"

"I'm here."

"Well?"

"This is really bothering me, Thorny. I'm listening to you tell me you've got the five hundred but Solly told me you sent it down the street to another firm. And that's not all that bothers me. I know damn well you never had the eighty thousand in the first place and now you tell me you do and you'll even kick in another twenty."

"I— "

"Now, I know Solly wouldn't lie to me. He's too stupid to do that. So that leaves you, Thorny. I think you're trying to feed me a line of bullshit and expect me to bite. No. What I think is you've already done the deal and you want to keep it all for yourself. That's what I think."

"You can— "

"Today is Wednesday. I'm going to expect three million *and* my original five hundred thousand by Friday. Like we agreed. Like *you* agreed."

"I never— "

"Otherwise, Solly is going to have to make the collection in a less conventional way. Are we clear on this?"

Walsh sagged in his chair. "It's coming into focus."

"I'm a reasonable man, Thorny. I think you've got the money now but I'll wait 'til Friday. That was the deal. Of course, if you don't have the money …"

"It's something else, isn't it?" Walsh said.

"What do you mean?"

"I mean this isn't about vacation money, is it? It's something else."

"I'll expect the three-and-a-half million by Friday."

"Jesus, Phil. I don't know how I can make this any plainer to you. The fact is I don't have the three million you're talking about. You can think whatever you want but I just don't have it. It's like I said—the deal went sour."

"That's not my problem."

Walsh sighed. "Alright, Phil. I'll tell you straight. I did try something. Found the perfect company and made a bet with your money but it went sideways. Something happened I never anticipated. If everything had gone the way it was supposed to, you would have had your money by Friday—maybe sooner. But it didn't. We both got screwed."

"Like *I* said, Thorny, that's not *my* problem."

"Why are you doing this to me, Phil? You're putting me under terrible pressure here. Unbelievable pressure. I'm about to get raped by the broker I did the trade with and now you. I told you I'd give your money back and another hundred thousand just for drill. What else can I do?"

"You're a smart guy, Thorny. You'll come up with something. You've still got two days."

"I can't think under pressure like this. I need time to breathe."

"Well, if I were you, I'd make every breath count. Otherwise Solly will—"

Walsh bolted upright. "Solly! That's it! You've got to let me use him. He can help me slow things down a bit. Give me some time."

"Solly isn't something I loan around."

"It's the only way you'll have any hope of seeing your money. Putting the hurt on me won't get you three million but I'll leave that up to you. You tell me which you'd rather have."

Phil fell silent again. Finally, he said, "What do you have in mind?"

- 17 -

Traci finished re-interviewing the three most recent rape victims at 7 P.M. Little else was learned but one of the perpetrators was remembered as having a lot of pimples—a remarkable feature considering his estimated age of forty-five. She spent another hour searching for the first four victims, then showing each the small photo of the combative prisoner. None of the seven women recognized him.

Exhausted, she returned to the station, changed out of her uniform then drove to her three-bedroom home in Beacon Hill. Sparky peered at her through the rear sliding-glass door as she entered the house. His tail wagged limply.

"Hey, big guy," she said as she opened the slider and allowed the yellow Labrador Retriever inside. "I'll bet you're hungry." She crouched and scratched the animal behind his ears. The dog gave a sheepish look. Traci glanced outside but saw nothing out of place. "What is it?" she asked. "Have you been a bad boy?" She moved for a closer look at the small backyard. The flower beds and lounge-chair pads were intact. She returned to Sparky and again crouched in front of him.

141

"I know. It was so-o-o hot today. I lose my energy, too, when it's hot. Come on." She moved to her kitchen. "I've got a special treat for you."

Sparky rose from his haunches and loped along behind her.

She opened the refrigerator and pulled out plastic-wrapped turkey slices, tore three into small pieces and mixed them into a bowl of kibble. She set the bowl on the floor and Sparky ambled over and sniffed at it. He nosed away the kibble, ate the turkey, then curled onto the cool floor near Traci's feet. She filled another bowl with cold water and set it beside the kibble. "Okay," she said. "I'll turn on the air. We'll both feel better."

She switched on the air-conditioner, then went into her bedroom. Three messages waited on her answering machine. Two were from her father, the other from a newspaper subscription solicitor. Nothing from David. She stripped off her clothes and slipped on a cool cotton robe before dialing.

"Hi, Dad. I just got home."

"Hi, honey. How's my favorite daughter?"

She laughed. "You always say that. Would you still say that if I had a sister?"

"If I'm talking to you, of course. So, how are you?"

"Just tired. How about you?"

"I'm still on the right side of the grass."

She laughed again. "You called twice."

"That's all? I was so excited I thought it was more."

"Hurry. Tell me."

"You're never going to believe this," he said. "Guess who has two tickets to the Dolphins' game on Sunday? On the forty-yard line, no less."

"Wow. That's great but I—"

"They said the game was sold out but you know me. Have I ever taken 'no' for an answer?"

"No, but—"

"I bought tuna for sandwiches and a six-pack. It's chillin' in the fridge as we speak. We're going to have a helluva good time this weekend, Traci. I'm really looking forward to your visit."

She moved her camera bag from a side chair and sat with her legs folded under her. "I have to go to New York, Dad. I'm still coming down but I don't know if I'll be there in time for the game."

"New York? You're going to New York when I've got *Dolphins* tickets?"

"I know but I was just told about it. Please don't be upset."

"Upset? Not a chance. It's going to be a great game, though. The Dolphins and Raiders. East meets west. The forty-yard line. Sure you can't make it?"

"There's nothing more I'd rather do and I probably will but this just came up and I really have to do it. I hope you understand."

"Don't give it another thought. Guess I could take Harold. Don't think he'd like tuna sandwiches, though."

"Thanks, Dad."

"New York, huh. Work or pleasure?"

"Work."

"You be careful up there. There's a lot of screwballs running loose in New York."

"Not to worry. I'll take Roscoe with me. I'll be okay."

"I'd take a couple of extra clips, too, if I were you."

She laughed. "It's New York, Dad, not Baghdad."

"I know, I know. When your mother was alive, I couldn't drag her to New York with a team of wild horses. She was convinced someone would push the big red button while she was there. 'Course the cold war's over now, and obviously nothing happened back then, either, but she just thought the Russians would somehow choose that particular moment to drop a bomb and that would be that. Can you imagine?"

"Sounds like something Mom would have worried about."

"It's all your fault, you know."

"*My* fault?"

"Absolutely. If you'd given her some trouble when you were growing up, she wouldn't have had time to think about the Russians and their bombs."

"If she'd only known."

"Ha! Well, I doubt whatever you did back then was all that bad, otherwise she would have heard about it."

"Probably. And I'm sure you aren't trying to get me to confess to anything now, right?"

"Naw. The proof is in the pudding. Besides, there's nothing you could possibly say that would spoil my image, honey. But just to be safe, we'll move on."

"Actually, I didn't do anything that awful, except maybe one time when I was visiting Uncle Willis and helping out with the wine crush a few years ago."

"Okay, okay. I'm closing my ears. You win."

"Gotcha."

He laughed. "That you did. Say, are you doing okay? Taking your vitamins and eating right?"

"I'm fine. Could use some more sleep but that's to be expected, I guess."

"When you're a public servant, there's a lot of emphasis on the 'servant' part."

"Don't I know it. Speaking of Harold, is he taking care of things okay?"

"Well enough, I suppose. 'Course the way he runs the pharmacy isn't the way I used to run it but I try to leave him alone and let him do his thing."

"I'll bet."

"I do. I really do. You'd be proud. Was in there this morning, as a matter of fact, and didn't say one word about the zillion banners he's got hanging all over from the ceiling. Doesn't look much like a pharmacy anymore, more like a circus sideshow. But he sends his checks regular, so he must be doing something right."

"Sounds like you still regret selling it."

"Sometimes I do but not as much lately. Probably shouldn't have bought another pharmacy after selling the Cambridge store. Probably should have just retired or taken up basket weaving or gotten into some other kind of business after moving down here."

"That would have been an even bigger mistake."

"Maybe … Hey, when are you going to let David marry you and make me a granddaughter?"

"Oh, Dad. I think you'd better sit on that for a while."

"Why? David's a fine young man. What are you waiting for?"

"I don't know. I just don't think I'm ready for marriage right now."

"You've been dating him for over three years, honey. How long are you going to make him audition for the husband role?"

"Three years might seem like a lot but to tell you the truth, if I added it up in the last three years I've probably spent a total of three months with him. He's never here. Always off to Paris or Taiwan or some other corner of the world."

"That's what importers do, honey. They travel. You could travel with him if you two were married."

"Then you wouldn't get your granddaughter."

"Because?"

"Because I'm not going to get pregnant and raise a child living out of a suitcase and David loves his work too much to quit. Besides, I've got goals of my own to consider."

"Hell, Traci, you can still be a woman's answer to Ansel Adams and raise a child at the same time. Think of all the wonderful things you'd be able to take pictures of if you went along with David on his trips. Did I tell you he sent me a postcard from Cairo? A great shot of the pyramids but you could have done them better."

"Well—"

"How about this? Get married to David, travel around with him and take your pictures and do a line of postcards. How about that?"

She laughed. "I don't take pictures, Dad. I capture moments, moods and feelings."

"Right, right. Feelings. Moods. Sorry. Didn't mean to minimize—"

"I know you didn't. It just wouldn't work if I went with David. I've gone with him before and there was never enough time. He moves around too fast for me. Never any time to find the flavor of wherever we happened to be. I appreciate your suggestion, though. It just wouldn't work."

"Then maybe it's time to give up on David. Maybe you need to look around a bit and see what else is out there. You're a pretty girl. You don't have any trouble meeting men. That clock's ticking, you know."

"I'm only thirty, Dad. I've got a lot of ticks left."

"I wouldn't wait too long, just the same."

"Don't worry. You'll get your granddaughter. I want her, too but first things first."

"Okay. I won't bug you again about that until next week."

"Fair enough."

"So, what's going on in New York that's more important than watching the Dolphins beat the hell out of the Raiders?"

"It's a symposium. I've got a bit of a problem in my precinct and several other departments are having the same problem, so there's a symposium in New York to discuss it."

"Sounds interesting. What kind of a problem?"

"A lot of indigent women are being attacked. It's really strange. My Lieutenant thought only one perp was involved but I found out it was more than one. What's strange is that the attacks seem to be so random."

"Men are beating up the women in your precinct?"

"No, no. Attacking them."

147

"That's what I thought you said."

"Oh. Attack is another word for rape. We call it attack. I don't know why but that's what police call it."

"So men are raping the women ... in your precinct. Indigent women."

"That's right. And it's happening in other cities, too. That's why there's a symposium."

"I thought you were a patrol sergeant. Did you get a promotion and not tell me about it?"

"No, Dad. I'm still in patrol. They just loaned me to detectives for a while and asked me to go."

"Because you're a woman?"

She laughed. "No, no. That had nothing to do with it. It all happened because I did some follow-up work on a few rapes in my district and found out there was more than one perpetrator. The detectives didn't do a very good job on their reports and I just wanted to find out what really happened."

"Hmmm. Is this something you did on your own or were you assigned to do it?"

"I did it on my own, initially, because it needed to be done and no one else was going to do it. It's really no big deal."

He paused. "You have to let it go, honey. I've let it go and you have to let it go, too."

"Let it ... What are you talking about?"

"You know what I'm talking about. You have to put it aside. Get it out of your mind. It'll eat you up if you don't."

"This has nothing to do with Mom. This is my job. I'm supposed to investigate crimes. It's completely different, Dad."

148

"I don't think so, honey. Not when you take the initiative. Not when rape is involved."

"It's completely different."

"Is that why you became a police officer? I never really understood why you chose that particular line of work in the first place. Not when you could have been so much more. Not after what happened to your mother."

"C'mon on, Dad. Let's not get into that again. We were having such a nice conversation."

"I'm just going to say this one last time, honey, and I promise I'll never bring it up again. But I have to say it one last time."

"What?"

"Just let it go. Get married, have lots of children and put the past behind you. Will you do that? Will you do that for your dear ol' dad? What do you say? Will you give up police work and make me a grandfather?"

"You're not being fair."

"Fairness has nothing to do with it. I'm just thinking about you. I'm thinking about your future. There's nothing more to be done. What do you think your mother would say if she knew you were a police officer and getting involved with rapists?"

"I would hope she'd be proud of me. The same way I hope you're proud of me."

"I am. I'm very proud of you."

"But …"

"There isn't any but. I'm very proud of you and how you've gotten along in a man's business."

"Dad!"

"Okay. Say what you want but I just wished you'd picked something else. Something a bit more ..."

"Feminine?"

"Ha! I didn't say that."

"You were thinking it."

"Well ... Just give it some thought, okay?"

"Okay. Hey. It just occurred to me. Maybe you know?"

"What?"

"We had a combative arrestee this afternoon, picked up from my beat—a real scrapper—and we had to put him in a padded cell. Nothing unusual about that, except a few things are nagging at me."

"And they are ...?"

"For starters, his rap sheet showed he's a regular resident in our fine institution and always combative. Eleven arrests in six months. Just petty stuff but a real fighter when collared. Then, poof ... nothing. Three months go by and not a peep from the guy until today."

"Maybe he was on vacation."

She laughed. "We're talking Skid Row, Dad."

"Then maybe he was in a different jail."

"Nope. Not there either."

"Well, maybe he just got religion and decided to clean up his act."

"Maybe. I haven't been on the Row long enough to know if that's a possibility but I don't think so."

"Okay. What else?"

"Well, I got a look at him before he was taken to the hospital for an M.T.— his arm got broken in an altercation at the jail—and he had some strange marks on his stomach. Deep blue streaks. Purple. Not tattoos.

150

Thin purple streaks, running every which way. Thought it was kind of strange. Any idea what it could be?"

"They didn't have any pattern?"

"None."

"How old is he?"

"Mid-forties."

"Anything else unusual?"

"Not much. Face was round. No scars or marks on it, though."

"Round face, huh?"

"Yeah. He was on the floor and squirming around a lot. I didn't see it that long but the shape stood out. I just remember thinking he had a really round face."

"Anything else about him? Any deformities?"

"Oh. Well, yeah. He did have kind of a hump on his back, near his shoulders. Probably from doing stoop labor."

"Maybe. I seem to recall coming across something like what you've described once or twice when I had the Cambridge pharmacy. Can't put my finger on it right now. Give me a few days. I'll think of it."

"Okay. My brain's in neutral right now, too, Dad."

"Hey. Mine's not in neutral, just stuck in low gear at the moment."

"That'd be the first time."

"Oh, well…"

She glanced at her watch. "It's really getting late, Dad, and I've got to get packed and get someone to watch Sparky, so better hang up."

"Okay, honey. Be careful in New York and call me when you know if you'll be coming down."

"I will."

- 18 -

Hotel Marriott Marquis, New York City Thursday

NYPD Detective Lieutenant Jerry Puttz ran a hand through the oiled locks of his curly black hair and waited behind the podium while three men sauntered into the back of the conference room. Each clutched a coffee cup with a jelly roll balanced on the lid in one hand and file folders in the other. They laughed aloud as they shuffled to one of the tables and sat.

"Nice of you and your friends to join us, Ski," Puttz said in a heavy Brooklyn accent.

"No problem, Jer. We was in the neighborhood." Detective Karpinski rocked his large body to one side, lifted a leg and broke wind with a loud report. His companions and the twenty other male detectives in the room roared with laughter.

"Knock it off," Puttz said. "Settle down." He glared at Karpinski. "In case you haven't noticed, bird brain, there's a lady present." He nodded at Traci, who was seated at a table near the podium. "I'm sure she's thoroughly impressed with your good manners. Maybe you'd like to belch for her after lunch?"

Karpinski dropped his head. "Sorry, ma'am," he said.

Traci turned around. "Karpinski, is it?"

"Yes, ma'am."

"Well, Detective Karpinski, you should feel free to express yourself the best way you know."

The men roared with catcalls and whistles. Karpinski grimaced. "Yes, ma'am," he said.

"Al-l-l right. Settle down," Puttz said. "Now that we're all here, does anyone have any questions?"

One of the men with Karpinski raised a hand. "Yeah, I do. My room sucks. It smells like stale cigarette smoke. And another thing, where the hell are the golf courses?"

Several men chuckled.

"Anybody else?" Puttz asked, looking around the room of twenty-three men and one woman. "Anybody here with an *intelligent* question?"

The group was still.

"Good, then we'll get started." Puttz organized his papers on the podium then looked up. "Each of you has been chosen by your respective departments to participate in this symposium because of an increase in Skid Row rapes in your city. About six weeks ago, when reports started coming in to NYPD, we thought it was just a blip, something to do with the moon or the heat or whatever, and that it would pass. But it didn't and they kept coming. Then we noticed other jurisdictions, like each of yours, were experiencing similar increases."

He turned to a small table next to the podium and switched on an overhead projector. A bar chart of selected felony crimes shone on a screen behind it. "For NYPD," he went on, "rapes in our low-life precincts are up four hundred fifty percent. In raw numbers, that's seventy-two versus only thirteen the month before." He aimed a red laser pointer at the bar on the chart entitled *Rape*. "To our surprise, though, aggravated assaults, batteries and four-fifteens in those precincts dropped precipitously, becoming almost non-existent." He moved the laser over the next three bars to highlight the low numbers of those crimes then turned back to the group. "Probably like most of you, we deployed extra units to those districts but we didn't know who we were looking for. Our stat people weren't much help either and couldn't find a pattern to focus on a particular perpetrator or perpetrators for us to shake. Vice put under-covers down there but they came away with bupkus." He switched off the projector and moved back behind the podium. "Right now, the problem is pretty much isolated to our bowery and that's where we'd like to keep it. But acting alone isn't fixing the problem. So, our brass came up with the pregnant idea for this symposium. They believed your collective wisdom ... with the possible exception of Karpinski's ..." He paused to allow an outburst of laughter subside. "... they believed that sharing information with other departments experiencing the same problem might help all of us come up with a solution." He glanced around the room. Everyone appeared to be listening. "That's it in a nutshell. That's what we're here for—not golf. Any questions so far?"

No one spoke.

"In a few minutes, you'll be broken up into four groups of six and this is what you'll be looking for." He raised the projection screen, revealing a green chalkboard with numbers from one to ten running down the left margin. Midway across the board was another column. A third set ran down the right margin. *PERPS* labeled the top of the first column, *VICTIMS* the second and *OTHER* identified the third.

"What you're going to be looking for," Puttz went on, "are commonalities in what you know about your perpetrators and your victims." He wrote *weather* in the first space under *OTHER* with a stub of chalk. "You're also going to be listing everything you know about the crimes themselves. For example, I've written 'weather' here." He rapped the chalk against the board. "We want to know everything about the weather at the time of the attacks. We want to know the air temperature, rain, no rain, sun or no sun, moon, no moon, clouds, clear skies, and anything else about it you probably didn't take the time to note in your crime reports."

The group laughed.

Puttz wrote *race* on the first line in the *PERPS* column, then sharply rapped the board again. "Over here, we want to know everything about your perpetrators. We want to know if they're Puerto Rican, Caucasian, African-American, Chinese, Hindustani, Martian … Whatever your victims told you, whatever they described, you put it down."

He took a swallow of coffee from a cup on the podium, wrote '*age*' on the next line and continued. "Now, I don't care if your perpetrator's ages range from three to a hundred and three. Just put it down. Is everyone with me, so far?"

A detective with bright red hair and a Wyatt Earp mustache shot a hand up. "What kind of a system is this, Puttz? That's not how we do it in Baltimore."

"No doubt," Puttz said, "but this is how we're going to do it now. An unconventional approach suits an unconventional problem." He looked around the room. "Anyone else?"

No one spoke.

"Okay. I think you're getting the idea. The point is to first detail everything you know about your perps and your victims. I want to know their hair color, eye color, length of hair, clothing, kind of shoes, color of shoes, teeth, no teeth, how tall, how much, how little, how everything. Got it?"

The group nodded.

"Then I want to know everything about the crimes. Time of day, day of the week, how long it took, the kind of force used—verbal, weapons, fists, hand grenades, whatever—anything that was said, and on and on and on." He tossed the chalk into the tray at the bottom of the board and returned to the podium. "Just to make sure we're all on board here, I want to do a little exercise." He focused on Karpinski. "How many cases did you bring with you, Ski?"

"Fourteen."

"Okay. Out of those fourteen cases, tell me the most nugatory fact that comes to mind."

"Nugatory? I got no bullshit facts like that."

The men at his table laughed.

"Trivial, Ski," Puttz said. "Seemingly unimportant."

"Well, why the shit didn't you just say trivial or unimportant?"

"Forget it, Ski. Just give me a fact, if one comes to mind."

"I don't clutter my brain with nuga ... nuga ... crap. I don't know no trivial facts, Puttz. Youse gonna have to ask someone else for one a dem."

The men laughed again as Traci raised her hand. Puttz quickly acknowledged her.

"Something I thought was kind of interesting," she said, "was what one of my victims told me about her attacker's breath."

"Good," Puttz said. "That's along the lines of what I'm looking for. What did she tell you?"

"She said his breath had a peculiar odor. Smelled like the breath of a dog was how she described it."

The men roared with laughter.

"That's a crime-stopper if I ever heard one!" one shouted.

"Yeah!" another man yelled. "Who woulda figured to look in that part of the animal kingdom?"

"Bestiality in reverse," the first man shouted back.

The men continued to banter and laugh.

"Settle down!" Puttz said. "Knock off the BS. Sergeant Ross just gave you a clue. Did any of your victims make a similar comment?"

"As a matter of fact, two of mine did," the red-haired detective said. "Thought it was kind of weird, myself, at the time." He rummaged through the sheaf of papers in his file folder and pulled out two. "Yeah. Right here." He waved the papers in front of him. "Both victims made about the same comment. 'Dog breath,'" he read from one of the reports. "'Breath like a dog,'" he read from the other. "I'm from Baltimore, ma'am. What department are you with?"

"Boston," she said.

"Boston and Baltimore," another man said. "Maybe we got a werewolf that don't like women in cities that start with B."

More laughter.

"Okay, okay," Puttz said. "That's about all I can take from you guys right now. I'm splitting you into groups, so listen up for your name and remember which group you're with." He read the list of names for each of the four groups. "We'll break for lunch at noon, then I want everybody back here no later than one o'clock. E.O.W. will be at seventeen-hundred. Tomorrow, we'll start at oh-eight-hundred, so try not to get too drunk tonight. Be on time. That especially applies to you, Ski."

"Don't worry about me, Puttz."

"Good. At ten-hundred tomorrow, we'll see where we all are, so pick a man—or woman—from your team to give a report on what you've got. Any questions?"

"Yeah," Karpinski said. "Can I be in her group?"

- 19 -

Walsh screamed into the pay phone outside his building. "Are you *insane*, Phil?! Have you completely lost your mind?!" He slammed his fist hard against the door and ignored the quizzical stares of the men and women hurrying past the glass booth.

"You're yelling at me, Thornton," Phil said. "I don't like that."

"I don't give a shit what you do or don't like, you moron! You're about the dumbest dick I know!"

"If you don't lower your voice, I'll hang up. I mean it, Walsh. Lower your voice or I'll hang up."

"Of all the dumb-shit things to do, you did the absolute dumbest!"

"Are you going to lower your voice?"

"Alright. I'll lower it, you dickhead. How's that? Is that low enough for you?"

"That's better. Now, did you have something to tell me?"

Walsh wiped the moisture from his lips. "Benny, you piece of crap! I'm talking about Benny."

"Are you referring to Mr. Weinstein?"

159

"Oh, no. Don't play dumb with me. You're not going to get away with that."

"You'll have to forgive me, Thorny. I'm—"

"Just shut up! What did I tell you to do? C'mon, Phil. Think. What did I tell you? Break an arm or a leg. Isn't that what I said? An arm or a leg. Just have Solly get his attention. That's all I asked you to do. *Persuade* him. Didn't I tell you that?"

"My recollection is that Mr. Weinstein was about to do something that posed an obstacle to your plan. You seemed more than concerned about that when we talked. I suppose 'frantic' would be the operative word."

"Frantic? You idiot I wasn't frantic! How could you—"

"I'm not—"

"Jesus, Phil, Benny had a wife and kids, for chrissake."

"That is regret—"

"Oh, God. You have no idea what you've done. No idea at all." Walsh again wiped saliva from his lips. "What the hell have I gotten into with you? Everywhere I go, that monster Solly ... Shit! There he is ... right across the street ... wearing that same shit-eating grin. Is that what it's come to, Phil?"

"Solly is there to protect my interests, Thorny. He only acts when they're threatened. Mr. Weinstein was a threat but *you* have nothing to fear from Solly ... if everything goes as you say it will."

"Your interests? What about *my* interests? The police will be coming after *me*, not you."

160

"There's no reason for the police to come to you. Solly is very efficient. Very thorough. They won't consider your involvement."

"The hell they won't! The hell they won't be coming after me. *I'm* the one who called Benny. *I'm* the one who made the arrangements. How do you know who he told he was going to meet? *I* have no idea who he told, so how the hell do *you* know? They'll be coming, alright. You can bet your ass on that."

"I seriously doubt it. But if they do you were in your office, right? You have a secretary who can vouch for that, right?"

"You don't know them, Phil. You don't know me. They'll know. I know they'll know. Jesus H. Christ! What have you done to me?"

"You worry too much, Thorny. If they come, which I seriously doubt, but if they do, they'll ask a couple of questions and that'll be that. It'll go away. But right now, you have a larger concern. You have— What was that?"

"What?"

"What are you doing?"

"Doing? Jesus, Phil, I'm not doing anything. Haven't you ever heard a pager before?"

"Ah, of course. I didn't think you'd be dumb enough to record this call. That would have been pretty silly, wouldn't it?"

"You're unbelievable. Really unbelievable."

"Well, I can tell you're a busy man, so I'll let you go. Work it through, Thorny. You're a smart guy. Work it through."

Phil hung up. Walsh stared across the busy street. Solly had not moved, his arms still folded across the barrel of his chest, the Cheshire Cat-like grin still etched across his enormous face. His cold, black rat's eyes stared back. Walsh shuddered then checked his pager. An Oregon prefix. He dialed the number.

"Deputy Patchett. May I help you?"

"This is Thornton Walsh, Deputy. I got a page."

"Oh, yes sir, Mr. Walsh. Sheriff Marsden wants to talk to you. Hold on, please."

A minute passed before the Sheriff came on the line.

"Mr. Walsh?"

"What is it, Sheriff?"

"Thanks for callin' back so quick. I wasn't expectin' to hear from you so soon."

"What's going on, Sheriff?"

"'Fraid it's Oscar, again, Mr. Walsh. You asked me to call if somethin' new come up an', well, somethin' did."

Walsh groaned. "Now, what?"

"Well, sir, we had to hook him up this time. He was causin' just one helluva mess and we couldn't let it slide … like before."

"Did he go back to the market?"

Marsden gave a quick laugh. "No. No, he didn't go back there. Not this time. This time we got a call 'bout a big mess over there at Broadway and Main an' your brother Oscar was right there in the middle of the intersection directin' traffic. He run Mrs. Hollingsworth's Jeep right into the mayor's secretary's pickup, is what he did. Some cars stopped but more cars came along an' he kept wavin' 'em into the intersection. It was just one helluva big mess by the time my men got over there and straightened things out. A *helluva* mess, Mr. Walsh."

"Was anyone hurt?"

"The mayor's secretary is okay but Mrs. Hollingsworth's got a bump. She'll be alright though, I reckon."

"That's a relief. What about Oscar?"

"Well, like I was tellin' ya, we had to hook him up. He's in the hospital right now."

"Hospital? What happened? Was he hurt?"

"Oh, he's okay. We just brought him there for observation an' evaluation, is all. We're gonna have a psychiatrist take a look an' see what's what. We can keep him there up to seventy-two hours, ya know, but I don't think we'll do that. Maybe just a day or two, is all. He's not that crazy. Just want to take a look-see."

"Look-see? At what?"

"Just see how he can get along. The doctors will talk to him and give him some tests, is all."

"Then what?"

"Then? I really don't know. I'll tell ya, Mr. Walsh, your brother needs someone to look after him. He showed me the medications he's supposed to be takin', clozapine, as I recall, an' somethin' else … haloperidol, I think. Serious stuff. But I don't think he's takin' 'em like he's supposed to. I really think he should be placed somewhere an' looked after. That's my opinion. Y'all got any thoughts along that line?"

"Damn, Sheriff, I don't know. I thought he'd be okay. I was hoping he'd function better out there. He loves Roseburg and he loves his job. All of his friends are there but I guess it isn't working out the way I'd hoped."

"Maybe *you* could take care of him, Mr. Walsh. Something's gonna have to be done, though, an' done soon. The sooner the better—before he gets into more serious trouble, 'cause that's where he's headin'."

"I know I should take care of him and I *want* to take care of him but I can't right now. I've got my own set of problems right now."

"Sure. I understand. We'll just lock him up, then. We can't have him wanderin' loose, that's for sure."

"You're going to put him in jail?"

"Got no choice."

"No, no. That's no good, Sheriff. You can't do that. That would put him over."

"Well, I don't see I got no other choice. This ain't a matter of starin' at women's breasts anymore. This is a matter of bein' a danger to hisself and our community. He committed a crime and under the circumstances, I can't release him on an O.R. No, sir. The county would have my star if I did that. No, sir. If you won't look after him or make other arrangements, I don't see as I got much other choice here."

Walsh let out a heavy sigh. "Alright, Sheriff. I know what you're saying. You're sure there's no way you'd allow him to go back to his house? It would only be for a few days or so ... until I got things worked out here in New York."

"I wish I could, sir, but I can't. Your brother's no hardened criminal or nothin' but there's just too much liability for me to allow that. If this was the first time he'd had a scrape or even the second, that'd be another story. But … well, I don't have to tell y'all."

"No. No, you don't. Alright. Let me think about this, Sheriff. Let me give this some thought and I'll get back to you."

"That'll be fine. Call whenever y'all want."

"Can I talk to Oscar? Can you give me the number for the hospital?"

"Sure. No problem there. I got the number right here."

Walsh took the number and placed the call. Several transfers later, his brother came on the line.

"Teetee?"

"Oscar. Are you alright?"

"Are you mad at me, Teetee?"

"You're my brother, Oscar. How can I be mad?"

"I'm sorry, Teetee. I don't know why I did that. It just seemed like something fun."

Walsh nodded. "I'm sure it did. I'm sure it did."

"This is a real nice place, Teetee. Lots of nurses coming and going, going and coming. Only one's pretty, though. The rest are fat. I think the pretty one likes me."

"I'm sure she does, Oscar."

"I really think so."

"Oscar, I talked to Sheriff Marsden and he said you'll probably only be in there for the day. Probably be getting out tomorrow, but he—"

Oscar laughed. "Hey, Teetee, you remember when we were kids and would go out in the backyard in the spring with a pail of soap water an' throw snails in and watch 'em fizz? You remember that?"

"Dammit, Oscar! Will you stop rambling and listen to me? This is serious!"

"Don't yell, Teetee. You sound like Dad when you yell."

"I'm sorry but—"

"I was just remembering how much fun that was with the snails, that's all."

"Oscar!" Walsh caught himself and softened his tone. "Oscar. I didn't mean to yell at you but this is important. I've got to talk to you and I can't when you ramble off like that."

"Okay. I won't ramble."

"Good. Now, the Sheriff says you'll probably be getting out of the hospital today or tomorrow but he won't let you go back to your house."

A whine came into Oscar's voice. "I can't go home?"

"No. And it's really better that you don't because I don't think you'll take your medicine like you're supposed to."

"I'll take it. I promise I will."

"But you forget, Oscar, and that's understandable. I forget to take my cholesterol medicine sometimes but there's a big difference between my medicine and the medicine you take. If I forget, it's no big deal. But you can't. You understand? You see what happens when you forget? You do those dumb things and you get in trouble. Am I wrong or am I right?"

"You're right, Teetee. You're always right."

"Okay. So, when you leave there, the Sheriff's going to let you stay at his station for a while ... just long enough for me to figure out where you can stay ... where you'll get some help. Okay?"

"Can I stay with you, Teetee?"

"I'm going to work on that, Oscar. Right now isn't good but maybe in a few days or a week at most. Alright? So, tomorrow, when you get out of the hospital, you'll have to stay with the Sheriff."

"I don't want to stay with the Sheriff."

"It'll only be for a little while. A week or so."

"Where with the Sheriff, Teetee?"

"In his station, Oscar. Just for a little while."

"Not in the jail!"

"Well, I don't know exactly where—"

"I can't stay in the jail!"

"Just for a little while. Probably not even a week. Probably just a couple of days ... at the most."

Oscar shrieked and Walsh jerked the phone from his ear.

"I won't!" Oscar screamed. He shrieked again. "Don't make me! I can't ..."

Walsh heard the phone drop, then several voices and a scuffle. A minute passed.

"This is Dr. Goldman," a voice said into the phone. "Whom am I speaking to?"

"What happened, doctor?" Walsh said. "Is Oscar alright?"

"He'll be fine. Yes. And who are you?"

"Thornton. Oscar's brother. I was just talking to him. What happened?"

"He became agitated, Thornton. He's quiet now."

"We were just talking."

"Apparently something was said that set him off. Do you mind telling me what that might have been?"

"Jail, doctor. If he's discharged tomorrow, the Sheriff's going to put Oscar in jail and that's … that's not going to be a very pleasant experience for him."

"I can't imagine it would be, Thornton. But that's pretty much the point of jails, isn't it?"

"That's not what I'm talking about. I know what jails are for. It's…. Let me back up a minute. Will you be evaluating my brother?"

"Yes, sir."

"Are you a psychiatrist?"

"I'm an MD."

"I was told Oscar would be evaluated by a psychiatrist."

"He will but there's a complete physical examination first … to rule out imbalances in his chemistry. I'll give him a thorough checkup then someone from mental health will see him."

"Oh."

"Perhaps I should explain," Dr. Goldman said. "Your brother is here on what's called a fifty-one-fifty hold. Obviously you know the Sheriff's department brought him in for an evaluation as a result of an incident earlier today."

"I was told about it, yes."

"Well, from notes I've read in his chart, your brother will be evaluated for evidence of delusional psychosis—probably schizophrenia from the behavior that's been described. Apparently—"

"Schizophrenia? Oscar's no schizo, doctor. He acts goofy at times and does goofy things but he's no schizo."

"Maybe not but that's not my call."

"And he can't be put in jail," Walsh said. "That would really freak him out."

"I'm glad you brought that up again. Has he been incarcerated before? Is that the basis for his mal-association with jail?"

Walsh glanced at his watch, then across the street at Solly. "I don't have time to go into all the details, doctor, and I don't know if you're the one I should be discussing this with but the bottom line is our dad used to lock Oscar and me in a closet when we were kids and did something wrong. Not for just an hour or so. Mostly all day. Sometimes a couple of days. He did it to Oscar more than me and it freaked him out."

"Your dad locked Oscar in a closet?"

"That's right."

"My God. How often was that?"

"I don't know. I moved away when Oscar was ten … went away to college and didn't go back home very often. There wasn't … there wasn't much reason to go back, at least not before dad died. So, I don't know. I don't know what was going on with Oscar while I was away but it probably didn't change much after I left."

"That would explain a great deal," Goldman said. "I'll pass that along to mental health."

"Listen, doctor, do you think there's any possibility at all that Oscar could stay in your hospital for about a week?"

"A week? I'm afraid not. Except for the outburst a few minutes ago, your brother hasn't exhibited any signs of disabling behavior. Of course, my field is internal medicine, not psychiatry. I've seen my fair share of fifty-one-fifties come and go but your brother doesn't seem to be much of a threat. He'll likely be released in the morning. I could be wrong, but that's my opinion."

"I was hoping—"

"As for jail, you'll have to work that out with the Sheriff. I'm told he's a compassionate man. Try talking to him. Maybe he can work something out."

"I've already tried."

"Well, that's his domain, not mine."

"Perhaps you could talk to him … explain about Oscar's background and why he can't be put in a cell. Would you be willing to do that?"

"I don't think—"

"You did say you didn't believe Oscar was a threat, right?"

"I did but that's a bit premature at this point, and I won't be the one to make that determination in any case."

Walsh slammed his fist against the phone's coin box. "Goddammit! Why the hell can't I get any cooperation from anyone? Why is it always no, no, no? Why the hell can't anyone say yes anymore?!"

"Sir, there's really no cause—"

"All I'm asking for is a little cooperation!"

"I believe I've explained as much as I can, sir. The only other suggestion I can make is that you consider some therapy for yourself. Good day."

The line fell dead.

Walsh slammed the handset against the coin box then threw it against the glass. It bounced off, struck his left shoulder, then fell limp and swayed back and forth at the end of its steel tether.

"Fuck off!" he screamed at two men who stood outside the booth and stared. "What are you looking at?!" They hurried away. He pulled a Palm Pilot from his jacket and switched to a list of phone numbers. He dialed one.

"Pride Foods," the secretary answered.

"Pride Foods?" Walsh said.

"Yes, sir," she said. "Our name has changed. We're now Pride Foods."

"Whatever. Let me talk to Cleat."

"Mr. Ledford?"

"None other."

"Whom shall I say is calling?"

"Thornton Walsh … and don't let him give you any of that 'unavailable' crap."

"One moment, sir."

She put the call on hold. A jingle extolling the company's pending new products played through the earpiece. Walsh was watching Solly and not listening.

"Thorny," Ledford said when he came on the line. "Now you know why I couldn't talk to you the other day. What do you think?"

"What do I think? I'll tell you what I think, you lowlife piece of shit! I think you're an asshole, that's what I think!"

He laughed. "I figured that's pretty much how you'd take it." He laughed again.

171

"A *real* asshole."

"You still got that block of ten thousand shares I gave you, right?"

"Fuck those shares! I stood by you, Cleat. I stuck my ass out for you. Remember, Cleat? Remember a year ago when you needed swing financing and the stock had to stay above fifteen? Keep it above fifteen, you said. Remember that?"

"Well, sure—"

"So what did I do for you? I touted your piece-of-shit company and kept the price up until you got that line of credit and this is what I get?"

"I know it sounds—"

"You know what that cost me, you dickhead? That little move cost me my job. Herschel's clients got creamed when the street got wind of your bottom line and the price collapsed. I got shoved into the shitter over that deal and Herschel flushed it. That's what I got, Cleat. Sent down. Sent to the fucking sewer!"

"I know, Thorny. I told you over and over how badly I felt about that. I tried to make it up to you. Gave you the ten thousand shares. It was all I could do."

"*All* you could do?"

"Came out of my personal account."

"So when I drove up to see you Monday, you didn't think maybe—just maybe—you owed me something? Maybe owed me just the *courtesy* of telling me what you were going to do?"

"Look, Thorny. I felt awful about blowing you off like that but I couldn't ... I couldn't take the chance

172

you'd say something and queer the deal. Run the stock up. I just couldn't take that chance."

Walsh turned away from Solly. "Four bucks a pop? You're not going to get away with it."

"Get away with what?"

"Give me a break, Cleat. You think I came in yesterday's mail? What do you think I do all day?"

"Look, Thorny. The deal's over, so why don't we get together and have lunch."

"Sure, Cleat. Set the table for a thousand, though. I've got a list of your shareholders and I'll be bringing them along."

"Wha— "

"I'll tell you what, Cleat. Let's cut the crap and get to the bottom line. I want to square the books and set everything straight between us. You want to do that?"

"I'd like nothing better."

"Good. Then this is what I'm going to do. Tomorrow, Friday, I'm going to make a quick stop at Chemical Bank, then take a drive up to see you."

"I'll look forward to it, Thorny. Things have changed up here. I'll show you around."

"Forget the tour. I'll just be staying long enough to pick up your check."

"Check?"

"For ten million dollars."

"What— "

"I'll have a certificate for two hundred and fifty thousand shares of whatever you're calling your company now, and you're going to buy it. Not at four, though. You're going to pay forty. That's ten million, Cleat, or I start talking."

"You're crazy, Walsh."

"Really? I've been to the grocery stores, Cleat. They tell me sales of Pride Premium are up seventy-eight percent. And I've talked to the networks. You've cut your ad budget down to twenty-five percent of what it was six months ago. So, how did you do it, Ledford? How do you move so much product without advertising?"

"What can I say? Pride Premium's a great product."

"Bullshit! I read the label. It's nothing but junk and you sell it for triple what other brands cost."

"It's—"

"I talked to your vendors, too. What about actinomycin-D? Does that ring any bells?"

"Acti...? I don't know what you're talking about."

Walsh turned around. Solly had not budged. "Don't play dumb with me, Ledford. I'm in no mood for bullshit. Nobody uses actinomycin-D in dog food, so I had to ask myself, what the hell is he doing with gallons of it? Fertilizing his lawn?"

"I really don't know what you're talking about, Walsh. Gallons? I don't even know what that stuff is."

"Okay, okay," Walsh said. "I can see we're going to have to get in the trenches. Forget Chemical. I'm going to hang up now, go back to my office and drop a dime on the FDA. Goodbye."

"Thorny, wait!"

"Fuck off, Ledford!"

- 20 -

Bill Ruecker scooted his chair away from the sleek gray and silver Titan 80-300 scanning transmission electron microscope in the Pride Foods product development lab. He pushed his glasses up and rubbed his eyes. They were red and sore from the strain of watching miniscule devices float aimlessly about on a tray in the scope's sealed chamber.

A hungry army of white blood cells almost completely ignored the slowly flapping, hinge-like machines—machines so small that thirty thousand of them laid end to end would not even cover the width of a human hair. Nanomachines. Machines built of precisely manipulated atoms. An incredible technology, Ruecker thought. He allowed a smile, relieved his work was finally showing results. He jabbed at a button on his computer keyboard and watched several pages of data shuttle from the printer.

The smile broadened and his head began to bob as he guessed at his bonus. It would be big this time. Real big! Little doubt about that. Much bigger than the one he got for his work on Pride Premium. Maybe enough

175

for a swimming pool. Maybe a pool *and* a big screen plasma TV.

He snatched the first few pages from the printer and checked the numbers. Active device counts stood at ninety-two percent. "Outstanding!" he said to the empty lab. He stood and arched his back, stretching taught muscles, then grabbed the phone and dialed.

"It's positive, Mr. Ledford."

"And …"

"And attacks dropped off to almost nothing. Eight percent."

"Well, that's good work, Bill. What did you use?"

"Paclitaxel. Tried no less than forty compounds and the only other one that works is sirolimus. Got the same results. I'd go with paclitaxel. Cheaper. Not as cheap as actinomycin-D but you can't argue with the results."

"Eight percent, huh? That should pass muster."

"It should more than pass, sir." The pool and TV jumped into focus. "I was surprised. Expected higher because of the unit volume and potential for coating overlap. I know we could get it down to four or five if you'd let me cut the batch volume."

"Can't do that but I *can* live with eight percent. That's for everything, right? Hot foods, too?"

"Yeah, uh … well, no." He stopped bobbing. "Hot foods are a different story. Hot popcorn oil really does a number on the paclitaxel, not to mention the enzyme coating. Really breaks 'em down fast. Same with coffee. Brew temps don't get nearly as high as popcorn oil but the numbers still aren't acceptable. Around forty-five percent for oil and thirty for coffee."

"Not *acceptable*? That's *worse* than not acceptable! What the hell have you been doing down there?"

Ruecker flashed on his home and grimaced. The image of the inviting, zero-horizon swimming pool and plasma TV began to fragment. "I've been working day and night, sir, that's what I've been doing. I can't change the physics of heat and that's what brews coffee and makes popcorn." He caught himself and lowered his voice, concealing his frustration. "But everything else works great. Dry seasonings, milk—if we add it after pasteurization—butter, toothpaste, pancake syrup: all eight percent. That's four hundred percent *better* than Pride Premium. Eight percent is as close to perfection as you'll get, Mr. Ledford, with the batch volumes you want, and you'll get at least that number in just about anything that isn't heated—except pickles, maybe. Don't know what vinegar acid will do yet. But I'll be working night and day on that too. I'll solve the problems, sir. Everything will be ready by next month's launch date. You don't have to worry about that."

"We don't have a month. Omni moved it up."

"I don't … How far up? What I mean, sir, is I don't think I can get it done any sooner. How far up?"

"Tomorrow. Friday. They want to start the blends Friday night."

"Friday *night*?" He brushed errant strands of red hair from his freckled face. "No, sir! That's not possible at all. I haven't even started my time studies. I don't have a clue about breakdowns over time and I haven't even started on pickles or vinegar-based salad dressings. Just the problems with popcorn and coffee alone are Herculean. No, sir. Tomorrow night's out."

"Forget the time studies. There's too much at stake here and I don't have time to explain it to you. You just keep working. I've got to make a call but then I'll be down to take a look. And by the way, Omni Foods is sending one of their food techs tomorrow afternoon and I want you to go over what you've been doing and answer any questions he might have. Got it?"

"Yes, sir."

"You just keep working and clean up that sty down there you call a lab. I don't want Omni thinking we run a schlock outfit."

"I'll clean up, sir, and I'll be here. Working away."

Ruecker slumped into the chair.

The pool and TV vanished.

- 21 -

"Morning, Alice," Walsh mumbled as he shuffled in. "Hope your day is going …" He caught sight of two men in dark ill-fitting polyester suits and scuffed dress shoes seated on the sofa. "… going better than mine."

"Mr. Ledford from Pride Foods called," Alice said. "I didn't know they changed their name. Anyway, he said to call him as soon as you got in." She gestured to the men. "And these gentlemen are here to see you." Neither smiled as they rose. "They're from NYPD."

"Are you Thornton Walsh?" the older of the two men asked.

"That's right. And you are …?"

"Detective Douvros." He nodded at his partner. "This is Detective Portillo."

Portillo squinted at the bandage and splint across Walsh's nose but said nothing. Walsh extended a hand but neither man made a move to shake it. He withdrew it and discreetly rubbed the sweating palm against his trousers.

"We'd like to talk to you … in private. Do you have somewhere …?"

"Uh, sure, detective." Walsh waved at his inner office and stood aside. "What's this all about?"

"Benjamin Weinstein," Douvros said.

"Ben? Is he in some sort of trouble?"

"Not anymore," Portillo said, his face expressionless.

"Good, good," Walsh said. "Have a seat in there. I'll be with you in a moment."

The detectives strode into the office and sat. Walsh closed the door behind them.

"Is anything wrong?" Alice asked.

"No, no. Everything's fine. What did Ledford say, Alice? What were his *exact* words?"

She gave him a curious look. "Just what I told you. That you should call him as soon as you got in." She paused. "Oh, yes. And that you shouldn't talk to anyone before you talked to him. Should I get him on the line?"

Walsh smiled. "Naw, not now. Let him wait. I'll see what the NYPD wants, then let you know."

"Very well."

Walsh entered his inner office and sat at his desk. "Sorry to keep you waiting. What can I do for you?"

"You had an appointment with Mr. Weinstein yesterday," Douvros said. "We'd like to know more about that."

Walsh leaned back. "Actually, I never kept the appointment. I called to cancel it but he already left, apparently. Why?"

"You didn't see him?"

"No. Why?"

"What time was your appointment?"

180

"I don't know ... uh ... Wednesday? Probably after the market closed sometime. I don't go out during trading hours." He leaned forward. "Maybe four-thirty, five. What's this about?"

Douvros narrowed his eyes. "Benjamin Weinstein was murdered yesterday," he said, not blinking.

"*Murdered?* My God! That's terrible. How?"

"We can't say. Your appointment was in his book but the time wasn't indicated. That's why we're here."

"Oh my God." Walsh threw his hands up. "I can't believe it. Ben is dead? Are you sure?"

"Ticket's been punched," Portillo said, nodding.

Douvros frowned. "Why did you cancel the appointment?" he asked.

"I don't recall exactly." Walsh began to fish through his desk for a cigar. "Guess I was busy."

"Can you tell us where you were yesterday?"

"Right here." Walsh didn't look up. "I was here all day. Ask my secretary if you want."

"We will," Portillo said.

"When was the last time you saw Mr. Weinstein?" Douvros asked.

"Last time?" Walsh found a panatela and tried to remove the wrapper but his sweaty fingers failed to grip the thin gold tear strip. "Last time was ... was ... damn cellophane! Men smoke cigars, not babies. They don't have to make these kid-proof." He bit down on the tear strip and jerked the cigar away, leaving a long section of the wrapper dangling from his lips.

Portillo smirked as Walsh spat three times before the section flew away and fluttered to the desk.

"Last time I saw Ben..." Walsh rolled the cigar tip in his mouth, trying to moisten it. "Last time ... was Tuesday, I think. Yeah, I'm pretty sure it was Tuesday. We had coffee ... at Chock Full o' Nuts." The exterior tobacco leaf kept sticking to his lips. He gave up and tossed the cigar into the drawer.

"What time was that?" Douvros asked.

"Uh ... Tuesday? I think we met around two, maybe two-thirty."

"Yeah? What did you talk about?"

"Nothing, really. Ben's wife is in a gardening club. We talked about that. And ... uh ... nothing earth-shaking. Just chit-chat and coffee."

"What else?"

"I don't know." Walsh waved a hand. "Indian Guides, maybe. Nothing important, if that's what you mean."

"That's exactly what I mean," Douvros said. "I think your discussion included more important topics than gardening and Indian Guides."

"Really? Why's that?"

"Not more than a minute ago you said you never left your office during trading hours. The market closes at four o'clock. Now you say you met with Mr. Weinstein on Tuesday at two or two-thirty."

Walsh looked away. No windows. *Not one goddamn window!*

"So, what else did you and Mr. Weinstein talk about, Mr. Walsh?"

The intercom buzzer rang. Walsh jabbed at the button.

"Sorry to interrupt, sir," Alice said. "Two men are here from the Amalgamated Association of Pipe Fitters and they insist upon seeing you immediately. I told them you were in conference."

"Tell them to wait, Alice. I won't be long."

"Yes, sir. And Mr. Ledford called—again."

Walsh smiled as he switched off the intercom and turned back to the detectives. "What was it we were talking about?"

Wham! The door flew open and two men burst into the room. Both were giants, both Samoan: six-five and three-hundred pounds apiece with scowling, pock-marked faces and bad crew cuts. Walsh jerked back. Portillo reached a hand under his suit jacket and turned around. Douvros jumped up and stepped away.

"You Walsh?" one of the giants snarled.

Alice stepped through the open door. "I tried to keep them—"

"That's okay, Alice."

"You that weasel Walsh?" the giant asked again.

"I am, and let me introduce you to my guests. This is Detective Douvros and his partner, Detective Portillo. NYPD."

"Oh, yeah?" the second giant said, eyeing Douvros. "I ate a cop for breakfast." He spat on the carpet. "One a you wanna be my lunch?"

Portillo stood and pulled his 9mm Berretta from its holster. He held it behind his back. Walsh saw it. The giants didn't.

"You some kind of dumb shit?" Portillo said. He took a step toward the man.

"Now, now," Walsh said as he rose from the chair. "Let's all take a breath and cool down here. Let's just relax a second." He walked around the desk and stood next to Portillo. "I'll just be a couple more minutes with these officers," he said to the giants, "then I'll be happy to see you." He walked to the door and gestured outside. "Please. Ten minutes."

"Fuck you, Walsh. We're not leaving 'til we get the money."

"Of course," Walsh said. "Of course. It'll just be another few minutes and I'll have a check cut for you." He waved again at the outer office. "Please. Just have a seat out there and I'll be right with you."

"Three minutes, pimple-lips," the first giant said. "You got three minutes."

The huge men lumbered out.

Walsh closed the door. Portillo stuffed the pistol back into its holster.

"I wonder if we could finish this another time?" Walsh said. "I'm kind of busy right now, as you can see."

"Those guys look like union muscle," Douvros said. "You want us to stick around?"

"Naw. Thanks, anyway. They're just a couple of clients. Got burned pretty bad in a few trades last week and they're closing their account. I can handle it. Thanks just the same."

"Alright." Douvros handed Walsh his business card. "Tomorrow," he said. "Come down to the precinct before five o'clock. We'll be waiting."

Walsh took the card and slipped it into his shirt pocket without looking. "Sure, sure. I'll be there. No problem. Thanks for understanding." He pulled the door open. The giants stood with folded arms near the outer door. Walsh escorted the detectives into the room. "I'll just be a second," he said to the Samoans. He stepped out with Douvros and Portillo. He walked with them to the bank of elevators and pushed the *down* button. "Think I'll pop down for a cigar," he said to their quizzical expressions.

"Looks like you busted up your nose pretty good," Portillo said.

Walsh again stabbed at the button. "No, no. Had a polyp removed is all. It's not broken." He swiveled his head back and forth between his office door and the elevators.

"That so?" Portillo said. "My sister had one removed six months ago and she didn't look anything like that. Not even a Band-Aid to show for it."

"Probably had a real doctor do it," Walsh said.

The elevator door opened and the men started in. Walsh gave a quick glance back at his office and saw the door swing open. One of the giants stepped out.

"Hey scumbag!" the man shouted. He started to run. "Your ass is—"

The elevator door closed and Walsh punched the button for the garage several times.

"Excuse me," Douvros said. He leaned in front of Walsh and pushed the button for the lobby. "Gonna pop down for a cigar, huh?"

The elevator began its decent.

"Keep 'em in my car," Walsh said. "Got a humidor in there." He wiped small beads of sweat from his forehead.

185

"You'll get cancer smoking those things," Portillo said, again studying Walsh's splint and bandage.

Walsh frowned and shook his head. "No kidding? I never heard that before. Cancer, you say?"

"That's right. My uncle died from cigars. He was fifty-two."

"What can I say?"

"I won't smoke. Say that."

Walsh turned around and stared at the man. "Tell me something, detective. You look like an intelligent man despite your occupation. Maybe you can tell me why perfect strangers believe they've got a license to criticize another person's habits and dispense medical advice? Any idea about that, detective? I mean, I didn't bring up the fact that your suit should have been cleaned three years ago, did I? Or that your breath smells like a bad fart and the stink from your armpits is about to make me vomit."

The door opened to the lobby.

"I oughtta make—"

"Come on, Lou," Douvros said, grabbing Portillo's arm. "We'll finish this tomorrow." He pulled his partner from the elevator.

"Before five o'clock, smart guy!" Portillo yelled through the closing door.

Walsh continued the ride down to the garage then raced over to the valet. He pulled a twenty from his pocket and clasped it into the man's palm.

"I need my car right now, Allen. Immediately!"

Allen glanced around at the faces of the dozen other men and women waiting for their cars, then discreetly opened his hand.

Walsh shoved another twenty into it. "Immediately!" he repeated.

"Right away, Mr. Walsh."

Allen hurried off to the key board as Walsh took a few steps back to check the elevators. Nothing. He returned to the drive line and shifted on his feet. A Mercedes pulled up and two waiting women in business suits sauntered to it. They were talking in serious tones and stopped next to the passenger door. A valet got out, accepted a tip from one of the women then went to the key board.

Tires squealed on slick cement thirty yards away as Allen wheeled Walsh's grey Lexus around a corner and up the drive line. He stopped behind the Mercedes and honked twice. The two women scowled at him and continued talking. Walsh stepped back for another check of the elevators. One opened, the Samoans rushed out. Walsh ran to his Lexus and jumped in the passenger seat. He leaned onto Allen's lap, jerked the door closed and locked it.

"Take it around the corner!" he shouted.

"What?"

"Drive around the fuckin' Mercedes, Allen! Go!"

Allen put the car in reverse. A Lincoln was stopped behind him. The bumpers collided.

Whaack! Walsh glanced up at his window. One of the giants struck it with the butt of a gun. The second was at the key board, pawing through the rows. The first giant again slammed the gun against the window. The pane shattered into a shower of a thousand fragments. Walsh turned away from the rain of shards. Women screamed.

187

"Get out of here, Allen!"

Walsh shoved the gearshift into drive and jammed his hand on the gas pedal. The Lexus lurched forward and slammed into the Mercedes, exploding both front air bags. The engine died. A thick hand grabbed his thigh and tightened around it. The colossus had him. He groped for the inside door handle. Walsh reached for the ignition key. It was covered by the now-deflated air bag. The giant found the handle, let go of Walsh's leg and yanked the door open.

The giant clamped both of his enormous hands around Walsh's ankles and pulled his body along the leather seat. Walsh flailed for a grip on anything to stop it. Then he wasn't sliding anymore. He glanced up. Solly had an arm around the giant's thick neck in a stranglehold. He was pulling him back, away from the Lexus. More women screamed. Solly's free hand pounded the giant's face and head.

"Get out!" Walsh yelled at Allen. The man was limp, dazed from the impact of the air bag. Walsh reached across and opened the driver's door. He pushed Allen out and slid behind the wheel. He ripped the air bag from the wheel and switched on the ignition. The car gunned to life. He threw the shift into drive and rammed the Mercedes. He backed up, rammed it again then careened around it with a piercing screech from the tires. The second giant ran toward Solly. A set of keys dangled from his clenched fist.

Walsh turned the corner. He sped along the spiral driveway from the basement garage to the Fifth Avenue street level and laid on the horn as he shot out of the building and into the daylight. A smartly dressed woman with a Saks shopping bag jumped out of the way. He wheeled the car to the right: a long row of stopped taxis. He slammed on the brakes. The light ahead changed to green. The line of cars moved. He accelerated, then braked, accelerated, then braked to a stop. Ahead, a man in a Con Edison vest and hard hat held up both arms. He motioned to the driver of a backhoe on the sidewalk to move the machine onto the street. The driver nodded. The backhoe rocked back and forth as it bounced down the curb and into the traffic lane. Walsh pushed down on the horn.

Wham! Something hit the Lexus from behind. Walsh was thrown against the seat. He shot a look in the rearview mirror. A blue Ford sedan and the two giants! *Wham!* They rammed him again. Walsh jerked the wheel to the right and stomped on the gas. He jumped the curb and sped down the empty sidewalk. The man in the Edison vest hollered something as Walsh raced by.

He checked the mirror again. The Ford hurtled along the sidewalk behind him. Walsh swung the car off the sidewalk when he passed the backhoe and drove into the empty traffic lane. He raced ahead, then turned right at the end of the block: more stopped traffic! He slammed on the brakes and checked the mirror. The Ford slid to a stop behind him and the doors swung open. Ahead, the signal changed to green. The line of cars inched forward. The huge Samoans filled the rearview mirror as Walsh inched the Lexus forward. Too late. One of the monsters was at the driver's side door. He tried to pull it open. The other giant reached through the broken window of the passenger door for

189

the inside handle. The man on Walsh's side kicked at the window with the heel of his boot. The boot bounced off. The passenger door swung open. The other man stuck his head inside. One of his massive hands clawed the air near Walsh's head. *Wham!* Another kick from the boot. The window held. Walsh's head swiveled back and forth, bobbing and dodging the clawing swings of the other giant, now halfway inside the Lexus.

"NYPD!" a voice bellowed from behind. "Step away from the car!" Both giants and Walsh turned to look. A tan sedan with a single rotating red light on the top was stopped behind the Ford. The two familiar figures of detectives Portillo and Douvros marched up, guns drawn and leveled.

"Back away from the car with your hands up!" Portillo shouted. The detectives stopped behind the trunk of the Lexus, one on each side.

"Better do what the man says, jerk-off," Walsh said to the giant inside the car, "or he'll have *your* ass for lunch."

The giant grinned then snapped a quick jab at Walsh's face, striking him on the nose. Walsh screamed and fell back. Bright, oxygen-rich blood flowed into the white bandage, turning it crimson.

"Get out of the car, scumbag!" Portillo yelled to the Samoan.

He slowly backed out.

Portillo peered into the car when the man was clear. "You alright?"

"Damn nose is broken," Walsh said.

Portillo smiled. "Get it fixed before tomorrow, 'cause I'm gonna bust it again when you come down to the precinct. Call *me* a fart-breath, will ya."

"Oh, God, it hurts," Walsh moaned as he dabbed a handkerchief at his nose.

"If it was me driving, I wouldn't have stopped. You can thank my partner your nose is all that's wrong with ya. Now get outta here before I hook you up along with these other two clowns."

Walsh sat up and drove away. He watched in the rearview mirror as the detectives led the Samoans to the tan sedan. He turned left at the next corner. Two more blocks and he stopped at the curb. He dialed from his cell phone.

"Let me talk to Ledford," he said to the secretary. "This is Thornton Walsh."

"Oh, yes sir," the woman said. "He's expecting your call. I'll connect you now."

Pause.

"Thorny," Ledford said, coming on the line. His voice smiled. "I'd almost given—"

"I'm in a rush, Cleat. What do you want?"

"You sound different."

Walsh pulled the bloody handkerchief from his face and tossed it on the floor. "Forget it. There's nothing different. Alice said you called. What do you want?"

"Well, hey. I called to tell you … what I wanted to say was I've been doing some soul-searching since we hung up earlier."

"Yeah?"

"That's right, Thorny. I wanted to say I screwed up, really messed up with you, and I want to make amends."

"Oh, yeah? How's that?" Walsh fished through the glove box for some Kleenex.

"You've always treated me square, Thorny, and then you somehow end up on the bottom. That's not right. Not for someone who's stuck his neck out for me more than once. I realize that now."

Walsh found some tissues and mopped the blood from his lips and cheeks.

"Are you there?" Ledford asked.

"Yeah, yeah. I'm here. I'm listening."

"It's just not right and I'm going to do something about it."

"Go on."

"Yes, well, uh … you haven't talked to anyone, have you? I mean about what you were saying earlier?"

Walsh tossed the bloody Kleenex to the floor next to the handkerchief and reached for more.

"I called. Yeah." Walsh smiled at the lie but it brought a sharp pain and he stopped. "Left a message. They haven't called back yet."

"You can't take that call, Thorny!" Ledford's voice cracked and then he lowered it. "I mean, that wouldn't be in our mutual best interests."

"What mutual interests? I have no interest here."

"That's what I was getting to. What I was calling about. Christ, I shouldn't be talking to you about this on a cell phone."

"Well, that's all I've got in here. Had the phone booth taken out last week."

"Jesus, Thorny. This is serious. Stop with the jokes, already."

"Alright, but hurry up."

"Sure. I'm talking about that block of stock ... the two hundred and fifty thousand shares."

"What about it?"

"I called Chemical Bank and they said they only show an Oscar Walsh as the beneficial owner of a block that size."

"He's my brother."

"Oh. Good. Good. That makes it easier."

"Makes *what* easier?"

"The sale. A lot of eyebrows would be raised if it was in your name but your brother—that's different."

"So, now you want to buy it?"

"That's what I'm getting at."

"At forty?"

"At forty."

Walsh sat back. "I don't know," he said. "I just don't know."

"Damn you, Thornton! Stop fucking with me!"

"Okay, okay." Walsh straightened in his seat. "Here's how it's going to work, Cleat. You're going to wire two million to my brother's bank in Oregon ... today ...now ... as soon as we hang up. Call Alice. She's got his bank's routing and account numbers. If you do that, I don't take the call from the FDA. You with me so far?"

"I am."

"Good. Then, tomorrow morning, sometime before noon, I'm going to be out to see you and you're going to have the rest waiting for me—in cash."

"Eight million in *cash*? I can't do that!"

"Then we've got nothing more to say to each other. Good-bye."

"No, wait. Wait a minute! Will you wait a damn minute?"

"What?"

"How about a wire for the balance. How about that?"

Walsh glanced at his watch. "It's two-thirty, Cleat. Plenty of time to call your bank and get them working on the delivery."

"You're a prick, Walsh! That's what you are, a goddamn prick!"

Walsh smiled but again the pain made him stop. "I'm not going to trade barbs with you, Cleat. Your insults aren't making any points, either. I'm calling my brother's bank in two hours. If the money hit his account, I'll see you tomorrow. If it isn't there, the FDA and the FBI will see you tomorrow. Either way, you'll get a visit."

He hung up.

- 22 -

Hotel Marriott Marquis
New York City
Friday, 8 A.M.

Lieutenant Puttz glanced around the room of bleary-eyed faces then stopped on Detective Karpinski's. His head was down, supported in his hands.

"Get a good night's rest, Ski?" Puttz asked.

Karpinski slowly raised his head. His mouth hung open and his eyes rolled up. "I think I'm gonna barf," he mumbled.

The men at his table laughed.

"What really bothers him, Lieutenant," one of the men said, "is a woman out-drank him last night."

Traci stood. She bowed to the cheers and applause of the men.

Puttz frowned and looked at Traci. "You feel any better than Ski this morning?"

"I feel great, sir."

"Good. Since you appear to be the only one in the room with a clear head, you can start ... unless someone else wants to go first..."

No one spoke.

Traci groaned, then gathered her papers and moved to the podium.

"Good morning, gentlemen," she said.

"Morning, ma'am," the men said, their voices barely audible.

"I'm told every speech should start with a joke," she said. She looked around the room. "Detective Karpinski, will you please stand?"

"Huh?" He raised his head a little.

"Please stand up," she repeated.

He sighed and struggled to his feet.

A moment passed.

"Thank you," she said. "You may sit down."

The men roared with laughter.

"Sorry, Ski. I couldn't resist."

Karpinski cracked a smile. "You're all right, ma'am." He nodded. "Youse can break bread with me anytime."

"Thank you. Maybe I will."

The men cheered. His tablemates slapped him hard on his shoulders.

"Okay," Traci said. She glanced at her papers then looked up. "Our group had ninety-three reported attacks that fell within the parameters for this symposium. I thought that was a lot but from talking to some of the other groups, it seems to be about average. One group had a hundred and twenty-seven. Another group had sixty-six. I don't know what the other group had but they're probably somewhere in—"

"We had eighty-nine," the lead detective from the remaining group said.

"I rest my case," she said. "Anyway, our group broke down everything according to the Lieutenant's guidelines and we came up with these commonalities." She held up her hand, her thumb and forefinger forming an *O*. "Nothing. Zip. Absolutely zero in common."

She glanced at Puttz. His eyebrows rose.

"Of the ninety-three victims," she went on, "twenty-five were Caucasian, twenty-five Puerto Rican or Jamaican, twenty African-American and twenty-three a smattering of Oriental, Latina and Middle-Eastern. That was roughly the percentage breakdown of each of our city's populations. No particular race was apparently singled out or targeted. Then we cross-checked their ages and found the numbers fit the bell curve for persons one might expect to find in any of our Skid Row areas. No common factor there either." She checked her papers again and continued. "Although most of the attacks occurred during the nighttime hours, which was expected, we found nothing to link them to a particular time of day, or weather, or day of the week or anything else. I admit I've had very little experience working sex crimes but, according to the experience of the detectives in our group, the majority of sex crimes—over eighty percent—are committed by persons known to the victims. However, out of our ninety-three cases, only ten perps were known to the victims. And of those ten, only two of the victims described their relationship as more than casual. The others weren't even speaking relationships. Just passing, familiar faces."

Lieutenant Puttz raised a hand. "Did you look at appearances? Anything common about their appearance? Hair color? Stature?"

"Yes, sir, we did. Our victims were about as nondescript as one might find anywhere. They ran the gamut from short to tall, slender to obese, dark hair to light, young to old, and on and on -- absolutely no pattern, no common physical characteristic."

"Let me interrupt a minute," Lieutenant Puttz said. He looked around the room. "Anybody here, any other group come up with something different?"

The men shook their heads.

Puttz stood. "Nothing?" His eyes narrowed. "No common traits?"

"Not here," the red-haired detective said.

"We didn't come up with anything either," said another detective.

"Manning?" Puttz asked the man from the remaining group.

"Bupkus," he said.

"You did find time to work your cases, I hope, before you went out to close the bars last night. Right?"

"Oh, yeah, Lieutenant," several men said.

"We were as surprised as you," one said.

Puttz shook his head and sat. "Go ahead, Sergeant."

"Thank you. So, with nothing to go on with our victims, we began to examine the perpetrators. We first looked at their ages and found they ran from the mid-thirties to, believe it or not, the mid-sixties. Actually, one man in his mid-sixties was identified in four of our cases." She smiled. "Guess that puts a hole in the theory that rape is a sex crime."

"Maybe not," one of the men said.

"What?" she asked.

"I said maybe not. Ever hear of Viagra?"

The men laughed.

"Yes, well … I doubt the free clinics are dispensing Viagra along with Methadone and penicillin but I might be wrong."

The men chuckled.

"Anyway," she continued, "we next focused on the perpetrators' physical characteristics—height, weight, race, musculature—and drew blanks there, too. Same with the methods of force used. But…." she pulled the last page of her papers from the bottom and set it on top. "… but we did begin to notice some peculiarities. Nothing as obvious as the man's age or race but more subtle things." She glanced at Detective Karpinski. "Nugatory things."

The men laughed.

Karpinski grinned.

"We talked a little about that yesterday and I'd almost forgotten but it turns out they were the only factors common to nearly all of our perpetrators."

Puttz straightened in his chair.

"As I said earlier," Traci went on, "we had ninety-three cases from the cities for our group. From those, we identified fifty-seven perpetrators with distinctive characteristics. Obviously, several were described in more than one report but of those fifty-seven slightly over three-quarters were described as having a lot of face and body hair, also acne—even the older men. Many were in some stage of baldness. Quite a few had thin skin, deep voices, halitosis was common, and the most identifiable characteristic of all—purple lines on their stomachs. Furthermore," she went on, "not as many but a still significant number of the men were described as having round faces—'moon-shaped,' some victims said—and their shoulders were large and soft. 'Fatty' was what several described."

She turned to Puttz.

He stared back at her, waiting. When she said nothing else, he stood. "That's it?" he asked.

"Pretty much as far as—"

"Balding, baritone, pimply-faced men with bad breath and blue lines on their stomachs?"

"Well …"

"I'd like to hear your recommendations," Puttz said, "if you and your group have any. Recommendations on how we're supposed to get a handle on this situation with the kind of crime-stopper information we've just heard?"

"We didn't—"

"How's about this, Lieutenant," Ski said. "How's about we cordon off the city and make every bald man with zits and bad breath give a DNA sample?"

The men roared with laughter.

Puttz grimaced.

"We didn't have time for recommendations," Traci said. "But I think the characteristics I've identified will be very helpful. They're very descriptive."

"What you've described, Sergeant, is something for the CDC, not the police."

"Not exac—"

"I'm a cop," Puttz said. He waved a hand around the room. "We're all cops ... here to discuss a cop problem, like rape. Rape is a cop problem, not a CDC problem."

"Sir, I do have something else."

"Well, then by all means, Sergeant, do go on." Puttz sat.

"Of our ninety-three cases, five arrests were made. Naturally, in the course of the arrests, the perpetrators were taken to area hospitals for AIDS testing. We checked the medical reports for each of those arrestees and found they all had elevated blood sugar levels. That may very well be a dietary thing and I believe we should ask the health departments in our respective cities to take a close look at the food served in the soup kitchens. High sugar levels might be a connection with our perpetrators and knowing their diets might be the key."

"Not likely," the red-haired detective said.

"Why is that?"

"Because we'd have a lot more perps, that's why."

"Not necessarily," Traci said. "Some men may tolerate high-sugar diets better than others. I really think it's worth looking at."

Puttz glanced at his watch. "Alright. Thank you, Sergeant. Let's take a fifteen-minute break and when we come back we'll hear from another group. Hopefully they'll have something for cops to work on and not more tips for the health departments and CDC."

201

- 23 -

"Hi, Lieutenant," Traci said into the phone. "I got your message. We're on a break."

"Having a good time up there in the Big Apple?"

She laughed. "I wouldn't exactly call it that."

"Didn't think you would. So tell me, are you getting a handle on the attacks or is it like most symposiums: a big waste of time and taxpayer's money?"

"Not a waste at all, sir. It's very interesting. Very revealing. We're split into four groups and I've already given the report for mine."

"How'd it go?"

"Not too bad. The others will be giving their reports when we get back but I don't think they'll have anything to add. I've already talked to them and pretty much know what they'll say."

"Then you might be able to slip away for a few minutes?"

"Slip away?"

"Run a little errand for me?"

"Sure, I guess so. I'll have to check first but I think it'll be okay."

"Good. Shouldn't take long."

"What is it?"

"The airport detail at Logan popped a guy for four-fifteen about an hour ago. Really agitated and had to be restrained. Nothing serious but the interesting part is the guy had a lot of money on him -- a hundred thousand, to be exact -- in cash."

"Wow! That's a lot of walking-around money."

"Exactly. The interdiction team checked him out and the guy's clean. No narc or mob connections as far as they could determine, just your average garden-variety screwball with a bunch of bucks."

"What's he doing with all that cash?"

"Good question. Interdiction says he's from Oregon. A logger, whatever that is. Had a few minors with the locals there but nothing to write home about. Got released from a fifty-one-fifty hold this morning, then he split. With all that cash, interdiction called his bank and guess what—the guy's loaded. The bank said he came into a lot of money recently. A *lot* of money. Two million. Wired in from New York."

"Really."

"As his story goes—and we have no reason to dispute it—the money came from his brother and they were supposed to meet at Logan. There's still plenty of time before their flight out to Barbados but the brother was a no-show when Looney Tune's plane arrived, so he was just sitting around and waiting. The poor guy had some heavy-duty prescription meds on him, which he apparently forgot to take, and that's probably why he came out of his tree and lost it."

"Have you talked to his brother?"

"Tried to. Supposed to be a hotshot stockbroker up there. Called his office and his secretary said she hasn't seen him today. Not like him to not check in with her, she said. Tried calling his apartment but the phone's disconnected."

"I can see where this is going."

"Thought you would."

"What about NYPD? Why not have them check on him?"

"I called and they'll do it but they said it'd be a while before they could get on it. I don't want to wait. I want to find out more about that money -- now, before Looney Tune goes to Barbados. That's where you come in."

"Wait a minute. If the brother is supposed to meet your guy at the airport, why not just have interdiction talk to him when he shows up?"

"Because there's a chance he won't. He isn't listed on any of the flight manifests to Barbados or anywhere else, at least not from Logan. He could buy a ticket at the last minute but that wouldn't give us time to interview him. Couldn't detain him without probable cause, you know."

"True."

"Interdiction's going to keep an eye out in any case but I want to be a little proactive on this one. Looney Tune might be more than meets the eye."

"Alright, Lieutenant. What do you want me to do?"

"It shouldn't take long. Just do a little checking. Go over to the brother's apartment and see if he's there. If he isn't, talk to a few people—neighbors and whoever. See what you can come up with. Get a little background on him. No crime's been committed as far as we know but we do want to have a chat with him. I want to know about the two million wired to the Oregon bank and where it came from."

"Okay. I'll do it. What about the man at the airport? Looney Tune, as you call him."

"Interdiction says he's better now. Took his meds and is calm as the proverbial cucumber. They'll keep an eye on him, like I said. He's still at Logan and waiting. He'll be waiting a long time, though. His flight doesn't leave for another nine hours. That should give you plenty of time to track down the brother."

"Nine hours? You said do a *little* checking."

"Yeah, well…. The brother's name is Thornton Walsh. His brother calls him Tee-Tee or something like that. Do whatever you think to dig him up. Okay?"

She sighed. "Okay, Lieutenant." She pulled a small notepad and pen from her purse. "Give me his address and the number for his office."

- 24 -

Traci found Detective Karpinski's unmarked Plymouth where he said it would be: in front of the hotel, parked in a red zone. The mike and connecting rubber-coated spiral cord to the police radio were slung over the rearview mirror—a universal signal to passing meter maids the car was off limits.

She slid behind the wheel then quickly got out when an overwhelming stench assaulted her nostrils. She found the offending sources—rotting, half-eaten burgers, fries and pastrami—and tossed them into a trashcan. She got back in the car, rolled down the window and unfolded a note from the hotel's concierge with directions to the South Bronx Free Clinic and Walsh's apartment in New Rochelle. The clinic would be her first stop. Twenty minutes later, she was deep in the Bronx.

She twice drove past the trash-strewn breezeway between two brown brick buildings before realizing it led to the clinic's dented metal door. She parked on the littered street then entered the facility.

Three Latino men and two Jamaican women with toddlers sat on uncovered wooden chairs in a small reception area. One of the men coughed repeatedly and scratched at open sores in the crook of his arm. The men glanced up as Traci entered then quickly dropped their heads and resumed absent stares at the cracked linoleum floor. Traci quietly closed the door and stood by it. Another door, past a cluttered metal desk, was open and muffled voices of a man and woman came from beyond it.

An unseen woman shouted from beyond the second door, "Take a form from the desk and fill it out!"

Traci moved to the open doorway and looked in. A short hallway led past several closed doors on the left to a large room at the end. That door was open. Inside the room, a gray-haired man in a white lab coat stood near a table, his back to the hall. A shirtless man lay on the table, face down. A Jamaican woman in a nurse's uniform peered through the doorway and spotted Traci.

"Take a form, missy!" she said, annoyed. "I'll be out to get you when it's your turn!"

"I'm Traci Ross. I called Dr. Kleinman earlier."

The man in the lab coat turned to look then beckoned with a hand. "I'm Dr. Kleinman. Come on back." He returned his attention to the man on the table.

Traci went into the room and stood to one side, behind the doctor. He was thumping the man's back and listening through a stethoscope.

"Normal to palpation," he said to the nurse.

She jotted a note in the man's chart.

The doctor walked his hands along the man's spine then squeezed thick layers of fat near his shoulders.

207

"How long have you had this?" Dr. Kleinman asked.

The man tensed from the pressure. "Don't know." He spoke in a low, husky voice. "No mirrors in the park john."

Traci moved from behind the doctor and her mouth fell open when the hump on the man's back came into view.

"Alright," Kleinman said. "Let's turn over."

The man struggled to turn on the narrow examination table. A kick from one of his legs made the difference. His eyes blinked open then shut again when assailed by the intense white light from the overhead examination lamp.

Kleinman grimaced. "Another one," he mumbled to his nurse.

The nurse leaned in for a closer look. Narrow purple streaks traced a stretch mark pattern across the man's abdomen. She nodded and noted the condition in the man's chart.

Traci's eyes widened. She took a step back.

Kleinman continued to probe and poke at the man's chest and arms.

"You're a long way from home, aren't you, Miss Ross?" Kleinman said, not looking at her.

"Yes, uh ... I ... uh ..." She continued to stare at the strange, but familiar marks on the man's stomach. He was Caucasian, about forty or so, with a thick carpet of black hair on his chest and arms. Thinning black hair on his head was messed and matted. Fresh pimples dotted his chin and forehead.

"Good job of tracking me down," Kleinman said as he poked. "I only come here twice a month. It's how I give back."

"That's … very …"

He turned around and smiled. "Not like your job, though. You give every day."

She forced a smile. "True enough."

"You wanted to see me about Thornton Walsh?"

"Yes, sir, but it can wait."

"What's ol' Thorny gotten himself into this time?"

"I'm not sure. I can wait, doctor. You're busy right now."

"That's okay. Milt doesn't mind." He spoke to the man on the table. "You don't care if Miss Ross and I talk, do you Milt?"

The man grunted a *no*.

"So, what can I do for you, Miss Ross? What do you want to know about Mr. Walsh?"

"He's apparently gone missing, doctor, and it seems you were the last to see him. Treated a broken nose?"

"One of the worst I've seen. Two breaks, actually. He'll probably look like Jack Dempsey when they're healed. Missing, huh?"

"Yes, sir."

He turned back to the table and the man. "Feeling any better, Milt?"

"Uh-huh."

"No more dizziness?"

The man grinned. "Just a little sleepy, doc." His words came in a slow, sing-song cadence. "An' a buzz."

"That's from the shot I gave you, Milt. It'll wear off after a while."

"Naw…. I like it."

Kleinman laughed. "I'm sure you do. Never had any complaints, yet."

"An' I won't be the first."

"I'm going to ask you to pee in a bottle for me, Milt, then Nurse White will give you a medicine to take. It's for a test and it'll take about an hour or so to show the results."

"Whatever you want, doc."

"Good. I'd like you to stay in the reception room during that hour. Will you do that?"

The man blinked his eyes open then shielded them with a hand. "Sure, doc. I got nothin' but time. What's the medicine for?"

"It's just something I want to use to find out what's going on with you. Nothing to worry about. Just a test."

"Sure, doc. 'S'okay with me."

"After about an hour, Nurse White will come and get you and you'll have to pee again. Okay?"

"Okay."

"So void your bladder the first time, get all the pee out then drink lots of water while you're waiting. Okay? Can you pee for me now?"

"Sure, doc. I can pee."

"Good. Go ahead and get dressed and my nurse will give you the bottle."

Milt muscled himself up from the table and onto the linoleum floor. He swayed slightly, steadied himself against the table then shuffled along behind Nurse White and out of the room.

Kleinman watched them leave as he pulled latex gloves from his hands and tossed them into a waste basket. "Let's go to my office," he said.

Traci followed him in and he closed the door.

"Thorny's missing?" he asked.

"It appears that way. He was supposed to meet …" She paused, then, "Doctor, can I ask you about something else, first?"

He smiled. "Want some free medical advice?"

"Oh, no, sir. Nothing like that. It's about some cases I've been working. The reason I'm up here … in New York. Nothing about me. I'm fine."

"Okay. What?"

"That man." She nodded in the direction of the examination room at the end of the hall. "The man with the streaks on his stomach."

"What about him?"

"It's something you said. 'Another one' was what you said. What did you mean by that?"

"Oh." He moved to a chair behind a desk and sat. Traci seated herself in another chair in front of the desk. "What I meant," Kleinman went on, "was Milt was the sixth man I saw here in the last day and a half with the same condition. Pretty unusual."

"How so?"

"Unusual because Cushing's disease is so rare. Extremely rare. Only about six people in a million get it and I think I've just seen all six … in this borough, anyway."

"Is that what he has? Cushing's disease?"

"Most definitely. Now to find out why. The dexamethasone suppression test will tell me. That's what my nurse will give him after he's urinated. We'll compare his cortisol level in an hour with the sample he gives me now and see if it drops."

Traci tensed. "How do you get it? Cushing's disease. Is it contagious? I was in a room with a man who had those same streaks two days ago. He probably had it. And now, again, today."

Kleinman laughed. "No, no. You have nothing to worry about." He leaned back and clasped his hands behind his head. "It's kind of a chemical chain reaction. People usually get it when their pituitary gets out of whack. The pituitary gland produces corticotropin and endorphins. Endorphins are okay. They make you feel good. But too much corticotropin and the adrenal gland goes nuts. It starts pumping out corticosteroids and androgenic steroids like nobody's business. Too much corticosteroids and you get Cushing's disease." He shook his head. "No. Not a disease. A syndrome. Cushing's Syndrome."

"You lost me with all that, doctor."

He smiled. "Bottom line? It's not contagious."

She relaxed. "That's a relief. Six in a million. Is that what you said?"

"That's right."

"Suppose I were to tell you I know of about three dozen men who have the same purple streaks on their stomachs?"

He brought his hands down and leaned forward. "Three *dozen*? I'd have to ask what planet you're from."

"At least three dozen … that I know of. Probably a lot more."

"All with Cushing's Syndrome?"

212

"*That* I don't know," she said. "The marks were only described in reports. They haven't been diagnosed as far as I know but I did see a man in Boston with those marks."

"Where are they—those men?"

"I don't know. We're trying to find them. They're all over the map. Boston, here in New York, Baltimore … a lot of places."

Kleinman leaned back again, thinking. "Well, if that's the case, then I'd say it's still unusual but not improbable, considering the populations of those cities." He narrowed his eyes. "Are you a nurse? I thought you said you were a police officer."

"Sergeant. No, I'm not a nurse. Are there any other symptoms? Besides the streaks?"

"Sure. Did you notice Milt's face, chest and arms? All the hair?"

She nodded.

"That's a symptom. More hair than normal on those areas. The voice changes too. Gets lower. Androgenic steroids do those things. They make a man's beard grow, put hair on his chest and give him a low voice. Too much androgenic steroids and the results get exaggerated. You get lots of body hair and a deep voice. *A really* deep voice. Another symptom, though not visibly apparent, is a heightened libido and increased sex drive. The pituitary shoots out luteinizing hormones, getting the testes in the act by making testosterone. That'll make him good and horny." He smiled. "Hallucinating isn't as common but that's what brought Milt in today. He was hallucinating and some

213

of his companions carried him in. Are they still in reception?"

She shrugged. "I guess so. Three men were there when I came in. Anything else? Other symptoms?"

He cocked his head up and thought a moment. "Oh, yes," he said. "Transient feelings of euphoria are often associated with it. That's from the endorphins. You may recall I said the pituitary puts *them* into your system as well."

"Vaguely."

"Well, it does. And quite a generous supply, I might add. There are other symptoms but I'd have to look them up." He nodded toward a full bookcase against one wall.

"I won't ask you to do that, sir. How about breath? Anything about that? Is a peculiar breath a symptom?"

"Peculiar breath?" He laughed. "Peculiar how?"

"Some men were described as having a foul breath. Dog's breath."

He laughed. "I don't recall anything like that. I may be wrong but I don't think I've come across anything like dog's breath in the medical journals."

"Pardon my ignorance, doctor … and I don't want to dwell on this subject … but how … why, I guess is the better question, why do some people get it?"

"Well, people can develop Cushing's Syndrome in one of several ways. It could be caused by a tumor in the pituitary, either cancerous or non-cancerous but it's usually caused by a small-cell carcinoma in the lung. That's much more common, considering the amount of air pollution. Smoking doesn't help either. Sometimes a benign tumor on the adrenal cortex will cause it. That's also very common. In fact, half the population develops such tumors by the time they're seventy but only a tiny fraction of those—about two in a million—are active and lead to disease."

She nodded in the direction of the examination room. "Does that man have a tumor?"

He shook his head. "I don't think so. I'm not a radiologist but I didn't see anything that looked like a tumor in the X-rays I took. I'll be sending him out for an MRI and CT of his pituitary and adrenal glands. Those scans will tell me more … I hope." He frowned. "It's a little perplexing."

"Why's that, doctor?"

"So many men … all with Cushing's yet no apparent reason for it. Each of the other five men I saw had unremarkable X-rays and their scans were also negative for tumors. Yet, the levels of cortisol in their blood clearly indicated pituitary stimulation. What's so perplexing is I can't find anything to account for it. Nothing organic. No tumors. Not in the pituitary or the adrenals. But dexamethasone makes those levels fall and that tells me the cause is definitely in the pituitary." He shook his head. "I've been in private practice thirty-one years, Sergeant. Granted, it's been in Manhattan but I can count on one hand the number of patients I've seen with Cushing's Syndrome in those thirty-one years. That's how rare it is. But, now … now I see six in less than two days and you say you're aware of dozens more?" He slumped back in his chair. "Guess I'll be doing some research."

The door opened and Nurse White poked her head in. "Mrs. Ferguson has to leave soon, doctor. Will you be much longer?"

Kleinman held up his fingers. "Two minutes."

"I'll let her know," Nurse White said. She closed the door.

"I'm sorry for taking up so much of your time, doctor," Traci said.

"Don't worry about it. This is a free clinic. Mrs. Ferguson will have to wait. You said you were looking for these men. May I ask why?"

"Sure. Several cities in the northeast—Boston, Baltimore, here, New York City and a few others— have seen a substantial increase in the number of attacks —rapes—recently. Detectives from those cities, including me, are here to compare information to see if we can find out why."

"And the men with Cushings, you think they're responsible?"

"I don't know that they *have* Cushings but the perpetrators were described in crime reports and a high percentage seem to share a lot of what you just told me. Different cities, but similar descriptions in many respects. The hair, the low voices, shoulders with humps, and their breath. Maybe all of them do have Cushings. Maybe not. But it's an interesting connection, don't you think?"

"Interesting? I'd say it's astounding."

Traci nodded. "Maybe so."

"Will you let me know?"

"I will."

"Good. But you did want to see me about Mr. Walsh, right?"

"Yes, sir. He was supposed to meet his brother in Boston earlier today but he didn't show. He probably just got hung up somewhere and I really don't think it's any big deal but I've been asked to do a little checking."

"Sure."

"The State Police don't have any record of an accident involving Mr. Walsh..."

"That's good."

"... but his secretary said she hasn't heard from him today. She's worried. Said it was unlike him not to keep her informed of his schedule. He always lets her know where he is and when he'll be in, she said. The last time she heard from him was when he called from his car yesterday afternoon. He asked her to call your office and squeeze him in—wanted you to look at his nose. She said you were probably the last person to see him. That's why I'm here."

"I see. That *is* a bit of a mystery." He wrinkled his brow. "Sure doesn't sound like Thorny."

"Did you see him yesterday?"

"Sure did."

"For his nose?"

"That's right. Broke it twice, as I said. The first time several days ago, the second time was yesterday. Came into my office in the afternoon. Didn't have an appointment, but we got him in."

"Did he say how he broke it?"

"Which time?"

"Both."

"Yeah, but neither story made any sense, really. The first time, he said a street panhandler clobbered him when he refused to give the man any money but I can't imagine Thorny being anywhere panhandlers congregate. He's a stockbroker, you know. Stock *analyst.*"

She nodded.

"Works for one of those big Wall Street firms. Not on Wall Street, though. A lot of 'em moved after 9/11. Moved uptown. Not far from my office."

"I know."

"Anyway, I didn't ask him where it happened or if he reported it to the police or anything like that. I was busy and he didn't seem to want to talk about it much."

"Probably embarrassed."

"Probably. Then the second time, yesterday, he gave me an even more implausible story. Said he got shoved into the door of a crowded subway."

Traci laughed. "I've ridden on your subways. Doesn't sound all that implausible to me."

He grinned. "It would if you knew Thorny. I don't think he's been on a subway his entire life."

"Oh."

"Right."

"Well, was there anything about his demeanor yesterday that was unusual? Anything inconsistent with what you know about him to suggest he might be having problems or be in trouble in some way?"

"Quite the contrary. The man was very upbeat. Joked around a lot, as usual. That's Thorny. Always joking around. Mentioned something about some deal about to break loose. Something positive from what I

218

gathered by his tone. Didn't ask him about it, though. He's always got some deal in the fire but never talks specifics. Always said he couldn't, so I didn't even bother asking. But to answer your question, no, I didn't see anything indicative of a man in trouble."

"Doctor?!" Nurse White said as she stuck her head back in the doorway.

"I'll let you go, doctor," Traci said. "You've been a big help and I appreciate your time."

Kleinman rose. "Not at all. Give me a call at my office if I can be of any further assistance. I always cooperate with the police."

"I appreciate that, sir. One last thing."

"Sure."

"I'm going to ask one of my colleagues, an NYPD detective, to call you about Milt and the other five men with Cushing's you talked about. They may or may not be involved in what we're looking into but he'll want to check them out just the same."

"No problem. I always cooperate with the police."

- 25 -

Traci left the clinic and got into Karpinski's car. She started the engine and sat, thinking. A minute later, she switched off the engine and returned to the clinic. The three men and Milt were seated on the chairs and talking in low tones. One of the Jamaican women and the toddlers were also there. Traci looked down the hallway. Dr. Kleinman was in the examination room with Nurse White and a woman whom Traci guessed was Mrs. Ferguson. Traci waited in the reception room for them to finish.

Ten minutes later, Nurse White and Mrs. Ferguson came into the reception area. Nurse White saw Traci and scowled.

"I'll just be a second," Traci said as she breezed past her. Traci found Dr. Kleinman in his office and stood in the doorway. He was dictating, but stopped and waved her inside.

"I'm sorry to bother you, again, doctor."

"No bother. Please…" He pointed to the vacant chair. Traci sat.

"Doctor, you said something earlier that didn't register with me at the time but I need to ask."

"Sure. What?"

"Please correct me if I'm wrong: I believe you said the blood levels of cortisol in the men you examined with Cushings showed signs of pituitary gland stimulation but you didn't find any cause to account for it. Did I get that right?"

"Very good." He smiled. "Yes, you did."

"Thanks. So my question, then, is there some other way to stimulate a gland—the pituitary gland in this case since it seems to be the one that's causing the problem?"

"Another way? Besides a tumor?"

"Yes."

"Well, I'm not sure..."

"How about if it was rubbed or massaged—like a heart? A heart can be stimulated by squeezing it as in CPR. Is the same thing possible with the pituitary, doctor?"

"The short answer is 'no.' They're completely different. One is an organ—the heart—and the other is a gland."

"I know, but is it possible?"

"*Manually* stimulate the pituitary? Is that what you're asking?"

"Yes."

"I'd say not. And the reason is this, the pituitary is inside the skull, and it isn't possible to compress the skull in the same manner the sternum or rib cage are compressed during CPR." He thought a moment, then said, "Of course, if the cranium was opened and the opening was large enough for the surgeon to insert his fingers, or if the gland was probed with an instrument through a small hole in the cranium, then it might respond in some way but I'm not sure."

"I see. Well, I guess that answers my question."

"It's an interesting question, Miss Ross."

"Sergeant."

"Right. Sergeant."

"Well," Traci rose from her chair, "that's all I wanted to know, so again, I thank you for your time."

"My pleasure. Come back anytime."

- 26 -

Forty-five minutes up the FDR and the New England Throughway, plus a few transitions in between, brought Traci into New Rochelle and Walsh's maple tree-lined neighborhood. She found his building and parked a few doors away. A Salvation Army truck was double-parked in front of the building, its back door open. A metal ramp sloped from the bed to the street.

Two young boys tossed a football in the street next to the truck. A Norman Rockwell moment, she thought.

She would have missed the huge form of a man in a silver Audi parked five cars ahead of her if one of the boys had caught the ball before it bounced off the Audi's windshield.

"Do that again, you little shit," the man in the Audi yelled, "and I'll spike your head into the sidewalk!"

"Sorry, mister," the boy said. He pointed to the other lad. "It was *his* fault."

"I don't give a shit. Keep the fuckin' ball away from my car!"

The boy ran over to his friend. They huddled a moment, then sauntered off after kicking a small pile of red and orange maple leaves in the gutter at the curb.

A lanky man of about fifty, dressed in tan twill trousers and a blue plaid Pendleton shirt, stood to one side of the door to Walsh's apartment building. Traci walked to the door and started in.

"Help you?" the man in the Pendleton asked.

She stepped aside as two men wheeled a polished oak desk on a dolly through the door from inside the building.

"And you are …?" Traci asked.

"I'm the super."

"Oh. I want to see Thornton Walsh."

"You missed him. He moved out."

The desk was wheeled up the ramp and into the back of the truck.

"When?"

The men closed and locked the rear door, then got into the cab.

"This morning."

"Do you know where he went?"

The truck began to rumble down the street.

"He didn't say. Even if he did, *I* wouldn't say."

She fished her badge and identification from her purse and held it up for him to see.

"Oh," he said, eyeing the badge. "That's different. Didn't mean to be rude but a tenant's business is private business."

"I understand. Do you know where he went?"

"Not a clue. He really didn't say."

"I see. I'd like to take a look at his apartment, if you don't mind."

"No problem, but there's nothing to see, officer."

"Sergeant."

"There's nothing to see, Sergeant." He pointed to the disappearing truck. "Almost everything he had is in there. Only a bed and dresser left in his apartment."

Traci turned to look. "Wasn't that truck from the Salvation Army?"

"That's right. Mr. Walsh gave it all away. Most of it, anyways, except for some dishes he said I could have. Had some real nice suits but I couldn't use 'em. He's a portly man, you know."

"Never met him, so I wouldn't know."

"You can take my word for it."

"Was his move something he'd planned?"

"Don't think so. Least if it was, he didn't tell me about it. Called this morning and said he was giving up his apartment. Said he'd already called the Salvation Army to come by for his furniture and clothes and things but said I could have whatever I wanted. Only took the dishes, though. The suits wouldn't fit and I didn't care for the rest of what he had." He nodded toward the truck. "They'll be back tomorrow for the bed and dresser."

"Did he say why he was leaving? Any reason?"

"Of course, I asked. He's been with me over eight years and a damn good tenant, at that. Never late once with the rent in the eight years. Nice guy, too. Funny. Always had a joke." He nodded. "Hated to see him go."

"So, why *did* he leave?"

"All I can tell you is what he told me."

"Which was…?"

"Which was he was afraid to live in New York any longer. His nose was busted up pretty good earlier this week, so I guess he thought his reason would make sense."

"It didn't?"

"Not even close."

"Why's that?"

The super squared his narrow shoulders. "You tell me, Sergeant. First off, this isn't the City. It's New Rochelle. Not much crime up here in New Rochelle. The guy lives here for eight years. A model tenant. Has a good job—respectable in a lot of ways—then all of a sudden decides to pack it in and leave because of a busted nose? Doesn't give any notice. Doesn't knock on my door and say: Gill, I'm moving out at the end of the month. It's been nice knowin' ya. Nothing like that. Just a phone call to say the Salvation Army is coming by to take his stuff. Does that make sense to you?"

"I suppose not."

"I mean, he reads the papers. He watches television. The crime is in the City. Sure, we've got some out here. Not like there, though. Little stuff. But hell, it's everywhere." He shook his head. "Nope. You'll never convince me he moved on account of crime."

"Then what do you think was his real reason?"

He brought a hand to his chin and cupped it between his thumb and forefinger. "I've been turning that question in my head ever since he called, and I'll tell you this: I can't come up with a thing. Nothing legal, anyways. Couldn't be a girl involved. Mr. Walsh never had a girlfriend as far as I know. At least I never

226

seen one come around. Always got hooked up in some casino in Jersey when the mood struck, if you know what I mean."

She nodded.

"I don't know what kind of money he made and I never ask my tenants about such things. Private, you know."

"Sure."

"Seemed like he always had enough, though. Always gave me a real nice tip at Christmas, so don't think it was money. That only leaves one thing to my way of thinking."

"And that is …?"

"His work, that's what I think. I think he was about to get busted like some of those stock brokers that touted certain stocks they shouldn't have—you know, Enron, WorldCom, stuff like that—and he was about to get caught. Maybe facing time in prison. Maybe a big fine *and* prison time." He shrugged and jammed his hands into his pockets. "That's all I could come up with."

"You're saying he was dishonest?"

"Hell, no!" He jerked his hands from his pockets and stuck them on his hips. "I'm not saying that at all. Nothing like that. I'm just offering a possibility." He waved a finger at her. "No. I'm not saying he's dishonest. I got no reason in the world to say that, so don't be saying I told you he was dishonest 'cause I'm not saying that." He stuck his hand back on his hip and shifted back and forth.

"I'm only trying to get an idea of what kind of man he was," Traci said. "That's all."

"He was a good man. Very well liked. Everybody here liked him. Paid his rent. All I said was his reason for leaving so sudden *might* have something to do with his work. I got no proof of that. As far as I'm concerned, he wanted to move for his own good reasons and that's that. Nothing else."

"Of course. That's good enough for me."

"Good." He stopped moving.

"Does he have any relatives nearby?"

"Naw. I don't think so. Only one I knew about was a brother in Oregon. Mr. Walsh talked about him a lot but I don't recall him ever talking about any other relations."

"Okay. I appreciate your help. Can I see his apartment now?"

"Yeah, okay. I got to get the key. It's in my apartment."

She followed him into the building as a blue Ford with a dented front bumper and two very large Samoan men stopped at the curb across the street.

The super pulled the key from a rack behind his door. "I'll take you up." He was closing the door when the phone rang. "Shoot. Let me get that," he said. "I've been waiting…" He stepped back inside and answered the ring. Two minutes later, he asked the caller to hold and beckoned Traci into the apartment. He cupped a hand over the mouthpiece and frowned. "This could take a while. My mom." He gave her the key. "Number 808. Take the elevator. I'll be up when I'm done."

She took the key and walked out, along the hallway and past a huge Samoan man with a swollen left eye who was checking the building's tenant directory. She rode the elevator to the eighth floor and found 808.

She stepped into the foyer, leaving the door ajar for the super. The drapes over a sliding-glass door at the far end of the bare living room were open. She crossed the floor for a look: a view of Long Island Sound dotted with sail boats canted by a strong westerly lay before her. *Nice*, she mused, *must have had a pretty compelling reason to give this up*.

She moved to the bathroom and opened the cabinet drawers. Empty. A wall medicine cabinet was also empty. Not even a Q-tip. The bedroom was across the hall from the bathroom and she went in. A queen-sized mattress and bed frame were against the wall on the right. A chest of drawers stood against the left wall and a large window straight ahead afforded another stellar view of the Sound.

She set her purse on the dresser and checked each of the drawers. Nothing. She moved to the window for another look at the view and spotted a small trash can between the bed and wall. Several mismatched socks and a white dress shirt lay on top. She grimaced as she plucked them from the can and dropped them to the floor. The shirt fell open, revealing blotches of red on the collar and pocket. She bent down for a closer look. Blood. Likely from his broken nose. Several crumpled papers were inside the can and she pulled them out. Three faxes: two listing locations of New Rochelle grocery stores and small markets, the other a list of several company names entitled *Pride Pet Food Vendors*. Handwritten notations of *Ledford. Noon. Friday* were scribbled in the left margin.

229

An enormous hand shot around her head and clamped over her face and mouth. She tried to yell as she grabbed at it. Another hand slammed the back of her head. The two hands squeezed together like a vice.

She kicked at her attacker's legs. No effect.

"Where's Walsh?" a man's gruff voice said behind her.

She tried to answer but the hand on her face stopped her words.

"Don't scream," he said. He started his hand away. She bit it.

"Bitch!" He threw her face-down on the mattress, jammed a knee into her back and slapped hard across the back of her head. "Don't fuck with me, bitch! Where's Walsh?"

"I … don't … know," she got out.

"You're in his apartment. Where is he?"

"I'm telling you I don't know. I'm looking for him too. I'm a police officer."

"Cop, huh?"

"That's right. Sergeant Ross. Boston Police Department. My ID's in my purse."

"How come cops are lookin' for him?"

"I can't tell you. It's an official investigation."

"Official, my ass. Where is he?" He again slapped her across the back of her head. She groaned. "Where is he?" He drove a fist into her back.

She cried out. "I … don't … know!"

"Fuckin' cops," he said. "Cops fuck with me plenty. It's payback time." He jerked her skirt to her waist and yanked her panties to her ankles, exposing her buttocks. He slapped it. "You're going to like this, bitch." He pushed down on her back with one hand then wedged his legs between hers, spreading them and pinning them to the mattress with her panties.

She tried to kick. Her flails were useless. She swung her arms in wild arcs behind her but struck nothing. He slapped her head again. Dazed, she stopped moving.

A dozen images flew in and out of her mind. Her mother, seven years before. The horror when police came in the night to say her mother was dead—savagely raped, then strangled and left in the park a block from their home. The years of sleepless nights, yearning to know the detail of her mother's final struggle to live, desperate to know her thoughts, to know if she knew the final fate awaiting her, if she suffered, if she had time to think of her sleeping daughter and of her husband who awaited her return from walking their dog. In an instant, she knew. Every question now answered as her own beast dug hands into her neck and shoulders, his legs immobilizing her. Her dad. Tuna fish sandwiches. Sparky. The bag ladies and men with purple stripes. A quilt of disconnected thoughts.

Thwunk! She heard a dull, mushy sound—the same sound she made with a mallet to tenderize cheap cuts of meat. The man on top of her fell onto her back, then rolled to the side. She could see him now: the Samoan from the hallway downstairs, minutes before.

Two hands shot past her face and grabbed the man's shoulders. They pulled him up, across her and off the bed. She turned her head. The hands belonged to another huge man with a crew cut and thick arms. The man in the silver Audi. He pounded his massive fists into the Samoan's face and head. She pulled up her panties and slid off the bed. The men fought on the floor between the foot of the bed and the dresser, blocking her path to her purse and her two-inch .38 Smith & Wesson pistol. Another powerful blow from the man with the crew cut and the Samoan fell still.

The man with the crew cut got up. "I hate people that pick on women," he said, then slammed his boot into the man's head. "You piece a shit!" he said to the unconscious man. He looked at Traci. "Did that dip-shit hurt you?"

She raced to collect her thoughts. Her legs wobbled and she slumped onto the edge of the mattress.

"Say the word, lady, and I'll put his lights out."

"No. Don't do that. It's okay. I'm okay. He didn't do anything."

"There's another one outside. Another piece a shit."

She tried to stand but her legs would not support her.

"You Walsh's squeeze?" he asked.

"No. I'm a police officer. Who are you?"

"What do you want with him?"

"I'm looking for him. What's your name?"

"Forget that. Come on. I'll get you out of here. His buddy'll be coming up."

"I can't. I have to call … report this."

"Forget it. He isn't worth it. Let's go."

"No. I …" She struggled from the mattress. "He tried to rape me." She moved to the foot of the bed and studied the battered man on the floor. "Is he dead?"

"Maybe." He kicked the man's stomach. A groan. "Sorry. Not yet."

"Who are you?" she asked again.

"I'm not going to jail over this slime ball, lady. Forget it."

"You stopped him from raping me. You won't go to jail. What's your name?"

"Solly. Okay? Let's go."

"Solly what?"

"Solly's enough."

"Thank you, Solly. I don't know what else to say."

"Forget it. I oughtta put his lights out for doing that."

She stood. "No, don't. Please?"

He looked down at the Samoan and drew his right leg back.

"Please?" she repeated.

"Ah, screw it. Alright." He set his foot down. "C'mon." He motioned to the door.

"I can't. I'm a police officer. I have to report this."

"No way I'm gettin' involved. You do what you want. I'm gone." He started toward the door.

She opened her purse and pulled out the gun. "You have to stay," she said. "You're a witness."

"No way." He took another step.

She cocked the hammer.

He stopped and turned around. "Fuckin' cops."

She held the gun steady another moment, then eased the hammer up and lowered the barrel.

He smirked. "See ya."

He went out.

Traci collapsed onto the edge of the mattress, the gun pointed at the Samoan. She waited.

The super strolled in minutes later and his eyes bulged at the sight of Traci holding the groaning Samoan at bay with her pistol.

Police responded to the super's call and took the Samoan into custody. She told them he might have a partner somewhere outside but, after a search, the officers concluded he must have left when he saw them arrive. Traci assured them she was shaken and sore but otherwise unharmed. She provided a detailed account of the assault, gave a sketchy description of Solly—omitting most of his distinctive features and his name—and said she would definitely return to New Rochelle to help their district attorney prosecute the Samoan.

The super offered to let her freshen up in his apartment and she accepted. As she washed, she debated whether or not to call her dad. No. She would consider telling him if they got together over the weekend. She put on fresh makeup, then left. Still shaken, she turned on the radio as she drove and found a classical music station. Beethoven's *Eroica* was playing. She turned up the volume. The powerful strains surged through the car and moderated her thoughts of the Samoan, the bag ladies and the trauma of her own near-attack.

Thoughts of David and the conversation with her dad slipped in.

- 27 -

Twilight had crept into the afternoon sky by the time Traci stopped Detective Karpinski's car in front of the lowered access control arm at the Pride Foods' guard shack. Solly stopped his Audi ten yards behind her. Though annoyed he had followed her during the forty-minute drive to the plant, a part of her welcomed his presence.

A wan and unimposing guard looked up from a magazine as Traci rolled down her window. "May I help you?" he said.

"I'd like to see Mr. Cleatis Ledford."

"Name?"

"Traci Ross."

The guard removed a clipboard from one wall and scanned a list of names. His mouth moved as he read them to himself. "I have a Vernon Roth," he said, still scanning the list.

"No, it's Ross. Traci Ross. I don't have an appointment. Here ..." She held up her police identification.

The guard raised his brows and set the clipboard aside. "For real?"

"For real."

He stepped from the shack and walked the four paces to her car. "Is there a problem? I wasn't told about any problem at the plant."

"No, no problem. Just a routine investigation."

"Routine, huh? Okay. I know better than to ask what you're investigating."

"Thanks."

"I wanted to be a cop once," he said, "even applied to Syracuse PD when I got out of the army. That's where I grew up." He pointed to his thick eyeglasses. "Couldn't get past the physical. The army didn't seem to care much about my eyes, but the PD sure did."

"They're picky that way."

"Tell me about it. Worked out okay, though. Ended up getting a good job with the post office and now I'm retired with a nice pension."

"Congratulations." She smiled and said, "I've got a few more years in the trenches before I pull the pin."

"Yeah, I hear ya there." He waved a hand over his uniform. "I just do this to support my golf habit."

They laughed.

"I've got to call you in," he said. "Just take a second. Mr. Ledford, right?"

"That's right."

"He's the president, you know."

"Actually, I didn't."

"Yep. Doesn't bother me any but I hear he's a real mean cuss to most others up here."

"Oh?"

He winked. "That's just between us cops. Not for the public to know."

"They won't hear it from me."

He grinned. "I'll give him a call." He stepped back into the shack.

Traci got out of the car and stretched. A minute later, the guard motioned to her, his hand cupped the phone's mouthpiece. "Mr. Ledford's secretary wants to know if plant security can handle it."

She went into the shack. "I don't think so."

"She says 'no,'" the guard said into the phone. A pause. "Okay, I'll hold on." He cupped the mouthpiece again. "She'll try to find him."

Traci looked around the small shack. Family photographs and clipboards hung above a dusty window. One of the boards indicated guard schedules, another detailed emergency procedures and phone numbers. The page on another board recorded the day's arrivals and departures. Her gaze drifted down the list, then stopped. Halfway down was an erasure. Only an arrival time was noted—no departure. She looked closer then stiffened. The markings under the new name were faint, but she was certain it once said *Thornton Walsh*. The arrival time was completely obliterated, but judging from the visitor before and the one after, she guessed it was close to eleven that morning. She flipped up the page. Thursday's record, the day before.

"Okay," the guard said into the phone. "I'll send her through." He hung up, then wrote Traci's name below the last name on the Friday visitor list. "He'll see you. Check in with security at the administration building. They'll direct you to his office." He tapped the clipboard. "And make sure you stop here on your way out." He gave a short laugh. "Otherwise there'll be a manhunt to find you."

"Manhunt?"

"Have to make sure everyone's accounted for. Company's real sticky about that."

"Security pretty tight here?"

"Yep. One in, one out. That's the way they want it."

"I noticed one of the names …"

"What's that?"

"Uh… Nothing. I was thinking about something else."

"Okay."

He gave her a map of the facility after marking an X on the administration building.

"One thing," Traci said as she took the map. She pointed at the Audi. "That guy in the car behind me is probably going to tell you he's with me."

The guard turned to look.

"It's a long story but he isn't."

"Ten-four." He gave her a quick salute. "I'll take care of him."

"Thanks." She got in her car and started down the plant access road. The control arm dropped behind her and she slowed to watch the scene unfold in the rearview mirror.

Solly moved up and stopped at the shack. The guard bent down and said something to him. A moment later, Solly's arm shot through the Audi's open window and his hand clamped around the guard's scrawny neck. The guard's body gyrated. He pressed his hands on the Audi's door frame in a futile effort to push away from Solly's iron grip. Then his feet left the ground and his head and shoulders disappeared into Solly's car. Seconds later, the guard flew backward out of the car and flopped on the ground. Solly got out, strode to the guard shack, then lumbered back to the guard with the shack phone, its long cord trailing. He tied the guard's wrists and ankles with a few quick turns of the cord, then dragged the man into the shack. The control arm raised and Solly got back in his car. Traci sped up as Solly raced past the descending control arm.

Persistent, she thought. She turned the corner at the end of the long access road then zigzagged around tall stacks of wood pallets. Several eighteen-wheelers were waiting near the loading dock. She squeezed between two and drove down the steep ramp to the front of the dock. She stopped. The Audi whizzed by at the top of the ramp. She got out.

"Hey! You can't park there!" a tall man in coveralls on the dock shouted.

"Police business!" she yelled back over the roar of the trucks and forklifts.

"I don't give a shit! Move it!"

She came up to the man. "I'm here to see Mr. Ledford."

"Yeah? Well, he ain't here. He's at administration. Other side of the plant."

Solly's car zoomed across the top of the ramp in the other direction. He didn't see her.

"Look, I'm late," she said. "Can you take me there?"

"You can drive yourself."

Traci gave a warm smile. "I'd probably get lost and I'm really late. I sure would appreciate it if you would take me there."

"Shit. Ledfoot, huh?" He rolled his eyes. "Alright but I want your keys. Your car can't stay here."

"Deal. I really appreciate it."

She gave him her car keys and he tossed them to another man. They got into an electric cart and drove through the enormous warehouse then out the other end. A short distance on the right was the administration building.

"I'll have someone bring your car around to the front here," he said when they stopped in front of the building. "Your keys will be with security at the front desk."

She thanked him and went into the building. A uniformed guard and a suited tall husky man with broad shoulders and a military haircut stood behind a fifteen foot-long, curved counter in the lobby.

The man in the suit smiled as she walked up. "You must be Officer Ross," he said.

Traci thought to correct him about her rank but decided such vanity no longer important. "Yes, sir," she said, instead.

"Welcome to Pride Foods." He extended a hand.

She shook it.

"I'm Mitch Vazzano. Chief of Plant Security."

"Pleased to meet you, sir."

The guard shoved a visitor's roster across the countertop and handed her a yellow identification badge. He noted the badge's number on the sheet.

"If you'll sign in, we'll get going," Vazzano said.

Traci wrote her name on the sheet, scanning the list of other names at the same time. No erasures. No Thornton Walsh.

"You'll have to leave your purse here," the guard said. "Pick it up on your way out."

"My gun is in there."

"Don't worry. I'll lock it up."

She passed the purse across the counter and the guard set it in a drawer. He locked it and gave the key to Vazzano.

"Right this way, officer."

Vazzano led her out of the lobby and a quarter of the way down a long hallway. He unlocked a door and ushered her inside a small windowless room with only a desk, two chairs and a filing cabinet. The walls were bare, as was the desk, except for a phone at one edge.

"Please have a seat," Vazzano said. He moved behind the desk and sat.

"I was expecting to see Mr. Ledford," Traci said, sitting.

"Certainly. As you might imagine, Mr. Ledford is an extremely busy man and he asked me to see if there's something I can do for you."

She shook her head *no.* "Not really."

"Perhaps if you could tell me what this is about, I could make a determination if Mr. Ledford is to be involved?"

"Involved? Alright. I can do that. I'm here on a missing-persons investigation."

"Missing persons? I'm not aware that any of our personnel have gone missing. May I have his name? Or her name?"

"It's a he and he's not an employee."

Vazzano leaned back. "I see. If that's the case then I don't know how we can help you."

"*You* can't. And I don't mean to be rude, sir, but you're wasting my time. I've had a very difficult day and I came here to see Mr. Ledford. My inquiry has nothing to do with any of your employees, so I don't know why I'm talking to you instead of Mr. Ledford."

"Yes, I understand your position but I still don't—"

Traci stood. "Sir, this is an official investigation, so if you'll just be kind enough to take me to Mr. Ledford—"

"You're with the Boston police department, is that correct?"

"That's right."

"If I'm not mistaken, Officer Ross, you have no jurisdiction up here. Would that be accurate?"

"As far as that goes, yes."

"Then unless you tell me more or give me a name, I'm afraid I'll have to terminate our discussion and send you on your way."

She paused a moment. "Fine. I'll tell you who it is but that's all."

"Very well."

"Thornton Walsh."

"Thornton Walsh." Vazzano said the name slowly, as though hearing it for the first time. His head and eyes drifted up. "Thornton Walsh," he repeated.

She laughed. "You'll have to do better than that, sir."

"I'm sorry…"

"Do you think I'm stupid? I know you know him. He had an appointment today—this morning—with Mr. Ledford. I saw his name on the visitor list in the guard shack. Somebody tried to erase it but they didn't do a very good job." She started toward the door.

"I really don't—"

"Bring her up," a voice said over the phone's speaker.

Vazzano leaned over the phone and pushed a button. "Yes, sir."

"Cute," Traci said. "Real cute."

- 28 -

James Cleatis Ledford looked up from behind a computer monitor on a wide, polished mahogany desk in his fourth floor office when Traci and Vazzano entered through oak double doors. Ledford stood, then went around to the front of the desk. A tall, slender, yet fit man in his mid-fifties, he wore the jacket of his navy blue three-piece suit buttoned and his jet black hair combed straight back—not a strand out of place. A wide smile framed his smooth, tanned face.

"I owe you an apology," he said. "Typically, police matters are handled by Mr. Vazzano or his staff and I thought he might best respond to your questions. It was my idea."

"No apology necessary, sir."

"That's most gracious of you."

"Yes, well … I know you're a busy man, so I'll get right to the point."

"Please have a seat," Ledford said, gesturing to a leather club chair in front of his desk. "May I have someone bring you a cold drink? Iced tea, perhaps? A soda?"

"Thank you, but no. I won't be here that long. I have to get back to New York."

"Of course."

Ledford moved to the chair behind his desk and they sat.

Vazzano remained on his feet at the side of the desk.

"As you've already heard," she nodded at the phone on his desk, "I'm trying to locate Mr. Thornton Walsh. I believe he had an appointment with you earlier today."

"Yes, he did. He's a securities analyst, you know."

She nodded.

"We were to have lunch and talk about the company's expectations for the next quarter. However, as you may or may not be aware, Pride Foods recently privatized and the meeting became unnecessary." He smiled. "Even though we stopped being a public company, Thorny and I go way back and I invited him up. Told him I'd treat him to lunch and give him a tour of the plant … for old times' sake. He was undecided but I left the offer open."

"I see. He never kept the appointment?"

"That's right."

"Then I don't understand why his name was on the list of today's visitors at your guard shack."

He laughed and waved a hand at Vazzano. "Looks like you're going to have to do some training, Mitch."

Vazzano nodded.

"This is how it works," Ledford said, "or rather how it's *supposed* to work in a perfect world. If we're expecting someone—a vendor or salesman or, in this case, Mr. Walsh—his name is phoned to the guard and they're supposed to write it down on a particular form. That speeds things up considerably because the guard doesn't have to make a lot of calls to get approval for visitors to come on the property when they arrive. In a *perfect* world, the guard just looks at the list, finds the name and lets him through."

"I see."

"Now, I'll be the first to tell you we don't hire Mensa candidates for guard work here but they generally do a pretty good job."

"I'm sure they do."

"Without knowing the facts, I'd have to say the reference you're talking about is likely the result of the guard writing Mr. Walsh's name on the wrong form, then erasing it when the error was realized."

"Possibly, but I didn't see his name on any of the other forms. Then again, I really didn't look that close. I'll check them on the way out. It's probably there."

"Of course." He looked at Vazzano. "Take a few minutes and go over those procedures again with the guards out there, will you Mitch? Do that right away."

"Yes, sir."

"It's bad for business when we're expecting someone and they get the third degree because their name wasn't properly noted."

"I'll take care of it, sir."

"Good." He turned back to Traci. "Anything else?"

"Yes. Can you tell me when the appointment with Mr. Walsh was scheduled?"

"Scheduled? Probably a week or so ago. I'm not sure, exactly. There's been so much going on lately with the change … Mitch, do you recall when Thorny made the appointment?"

"A week or so ago, sir."

Ledford nodded. "That's probably right."

"And he didn't cancel it?" Traci said.

"I don't believe he did," Ledford said. "Did he cancel it, Mitch?"

"I don't believe he did, sir. Just a no-show."

"Yes. That's my recollection as well. But not unusual. Not for Thorny." Ledford laughed. "He was always threatening to come up to my home for dinner and kick my butt at cribbage but more often than not he wouldn't make it. Something always came up—or so he would say."

Traci shifted in her chair. "Is that your standard practice?"

"What's that?"

"It sounds like Mr. Walsh's appointment was scheduled through security. Is that how it's done?"

"My gosh, no," Ledford said. "My secretary would have handled that but Mitch would be advised of all expected visitors—my guests as well as those for other departments at the plant. That's part of his function here at Pride. He gets a daily list." Ledford leaned forward. "We're doing some very interesting work here, Miss Ross—very interesting—and any number of people would very much like to be privy to that work. No. We keep Mitch and his staff apprised of our guests, just to make sure they're our friends." He laughed again. "You'd be surprised how clever they can be, right Mitch?"

"Yes, sir. Very clever."

"I can imagine," Traci said.

"I'm certain you can."

"Do you recall when you last spoke to Mr. Walsh?" she asked.

Ledford cocked his head to one side. "Probably … well, that would probably have been around the first of the week. Monday or Tuesday seems right--a few days after I became aware of his appointment. As I said, it's been a very hectic week with the company and the change."

"Sure. Not Thursday—yesterday—but Monday or Tuesday. Is that your recollection?"

"Well, now, if you have some reason to believe Mr. Walsh and I spoke yesterday, then I would have to defer to your evidence of that. My recollection is Monday or Tuesday, but it may have been later, as you say." He began to drum his fingers lightly on the desk.

"It would be helpful if you could pin it down better but I understand how time can slip away when you've been so busy."

"It doesn't slip. It evaporates."

"Yes, it can do that." She paused, then said, "Sir, do you recall Mr. Walsh's frame of mind the last time you talked?"

"Frame of mind? Just ol' Thorny. Nothing stands out to the contrary as I think back. Always a good-natured guy. Likes to tell jokes. Should have been a salesman."

"You said you two have known each other for a while. Was that more a personal or professional relationship?"

"Half and half but it began as professional. He was one of only a handful of analysts who cared about Pride back then and that kept us in touch. The personal relationship just evolved from there. Thorny's a very likeable guy."

"So I've heard but I'm still a bit confused … about Mr. Walsh's name being on the visitor roster."

"Yes?"

"If his meeting with you was scheduled a week or so ago, as you said, and you spoke with him Monday or Tuesday, as you believe, and your conversation then essentially made the meeting moot, why would his name be called to the guard shack?"

"Yes, well—"

"Why notify the guard at all if—"

"I think I can answer your question," Vazzano said. "Visitor names are called in to the guard shack right after an appointment is scheduled. That would have been a week or so ago when Mr. Walsh made it. What probably happened was the guard noted the appointment on a separate piece of paper, set it aside, then logged it on today's sheet—the day Mr. Walsh was expected."

"But it was on the list of today's *visitors*—people who *actually came* to your company--somewhere in the middle of that list, not on that other form you're talking about."

Vazzano crossed his arms. "I think that's already been explained, Officer. The guard wrote Mr. Walsh's name on the wrong form. It's as simple as that."

"The wrong form," she said, nodding. "Right around eleven o'clock. After about a dozen other people arrived at the plant. Is that what you're saying?"

"That's what I'm saying, officer. I don't know why you're having a problem with it."

Ledford stopped drumming and glanced at his watch. "Anything else?"

"Just one more thing, sir."

"Certainly."

"I'd like to take a look around your plant, if you don't mind. It's something I have to do. Routine in these circumstances. My lieutenant would be upset with me if I didn't."

"Done." He slapped the desktop lightly and rose. "Mitch will take you. Give her the VIP tour, Mitch."

"Yes, sir."

"Oh, by the way, officer," Ledford said. "Do you have a pet?"

"I do. A yellow Lab."

"A wonderful animal. Give her a case of Premium, Mitch."

"Yes, sir."

"In fact, load up her car."

"I'll take care of it."

"Thank you, sir," Traci said, "but I really can't."

"Nonsense. You made that drive all the way out here and I'm not letting you go away empty-handed. Pride Premium is a best-selling dog food. I'm sure your Lab will love it."

"Actually, he prefers kibble."

Ledford winked at her. "I'll tell you what. You give him a can of Premium and I *guarantee* he'll love it. Won't settle for anything else. If he doesn't, *I'll* eat it."

She laughed. "I wouldn't make you do that but I still can't accept it … unless you would consider it a donation."

"Consider it as such."

"Okay. Since that's the case, I'll give it to my colleagues in New York to pass around to animal shelters in their precincts. I'm sure it'll be appreciated."

He gave a warm smile. "Wonderful."

- 29 -

Traci and Vazzano left the building through a rear door and rode an electric cart to the production building, cavernous structure with a forty-foot-high ceiling where dozens of men and women in white smocks, hair nets and filter face-masks tended to enormous, ear-deafening machinery.

Bulk product flowed from huge, eight-foot-diameter mixing vats behind the machines, was processed in the bowels of the massive equipment, then dispensed at the front in measured quantities into variously shaped containers. The filled containers quickly moved along whirring conveyer belts to the waiting arms of more workers, who methodically stacked the containers onto pallets. Forklifts shuttled into the building, scooped up the full pallets of Pride Premium dog food and other products, then ferried them to the warehouse.

They stood for a minute and watched the activity.

"Quite a scene," Traci said. "I'm impressed."

"It isn't all for our use. We do a lot of contract filling, too."

"Contract filling?"

"That machinery you're looking at is extremely expensive, costs in the millions of dollars. Some companies won't make the investment. What they do instead is send us a list of ingredients—or send the ingredients themselves. We mix them up, put it in cans or sacks or whatever packaging they want, then ship the finished product back."

"I see."

Vazzano pointed to a ten-foot-wide, twenty-two-foot-tall machine topped by a large hopper in the center of the floor. "We're filling boxes of corn meal for Dominick's on that line. Caramel popcorn for Right Snack is going into boxes on the line to the right of it."

"Very interesting."

"Contract filling is a big part of our business and we like to keep those lines running twenty-four-seven."

"Looks like you've got six that aren't pulling their load." She gestured to the idle machines on the left side of the floor with several men in and around them.

"Those we keep for Omni Foods. There's a production change and the engineers are getting them ready. They'll be pulling their weight when they start up tonight."

"That's a lot of lines. Omni must be a big customer."

Vazzano didn't respond.

"Assembly lines have always fascinated me," Traci said. "My dad used to show me videos of an old TV program called *Industry on Parade*."

"Never heard of it."

"It was about different companies and what they did. They showed a lot of bottles or cans moving along conveyers, hardly stopping long enough for food to drop into them, then they were sealed and labeled and put into boxes—all done by machines."

"That's pretty much what we do here."

"What was really interesting was the program showed how everyday things were made."

"Yeah? Like what?"

"Well, like toilet paper."

He wrinkled his nose. "Huh?"

"Sure. It's something everyone uses every day but did you ever stop to think about how they get all that paper so neat on that small roll of cardboard?"

Vazzano frowned. "No, never thought about it."

"Well, that's what the program was about."

"Toilet paper, huh. Doesn't sound like a program I'd watch."

"Could we get a little closer? I'd like to see how they work."

"Sorry. This is as far as you can go. Insurance doesn't cover visitors and some of the products have secret formulas and ingredients. Our customers wouldn't like it if we let outsiders wander around."

"I understand."

Another forklift raced into the building.

"If I worked here, that's what I'd want to do," she said.

"What's that?"

"Drive a forklift."

"Really?"

"My uncle has a small vineyard and winery in Concord—only bottles about eight hundred cases a season—and I spent a few summers with him, helping out with the crush."

"Is that so?"

"It was hard work but the most fun was when he'd let me drive the forklift and move barrels around. I got pretty good at it."

"Drive a—"

A voice crackled over a walkie-talkie hooked to his belt.

"Excuse me," he said.

He picked it up and held it to his ear, listened a minute, then stuck it back on his belt. "Something's come up I have to take care of," he said. "One of my men is coming over to take you around from here."

They went outside.

When a guard rode up, Vazzano left.

"Where would you like to go?" the guard asked.

Traci looked around. "How about that building over there?" She pointed to a long, single-story brick building seventy-five yards away.

"That's the hole. Doesn't look like much from here but we call it the hole. Has five subterranean floors."

"Really?"

"Yep. In the winter, people on the lower levels never see the light of day. Go in when it's dark and come out when it's dark. Glad I don't work there."

She got in the cart and they drove toward the building.

"What kind of work do they do in there?"

255

"Research. Come up with new products and stuff. Like the twenty cases of Pride Premium I just put in your car."

She laughed. "Is there any room left for me?"

"Yeah, there's room. And they got a cafeteria in there, a big lounge and a pretty good gym."

"Sounds nice."

He shrugged. "I wouldn't know. Only heard about it. Just the moles that work there can use it."

"They probably need it if they don't see daylight."

"Probably."

They arrived at the building and went in through a set of double solid-core doors.

Traci's guard waved 'hello' to another uniformed guard seated at a small table inside the lobby.

"This is it for me," Traci's guard said. "Chris will take over from here. I don't have clearance for the hole."

"Seems like a lot of security for a food company."

"Yeah, I guess so."

Chris stood when they came up to his table.

"She wants to see what's here. Downstairs, too."

Chris glanced at the ID pinned to Traci's blouse. "Yellow can't come in here."

"Yeah, she can. Vazzano said so."

Chris pointed a finger at Traci's badge. "Then she'd have a red card. Hers is yellow."

"Hey, man, I don't hand out the badges. All I know is two minutes ago Mr. Vazzano told me to take this lady wherever she wants. She wants to see the hole, so show her the hole."

"Vazzano said that?"

"Told me personally."

"Good enough by me. I won't argue with the boss-man."

"I'll hold the fort for you here." He went around and sat behind the table.

Chris and Traci crossed the lobby and passed through a metal door. They walked along the ground level corridors, where most of the doors to windowless offices were open. Only a few of the offices had employees inside. They appeared to be busy putting things away in preparation for leaving.

"Is there something special you wanted to see?" Chris asked.

"No, just want to look around."

"Haven't had anybody come here just to look around. You with the company? I haven't seen you here before."

"It's kind of a special situation."

"Good enough by me. None of my business, anyway."

He swung open one of the double doors to the cafeteria. Three men and two women were inside, seated at tables, eating and talking. A heavy aroma of freshly-popped popcorn hung in the air. Narrow windows near the top of one wall were painted black and only the light from an array of overhead fluorescent fixtures illuminated the room.

"Want anything?" Chris asked.

"No, thanks. Why are the windows painted?"

"So people can't look in."

She laughed. "What would anyone want to see in a cafeteria?"

"Nothing as far as I know."

They continued along the hallway and paused in front of a set of double glass doors. Inside, a man and a woman pedaled furiously on stationary bicycles. A television blared. Neat stacks of free-weights, barbells and other equipment were set in place on the carpeted floor. As in the cafeteria, a high row of windows were blacked out.

"Very nice," Traci said.

They rode an elevator down to the first subterranean level. More offices and open doors. Nothing ominous. They went to the second lower level. More offices but the doors were closed. Signs on some indicated *Infirmary*, *Procurement*, *Supplies*.

"Lower we get, the tighter the security," Chris said. "You'll see what I mean."

They walked the floors of the next two levels. On the fourth, only numbers distinguished one door from the next. Card readers were mounted on the wall next to each door.

"Any way I could take a look inside some of these?" she asked.

He laughed. "No problem. Which one do you want?"

"Doesn't matter. How about this one?"

Chris pulled a plastic card from his shirt pocket and slid it through the card reader. The door clicked and he pushed it open. Traci started through the door but Chris thrust an arm in front of her. "Can't go in," he said. "You can only look from here."

"Sorry." She peered inside. A cloth-paneled partition four feet inside blocked her view. "I can't see anything."

"That's the idea."

"But Mr. Vazzano said I could go where I wanted."

"You can get in the building but not the offices. Not even Ledfoot could let you inside L-four and L-five offices and *he's* the *president*."

"Oh. So far I haven't seen much of anything."

"That's what the hole is all about to visitors—unless they've got a better reason to be here than just look around."

"There's one more level, isn't there?"

"That's right but you won't be able to see anything there either."

"I might as well have a look as long as I'm here."

"Good enough by me," Chris said.

He used his card to allow the elevator to descend to the fifth subterranean level. A slim uniformed guard stood up from behind a short horseshoe-shaped table with two closed-circuit television monitors on it. Floor-to-ceiling panels of clear Lexan extended from the sides of the elevator and five feet beyond it, then narrowed to the first of two glass doors that enclosed a chamber twice the size of a phone booth. The second door led to the guard station.

"Everything down here is clean," Chris said. "We can only go through one at a time." He flipped a switch on an intercom mounted on the Lexan near the elevator. "Got a visitor."

The guard gave a curt wave. He pushed a button on his console and the first door slid open. He beckoned with his hand.

"Step inside, ma'am," Chris said.

Traci stepped in. Below her feet was a metal grate. She saw another grate in the ceiling above her.

"Raise your arms and stand with your legs apart," Chris said.

Traci lifted her arms and widened her stance.

"A little wider," he said. "Try to take up the slack in your skirt."

She moved her legs farther apart.

"There'll be a rush of air for a few seconds," he said. "It'll blow off any dust or other foreign material."

The door behind her hissed closed then a loud whoosh of air blew up from her feet, billowing her skirt to her waist. She blushed as she tried without success to push it down with her hands. Seconds later, the air stopped.

The guard in front of her grinned. He pushed another button and the second door opened. She stepped out.

"Sorry about that," he said. "You didn't have it tight enough."

"Should have worn pants."

"I've told them a hundred times to reverse that air flow. Happens all the time to visitors. Anyway, welcome to the hole."

"That's some welcome."

Chris followed in seconds later.

"You'll have to sign our guest list," the guard said. He gave her a pen and a clipboard with a single slip of paper on it. She wrote her name and arrival time.

Chris spotted the guard's curious glance at Traci's ID as she wrote. "I know, I know," Chris said. "You don't have to ask. Vazzano said she could come down here. She won't be going into anything."

"Then what's the point?"

"Just looking around, she says."

"Looking around? You can look all you want, ma'am, but there's nothing to see."

"I'm sure you're right. I won't be long."

"Take all the time you want."

Traci and Chris walked away, down a short hall, then turned left at a *T,* where closed-circuit television cameras monitored the three directions.

"What's so special about this level?" she said.

The guard put a finger to his lips. "All the super-secret stuff happens here. I used to be a guard at some secret facilities before, like Lockheed's Skunk Works in California, and this place is right up there."

"Looks like it but what kind of secrets could a food company possibly have?"

"Pride is more than a food company but as far as their secrets go, that I couldn't tell you. Wouldn't be very secret if I knew, would it?"

"Mr. Vazzano said Pride does things for other companies, like contract filling, but he didn't mention anything else."

Chris tossed his head up. "Couldn't tell you about that either 'cause I don't know. Saw some uniforms in here the last couple of weeks. Maybe we're developing new field rations for the military. Could be a big contract if that's what we're doing. If I were to guess, that would be my guess."

They turned left at the end of the hall. No cameras and none of the doors were marked.

"How do the people know which office is theirs?" she said.

"Guess they count the doors as they walk."

"Probably. Are there any restrooms down here? I need to use one."

"Sure. And, yes, you *can* go inside that room."

She laughed.

They made another left turn. No cameras. A guard stood outside one of the doors near the hallway's two-block-long midpoint.

"She needs to use the head, Frank," Chris said when they came up.

"Afternoon, ma'am. Right there."

He unlocked the door across the hall from him and she went in. A minute later, a deafening wail from a siren blared for several seconds over a loudspeaker inside the bathroom. The door opened and Chris called out. "Stay in here, ma'am. I'll come back for you." She quickly washed, then stepped out. Frank and Chris were sprinting around the corner at the end of the hall.

The moment they were out of sight, she knocked on the door Frank had been standing near. No reply. She knocked again, harder. Nothing. She wrenched on the knob. No luck. Footsteps. Around the corner on her left. Two people walking. Men's voices. She stepped back from the door.

"Okay, okay!" an irritated, high-pitched voice on the other side of the door shouted. The lock latch clanked and the door opened. A young, red-haired man with freckles and wide, blood-shot eyes stuck his head out and looked around the empty hall. "Where's Frank?"

"Had to go somewhere. Can I come in?" She glanced along the hall to the right, then the left. More voices.

"You from Omni?" the man asked.

"Omni? Yeah. Right. Can I come in?"

He swung the door open.

"I was expecting a man. Bill Ruecker here. And you are...?"

Traci shook his limp hand as she stepped inside the room and quickly closed the door. "Traci Ross, Bill. Nice to meet you." Her gaze wandered around the large room. Three long tables, holding a variety of unrecognized equipment, were aligned in a row in the center of the large room.

"Mr. Ledford said a man would be coming," Ruecker said. "Least that's what I thought he said. No matter." He smiled approvingly as he looked along her body. "You'll do."

"Thanks." She smiled back.

Ruecker checked his watch. "Come on. It's late and we've got a lot to go over." He took a few steps, then stopped. "Maybe you don't need everything. You need everything? You want to know all that? Mr. Ledford said to go over everything."

"Well ..."

"Tell you what. Just stop me if I start to get into stuff you already know. Okay?"

"Sure. That's fine."

She followed him past the long center lab tables to a short table next to the scanning electron microscope. Dozens of computer printouts were scattered on the table. Ruecker began to rifle through them.

"No end to this," he said without looking up. "*Unbelievable* project. I've worked on tough projects before but *nothing* like this. And I get *no* help. *Zero.*" He looked up at her. "Ledford won't give me any help. There's probably only three people in the whole company that know what I'm doing down here." He held up three fingers. "Three! And that includes *me*. I've had to do all of it myself. Can you believe it? *One person.* It's been *brutal.* How many on your staff at Omni?"

She picked a number. "Eight."

"Eight?" He let out a high, shrill laugh. "With eight I could conquer the world! Got any openings?"

"Not right now."

"Too bad. This is a sweatshop. Nothing's ever good enough and everything's a rush. Hurry, hurry, hurry. Rush, rush, rush."

"We have our moments, too," she said.

"*Moments?*" He threw up both arms. "*Moments* I could deal with. I have *weeks--months* of unbelievable pressure--like now. You guys at Omni want to start blending and filling tonight and I haven't even done the time studies." He waved his hands in narrow circles and pointed with his index fingers. "You're pushing too fast. *Way* too fast." He turned back to the papers. "The dog food was a fluke. A golden BB. I got lucky. Real lucky. But who cares if it breaks down right away in dog food?" He turned back to her. "Right? Am I right or am I right?"

"Right as rain," she said.

"You bet. But peanut butter, that's a different story. Right?"

"You bet."

"And all the other stuff you guys want to use it in. Different story altogether." He turned back to the papers and resumed his search. His head began to bob from side to side as though to the beat of a rock tune playing in his head. "There you are, you little beauty." He snatched a printout from the pile and handed it to her. "Take a look at that." His shoulders began to sway in sync with his head.

She eyed the paper and the columns of numbers.

"Pretty impressive, huh?" he said.

"I ... uh ..."

He reached across the paper, pointed to a number at the bottom of the second column and beamed. "See that? Ninety-two percent. Is that incredible or *what*?"

"That's ... incredible, alright."

"I knew you'd appreciate it." He stopped bobbing. "Ledford just gave it a big yawn but I knew you guys at Omni would appreciate it."

"Yes. It's ... very—"

"Here. Take a look." He motioned to the electron microscope. "I've got some in the tray." He slid a chair to the front of the machine and she sat. He jabbed a finger in the air several times near the eyepiece. "Just take a gander at that."

She moved her head to the eyepiece and looked through the lenses. Hundreds of tiny nanomachines slowly flapped in a tray filled with a thick, syrupy liquid.

"What—"

"Butter," he said. "That's your butter. Omni First Quality, I think you call it." His head and shoulders began to bob again. "It's the same for your envelope glue. Same for your crackers and soft cheese spreads, same for your mayonnaise and, of course, your seasonings. *Seasoned Greetings*. What a name." He laughed. "They'll be in for one helluva greeting, right?" He kept bobbing. "So, what do you think?"

She looked up and smiled at him. "You've gotten ahead of me ... What's your name again?"

"Bill." He grinned.

"Actually, Bill, I'm new. They only told me this morning I was coming here."

He stopped moving. "This morning? Why would they send ...? Oh-h-h. That's why Ledford told me to go over everything. Damn." He checked his watch again.

"Look, Bill," she said. "You're in a hurry. You don't need to explain everything. Just tell me what I'm looking at"—she nodded at the microscope—"and how it relates to Omni. Alright? How would that be?"

"Relates to Omni?" He narrowed his eyes and glanced at the ID card on her blouse. "Maybe I'd better call Mr. Ledford." He reached for the phone.

She touched his arm. He pulled it away. His other hand hovered over the handset.

"This is fascinating work you've done, Bill," she quickly said. "I can see that already. To tell you the truth, eight of us at Omni couldn't have done what you did all by yourself. You're an amazing man."

He stared at her.

"I'm serious," she said. "Really remarkable." She turned away and peered into the lenses. "To think you did this all by yourself."

He allowed a thin smile. "You sure you're from Omni? Maybe I should check your ID."

"It's in my purse, Bill. You know security keeps purses at the front desk."

"Yeah. Yeah, that's right." He bobbed slightly. "Okay. What do I care? I'm just a biochemist. They wouldn't let you down here if you weren't who you say you are."

"Exactly."

"Everything okay in here?"

Ruecker turned around. Frank, the guard, stood in the open doorway.

"Yeah, why?" Ruecker asked.

"Just checking. Some big guy got past security at the gate a while ago. Tied up the guard. He's on the property somewhere and we're trying to find him."

Traci smiled. She was sitting, her body blocked from Frank's view by the equipment on the three lab tables.

"Well, no big guy in here," Ruecker said.

"Okay. Just checking. And keep your door locked. It wasn't locked when I tried it just now."

"Yeah, yeah—"

Ruecker started his mouth open as Frank closed the door.

"Ah, screw it," he mumbled. "What do I care?"

"Say again?" Traci said.

"Nothing. Damn interruptions." Another check of his watch. "I'm really running short. Got to get things ready for the one-A.M. blend."

"I'll try not to keep you." She turned back to the microscope's eyepiece. "What were you saying about this?"

"Oh, yeah. That's butter. Butter and the magic bullets. See 'em flap?"

"Like laundry in the wind," she said.

"Ha! Laundry in the wind. That's good. Real good. Laundry. Wait'll I tell Mr. Ledford. He'll get a kick."

"Why are they in butter?" she asked, not looking away.

"Why? That's the genius of it. They're nanomachines. Very *special* nanomachines."

"Machines ... in butter?"

"The coating's the secret. You can't just put something in a person's system and expect it to stay there, right? Nothing like those machines, anyway. White blood cells would attack 'em like Attila's Huns. Turn 'em into big globs. They'd be useless in minutes. But with paclitaxel, it's a different story. Yes, ma'am. Completely different. That's what's on 'em. Tried dozens of compounds but paclitaxel works best—the same thing they use on stents to prop open arteries. Keeps the white cell soldiers away, and then ..." He tapped her shoulder. "Are you ready for this?"

She turned around. "All ears."

"Then I put a layer of enzyme on top to tell 'em where to go. Not just any enzyme, though. Gland-specific. Turns the little beggars into homing pigeons."

"Really?"

"You bet. Don't want 'em running around without direction, do we? No telling where they might go."

"Of course."

"Pop in those little guys and they go straight to the big P. They don't pass Go and they don't collect two hundred dollars."

"Big P?"

"Pituitary. Men on a mission. Darts to the ten ring."

"And then?"

"And then? They stay there. Lock on. Like keys in a lock. That's what the enzyme does. It's the key to the lock. Lets the machines lock right into the gland's cell surfaces and stay there, just flapping away, massaging." He curled the fingers of his hands and made a wiggling motion. "*Stimulating* it into doing what it does best."

Traci stiffened. "Which is …?"

"Bip, bip, bip and voilá! Smile time. Feel-good time. Just-what-the-doctor-ordered time."

"I don't—"

"C'mon. You don't have to be coy with me. We both know what this is all about, right? Good-time Charlie keeps 'em comin' back for more, right?" He started to bob and weave again with his head and shoulders. "Pretty neat, huh?"

"Yeah, uh … I–"

"That's how we move so much of that crap dog food. Pride Premium. Ha! *Premium*. What a joke."

Her mind spun.

"But, what the hey," Ruecker said. "Who cares. We move a ton a minute—just like what you guys at Omni want to do with that butter there," he gestured at the microscope, "and with your mayo, and your peanut butter, and the seasonings, and the pancake syrup, and ..." He stopped moving and leaned in close to her. "Forget about your ketchup. Acid's a killer. Tell your people tomato-based products won't work. Same with your pineapple drinks." He glanced around the lab then leaned closer still. "I told Mr. Ledford I could make it happen but I'll tell you a little secret: I can't." He straightened. "Ha! No one can. Same with vinegar-based salad dressings. Won't happen. No way. No how. The acid eats the enzyme and the paclitaxel. Nothing stops it. Tell 'em at Omni, okay? No way *I* can say anything."

"Sure, Bill. I'll tell them.

"Excellent."

"What's happening at one A.M.? You said you were going to do something with it then."

"Yeah, you bet. Shoot it in with whatever you guys got mixing up over in production tonight. Shoot the juice and let her rip." He punched a fist in the air.

Traci stood and forced a smile. "How do you do that, Bill? Shoot it in?"

"Naw, pump it." He pointed to a tightly spaced row of six half-inch-diameter stainless steel tubes affixed to the wall behind the microscope. The tubes ran up the wall and disappeared into the acoustic ceiling panels. The lower ends of the tubes terminated at the back of a closed, twelve-inch-square chamber. Ruecker pointed to the chamber. "The nano-machines are kept in there in a constantly agitated solution of distilled water and glucose. At one A.M., *boompa-boompa-boompa*, the solution is pumped out through those tubes and sprayed into the Omni vats. Easy, huh?" He started to sway again.

"Yeah, nice. But—"

"I know. I know what you're gonna say. You're gonna say what if? Right?"

"No, not—"

"It's handled. Ledford made sure of that. That's why it's piped over. No one sees or touches it."

"Ah." She nodded as though she understood.

"Exactly. Nothing can go wrong but if it *does*," he gestured with a sweep of a hand over his desk, "then it al-l-l goes away." He gave a smug grin.

"Goes away?"

"Well, sure."

"Away where?"

He stopped swaying and threw his hands up. "How would I know? It just goes away is all I was told." He shrugged. "Where or how it goes is somebody else's business. I'm home and in bed at one A.M., so what do I care?"

The lab door opened. Frank and another man stood in the doorway.

"You've got a visitor, Bill," Frank said. "And lock your door! It's still unlocked." The other man smiled as he crossed the room. Frank pulled the door closed.

The man extended a hand. "Vern Roth," he said. "Omni Foods."

Ruecker wrinkled his brow. "You're a little late," he said, shaking Vern's hand. "I was just wrapping it up with your colleague."

Traci offered her hand and a warm smile.

Roth tilted his head down and eyed her over the top of his glasses. "Colleague? What's your name?"

"Traci Ross. Say, I'd love to stay but I've got to get back." She started toward the door.

"What department are you from?" Roth asked.

Traci reached the door and opened it.

"Hey!" Ruecker yelled.

Frank stuck his head in the door as Traci bolted past him and ran down the hall.

"Get her, Frank!"

"What?"

"That girl! Get her!"

Frank took off, pulling a walkie-talkie from his belt as he ran.

Traci reached the end of the hall and turned the corner on the right.

Two strong hands grabbed her.

Vazzano!

- 30 -

A moonless night had swallowed the Pride Foods property by the time two security guards handcuffed Traci and escorted her from the Level-2 utility room to an electric cart outside the research building. Her struggles against the cuffs during the short ride to the administration building only tightened them, and her shouts of protest were swallowed by the din of scurrying forklifts and growling eighteen-wheelers at the distant production and warehouse buildings.

"You take her from here," the senior guard said when they reached the building. "Vazzano said to smack her if she gives you any crap."

"Where you going?" the other guard asked.

"Gotta help find that big guy that got on the property."

"They haven't found him yet?" the young guard asked.

"Not yet. But he'll be one sorry ass when we do."

Traci and the young guard got out of the cart and the other one drove off.

She was pulled along to Ledford's office then pushed inside. The guard removed her cuffs, went outside and closed the door.

Ledford was seated at a small conference table, without his coat or tie. He stood when she was thrust into the room. Vazzano and another man—short and stocky with thinning dark hair and a white bandage across his nose—were with him. They remained seated but turned around when they heard the commotion. Silverware and plates of food were on the table. Traci stayed by the door.

"Please have a seat, Miss Ross," Ledford said. "We've just started."

"You're in a lot of trouble," she said. "I don't know where you get your nerve but you're in deep, deep trouble."

"I think not, Miss Ross. You were trespassing in a secured area. You're the one with a problem here but let's put that aside for the moment." He motioned toward an empty chair at their table. "Please, have a seat and eat the salmon before it gets cold."

"Eat it yourself! I'm leaving!" She tried the door. The knob would not yield. "You'd better let me out of here!" She yanked on the knob.

"In due course," Ledford said. "If you prefer not to eat, then sit and we'll talk."

"Screw you!" She marched to his desk and picked up the phone.

"The switchboard's closed," Ledford said. "You'll need a code for an outside line and I'm afraid I've forgotten it."

She punched several buttons and listened. No dial tone. She slammed the phone down. "Why are you keeping me here?"

"If you'll have a seat, I'll be happy to explain."

"Tell me now or I'll start screaming!"

He laughed. "Scream if you wish—no one will hear. However, you *will* spoil our dinner." He sat and picked up his fork.

She flashed on the isolated access road to the sprawling plant, the hundreds of acres of forested land surrounding the property and the nearby fleet of noisy trucks.

"There's someone I'd like you to meet," Ledford said. "Please…" He again waved at the vacant chair.

"I'm not meeting anybody! This is kidnapping. This is serious. I'm a police officer!"

"No one has been kidnapped. You've only been detained."

"Bullshit! You have no right. You have no authority to detain me! Open that door this instant!"

Ledford leaned back in his chair. "You're trying my patience, Miss Ross."

"Screw you!"

He gave another short laugh. "My, we do have a temper, don't we? Alright, let me put it this way. I imagine you earn—what, maybe sixty thousand a year as an officer of the law? Would that be about right?"

"That's none of your business."

"Of course, but what would you say to a salary of five times that amount? Would that be of interest to you?"

275

Traci furrowed her brow. "What are you talking about?"

"Coming to work for me." He set his fork on the plate. "I could use someone with your fire and tenacity."

She said nothing.

"Ah. I see I have your attention."

"You don't have squat."

"But you're thinking about it."

"I don't work for kidnappers. Forget it."

"Five minutes of your time, Miss Ross, that's all I ask. Then you'll be free to leave or stay. Five minutes."

She was silent.

"What do you say? Just five minutes?"

She ran a hand through her hair. "Alright. Five minutes. That's it!"

"Certainly." He motioned to the chair.

She sauntered over and sat.

Vazzano resumed eating. The other man leaned back and lit a cigar.

"Are you sure you won't try the salmon?" Ledford asked.

"No thanks. Just get to it. The clock's running."

"Of course. But first, I'd like to introduce you to our guest. Miss Ross ... meet Thornton Walsh."

The man nodded and blew a cloud of smoke toward the ceiling. "A pleasure, ma'am."

Her mouth fell open.

"You really should try the salmon," Walsh said. "It's delicious."

Traci glared at Ledford. "You've got a real problem with telling the truth, don't you?"

276

He didn't respond. She turned to Walsh. "I've been trying to find you."

"So I'm told. Sorry for any trouble."

"Your brother's waiting for you at Logan airport."

"He was but not anymore. Talked to him a couple of hours ago." Walsh laughed. "He told me about the scuffle at the airport ... forgot to take his medication. He does that sometimes. I hope he didn't give your officers much of a hard time."

"Not too much."

"Good, good. Cleat fixed him up at the Logan Hilton and he's kicking back. I'll be picking him up tomorrow."

"Have a nice trip."

"Trip?"

"Barbados. Isn't that where you're going?"

Ledford looked up.

"Barbados? No, no. We don't have plans for Barbados."

"That's not what your brother said."

"Ha! Can't imagine where he got that idea. Must have read about the place in one of those in-flight magazines during his trip out from the west coast. He gets confused. No. I was to meet him earlier today, then take him back with me to New York but I was ... uh ... held up ... here ... with Cleat. Barbados? That's a good one."

"Back *where*? I was at your apartment. You moved out, gave your things to charity. I talked to your super."

Ledford stopped eating and eyed Walsh.

"Oh, that." Walsh blew another cloud of dark smoke. "To tell you the truth, I couldn't stand the dump. Couldn't think of a nice way to tell Gill I wanted to leave. It's nothing. You really should try the salmon." He jabbed his cigar toward the fish on her plate.

She turned to Ledford. "Did you have something to say or are you wasting more of my time?"

"I apologize for the subterfuge earlier, Miss Ross—"

"I'm not talking about that. I don't care about Mr. Walsh and his brother anymore, and I don't care about your lies. I gave you five minutes. You're down to four."

"Very well." He folded his napkin and set it to the side of his plate. "What brand of toothpaste do you use?"

"What?"

"Please. Indulge me, if you will, and answer the question."

"Toothpaste? Alright. Crest. Why?"

"Not Colgate."

"No, Crest."

"Have you ever tried Colgate?"

"Probably."

"But you didn't like it."

"I told you I use Crest!"

He nodded. "So you did. Then tell me what is it about Crest that made you choose that brand over Colgate or any others you've tried."

"This is ridiculous." She crossed her arms. "You kidnap me, lock me in a closet, have me handcuffed and dragged up here, and now you want to talk about toothpaste? You're crazy."

278

"Now you're wasting *my* time, Miss Ross. I'm going to add your delay back to the five minutes."

"Oh, brother. You're something else."

"One more time, please. Why do you prefer Crest over Colgate?"

She flicked a hand out. "I don't know, maybe the taste. I haven't thought about it. It isn't something I think about every night and morning when I brush my teeth."

"Of course. So is it possible, Miss Ross, that you could prefer particular products for reasons you're not aware of? Is that a possibility?"

"I don't know, maybe."

"Suppose that *could* be the case. Suppose you preferred a certain brand of marmalade, for example, not because of its taste, not because of advertising or a celebrity's endorsement or price or any of the other factors people customarily use to select one brand over another. Would that be an interesting situation?"

"Bizarre would be more like it."

"Again suppose, if you will, a product you preferred was actually inferior to the other brands, that it cost more to buy, was less effective and made with cheaper ingredients but you wanted it anyway. What would you say to that?"

"Why would I do that? Why would I pay more for an inferior product?"

Ledford leaned forward. "Because it made you *feel* good."

"Made me feel good? What's in it? Drugs?"

"Not drugs. The food business is extraordinarily competitive, Miss Ross. The instant a competitor saw they were losing market share they'd scramble to find out why. In the natural course of things it wouldn't be long before they'd analyze the competing product, eventually with a mass spectrometer to find out what's in it. No. Not drugs. They'd be revealed in a heartbeat. Something else."

Her eyes widened. "The flappers? Those things I saw in the hole? 'Keeps 'em coming back for more,' Bill said."

Ledford smiled. "That's right. Those miniscule, undetectable nanomachines—flappers, as you call them—that gently, rhythmically stimulate the pituitary gland to secrete endorphins into the bloodstream and make the consumer feel good."

"Now I know you're crazy."

"Hardly."

"You put those things in your dog food, didn't you?"

"We did."

"In all those cans you had put in my car."

"That's right."

She waved a finger at him. "*You're* an animal, Ledford. Do you have any idea what you've done? Do you know who's eating that dog food besides dogs?"

"Besides dogs?"

"Derelicts. Derelicts are eating that stuff and they're developing Cushing's Syndrome. And I've got a flash for you, Ledford, endorphins aren't the only things getting in their bloodstream. Testosterone gets in, too, and the derelicts can't cope with it. They're raping women because of it."

He nodded slowly. "Interesting."

She felt a shoe tap one of hers and she moved her foot away.

"And you want to put those things in food people eat?" she said. "I take it back, sir. You're not an animal. You're the devil."

"The devil?"

"And more."

He leaned forward. "Let me ask you this, Miss Ross, have you ever had a headache?"

"I've got a big one right now."

"And when you get a headache, do you take anything for it? An aspirin. Tylenol …?"

"You're nuts."

He smacked the table with his fist. "Answer the question, dammit! I've still got three minutes! Do you take aspirin when you get a headache?!"

She sighed. "Sometimes."

"That's better. Now, on those occasions when you do, does the aspirin or whatever preparation you take relieve your headache?"

"Not always."

"Don't fight me on this, Miss Ross!"

"I'm not fighting you! Sometimes they work, sometimes they don't."

"Very well. The point I'm trying to make is you don't give any thought to the mechanics of aspirin, do you? You have no idea where it goes, why it does what it does, or what happens to it after you swallow it. Isn't that true?"

"Why would I?"

"And in addition to taking aspirin to relieve your headaches, you've probably taken it to relieve aches and pains after a hard day of chasing crooks. Would I be correct in that assumption?"

"I have. Yes."

"And you've also probably taken it to reduce a fever when you catch a cold, and to lessen the pain of menstrual cramps during your period, and when you get a toothache. Am I right?"

"I've taken it for those things."

"Of course. Aspirin and similar products do an excellent job of relieving pain and making people feel better. Wouldn't you agree, Miss Ross?"

"Are you trying to equate aspirin to your nanomachines?"

"Aspirin is an analgesic, Miss Ross. Analgesics interfere with systems responsible for pain and they reduce inflammation—both desirable benefits. However, analgesics can also cause ulcers, diarrhea, abnormal breathing, tinnitus—even brain hemorrhage. Every silver lining has a cloud, Miss Ross. Benefits are not without their risks of side effects."

"From your point of view, maybe."

"Isn't yours rather shortsighted?"

"Not in the least."

"Oh, yes it is. Companies spend millions advertising their products every year. Wouldn't it be better for the economy if that money was paid to shareholders as dividends—money they could spend as *they* saw fit?"

"Odd you would bring that up since you don't have shareholders anymore."

"But we do have employees—hundreds of them, and hiring more every day. Employees earn wages and we pay them handsomely, which would not be the case if we had to spend that money to advertise our products."

"Or, from what I gather, use quality ingredients."

"Let's just say 'less expensive.'"

"And I'm sure you've figured out just which companies will get your machines, too. The highest bidders? Maybe like Omni Foods?"

"Omni is a very forward-thinking company."

"Greedy sounds more like it but it doesn't matter because what you're doing is wrong. You're messing with people's glands, fooling people into thinking they're buying something of value."

She felt another, more forceful tap on her foot.

"Aren't they getting value when they feel good?" Ledford said.

"They don't when they pay more for second-rate products that make them sick and turn them into criminals."

"You're minimizing the benefit. Additives supplement product ingredients all the time."

"But yours are machines."

"Technically, yes. But they aren't tractors or chain saws or something of the like. In reality, nanomachines are nothing more than manipulated molecules —atoms arranged in a particular way to make the molecule perform a specific task. But what's the difference, Miss Ross? Tell me the difference between an aspirin that interferes with pain systems and our devices that make a gland do what it does anyway?"

She pushed her chair back and stood. "You just don't get it."

"Get it? *You*, Miss Ross, don't get it. What you're failing to see is the big picture. A company's very existence depends on profits, and the nature of the food business squeezes those profits to unbelievably slim margins. Anything can and *will* make the difference to tip the balance one way or the other. Pride Foods---this very company---is no exception. Kennel Ration, Friskies, Purina—you name it—they were crushing us with huge advertising budgets and bringing us to our knees. Hundreds of our people stood to lose their jobs—men and women with families to feed and mortgages to pay and prom dresses to buy. They are productive people, Miss Ross, not derelicts or society's parasites. They are people who depended upon their company—this company—to sustain them."

"You're so full of it, I can't believe it. You think an appeal like that is going to get mileage with me? Don't bother slinging that altruistic crap. It won't stick."

Walsh lifted a hand. "Can I say something?"

Ledford slumped back. "Go ahead."

"I was skeptical, too, at first, Miss Ross. To tell you the truth, I couldn't believe it when Cleat told me what he was doing. But I've been here for the better part of the day, toured his plant, talked to his people, looked at his books." He shook his head. "I have to tell you, he's got a tiger by the tail. I admit I wouldn't know a gland from a can of Spam but I've seen the results. Six months ago, I wouldn't have given two cents for Cleat's chances of surviving the end of the year but now ... hell, it's astonishing! What Cleat's come up with is truly revolutionary. It changes everything about product marketing and in a big, big way. We've all seen companies try to outdo each other—change their packaging, put on labels like 'new' or 'improved'—but it's still the same ol' shit, right? Not with Cleat, though. Not anymore. What he's done is make it possible to change the way a product is sold without the expense of actually trying to sell it. It's an *enormous* opportunity. I don't care if the company sells Fig Newtons, denture adhesive or suntan lotion. Virtually anything someone eats or rubs into their skin that's been augmented by Cleat's nanomachines will give the company that makes it a population of consumers with unbelievable brand loyalty. Those people won't care one whit about all the advertising they hear and see from competing brands. They'll just keep buying Cleat's products because they *feel good* when they use them. Quite frankly, Miss Ross, that's exciting and I'm glad to be a part of it." He looked at Ledford. Ledford smiled.

She felt another sharp kick on her shoe.

"Stop doing that!" She glared at Walsh.

He flushed. "Was that me? I'm sorry, ma'am. Sometimes I think I've got two right feet."

She stepped back from the table. "Just what *is* your part in this?"

"Actually, I haven't started yet but I'll be the hook-up guy."

"Hook up?"

"Arrange marriages. I spent a lot of years on Wall Street, Miss Ross, and I've dealt with a lot of people. Anyone on the Street as long as me gets to know who the players are, gets to know which CEO's will push the line, hears the ones who scream the loudest for an edge.

That's where the hook-up guy comes in. I'll arrange marriages between Cleat and those screaming CEO's."

"Some marriage. What are the vows? 'Till prison do we part?'"

"You should feel fortunate Cleat's offered to bring you on board," Walsh said. "You'll make a ton of money, drive a nice car, live in a big house, travel the world ..."

"That's all wonderful and good but one thing gets in the way."

"What's that?"

"My conscience."

"It's a huge opportunity, ma'am. Think about it."

"I already have." She turned to Ledford. "Is the government in on this, too?"

"The government? Whatever gave you—"

"Dammit, Ledford!" she shouted. "Will you give me a straight answer for once!"

"But, I don't—"

"Cut the crap. One of your guards told me. Said the military has been here ... started showing up a few weeks ago." She jabbed a finger in the air at him. "Tell me the truth. What does the military want with your machines? Are you putting them in their rations?"

"I'm afraid that's classified, Miss Ross. Nothing I can discuss."

"What you're doing, sir, is wrong. It can't happen."

"Oh, but it has," he said. He checked his watch. "Production is already underway."

"Then I'll have to stop it. You've made a lot of people sick, ruined people's lives, created a police problem."

"Those people you're so concerned about are derelicts. Let's keep that in perspective. So what if a few extra milligrams of testosterone are released? Derelicts shouldn't be eating dog food, anyway. I pay enough in taxes. Those soup kitchens should be serving caviar and prime rib with what I pay. However, your information has been noted and I'll bring it to the attention of our chemist."

Traci threw up her arms, exasperated, then walked to a large picture window at the side of Ledford's desk and looked out. Her car was parked in the lot below, as promised. The silver Audi was nowhere in sight.

Her gaze moved to Ledford's reflection in the window as he turned to Vazzano.

"Have Ruecker up here in twenty minutes," Ledford said. "I want to know if we can cut back on the coating, see if dissipating it faster mitigates the testosterone effect she's talking about."

"I believe he's already left for the day, sir."

"Then get him back here!"

"Yes, sir." Vazzano pulled the walkie-talkie from his belt and issued the order.

"Mr. Ledford?" A voice spoke over the intercom.

"What?!" Ledford snapped.

"This is Arty at the front desk, sir. Mr. Westfield from Omni Foods is here. Shall I bring him up?"

"No. No. Have him wait. I'll be down momentarily."

"Yes, sir. I'll let him know."

Ledford drew a deep breath then let it out in a heavy sigh. He turned to Traci. "This isn't going well, is it? I don't believe I've gotten through to you, have I,

287

Miss Ross?" She remained at the window and did not turn around. "I was hoping you'd see things differently … hoping you'd want to become part of our team and help us. But, I'm afraid I don't see that happening."

"You've got that right," she said, still gazing out the window. "As soon as I get out of here, I'm calling the FBI."

"Don't be naïve, Miss Ross. Systems are in place. The authorities may come but they won't find anything." He cradled his chin in the web of his hand and stroked his cheek with his fingers for a moment. "Yet, your position as a police officer makes things a bit cumbersome. However," he pulled his hand away, "we'll work that out."

She turned around. "Work what out?"

Ledford nodded to Vazzano, who made another quick call on his walkie-talkie. Traci turned back to the window. Someone got into her car and began to drive it away.

She spun around. "What's going on? What are you doing with my car?"

"You won't be needing it, Miss Ross. It'll be dropped off in New York somewhere."

The office door opened and two guards stepped inside, their pistols drawn and leveled.

"Take her back to research," Ledford said. "That one too." He waved a hand at Walsh. "Lock them in Level-2 storage."

"Wait a minute," Walsh said. He rose from his chair. "We had a deal! I went along … did my part."

"Deal? You're a loser, Walsh. I don't make deals with losers."

Walsh shook a fist at the man. "You won't get away with this, Ledford!"

He laughed. "Oh, but I already have."

- 31 -

Traci and Walsh were led out of the building, urged along by periodic jabs in their backs by the guards' pistols. One guard holstered his weapon and slid behind the wheel of an electric cart parked at the back door. The other guard directed Walsh, then Traci, to sit on the bench seat next to the driver, then he stepped onto the cart's rear bumper and gripped the edge of the plastic canopy. He held his gun at the ready in his free hand, too far away for Traci to make a grab for it.

Mercury-vapor lights atop tall standards in the rear parking lot were off at that hour, and busy forklift drivers eighty yards away were oblivious to the small cart and its passengers as it began to roll across the pavement in the darkness.

Fifty yards away on Traci's right, a pair of headlights flicked on and the vehicle began to move, slowly vectoring toward them. At thirty yards, it accelerated.

"Who the hell...?" the guard on the bumper behind Traci said.

"Asshole," the driver guard said. He sped up and angled to the left.

Traci squinted at the blinding headlights bearing down on them. The driver guard made a sudden hard turn to the right. She grabbed at the edge of the canopy for support. He stomped down on the throttle pedal. No effect. The cart's governor was already pegged at its top speed. The headlights swerved to the left, now unmistakably aiming at the cart and closing the gap between them to ten yards. The headlights switched off. The guard made a wild swing to the left, wrenching Traci's grip from the canopy and throwing her off the seat. She sprawled to the asphalt. A second later, the car skimmed the cart's front bumper, spinning the cart around and banging the passenger side against the car's rear door. The guard on the bumper flew off, sailed over the car's trunk and disappeared in the darkness.

The car slid to a stop. The driver got out.

Traci immediately recognized the man's huge form.

Solly strode to the driver guard and a single blow from his fist knocked the man unconscious. Solly jerked him from the seat and tossed him onto the asphalt.

"Get out!" he told Walsh.

Traci struggled to her feet.

"Get in the car, ma'am!" Solly shouted.

She started toward the car, her steps unsteady. Solly pulled Walsh from the cart then pushed the dazed man into the Audi's back seat. Traci reached the front seat and got in as Solly squeezed in behind the wheel. He left the headlights off as he sped past the forklifts. Traci thought she spotted Ledford and another man she guessed was Westfield of Omni Foods getting out of a cart at the entrance to the production building. Solly continued around the warehouse, past a waiting line of eighteen-wheelers and toward the access road.

Traci turned in her seat. "Are you alright?" she asked Walsh.

He rubbed at his forehead where it had struck the cart's Plexiglas windshield. "Yeah ... uh, I guess so."

She turned to Solly and managed a smile. "You have an uncanny knack for showing up at the right time."

"That's what I get paid for."

"Who's paying you?"

He only gave her a quick glance then turned back to the road.

"Guess it doesn't matter," she said. "Once again, I'm grateful."

"Where are we going?" Walsh asked.

Solly guided the Audi onto the narrow access road.

"Where are we going?!" Walsh repeated.

An eighteen-wheeler's headlights wove toward them. Solly pulled to the shoulder and stopped.

"I've gotta go back!" Walsh said. "Cleat's got my money! And Phil's!"

Solly turned around. "Shut the fuck up, funny boy!"

"Why do you think I'm out here, Solly, for the fresh air? Cleat's got my money. He was supposed to give it to me but he screwed me. He's got Phil's three million too. I *saw* it! It's in his safe!"

"I've got to go back, too, Solly," Traci said. "We all do. We have to try to stop what they're doing."

"No way," Solly said. He stared straight ahead. "Walsh is going to Atlantic City. That's what I was told and that's what I'm doing. You do whatever you want."

"You can do that, Solly," she said. "Take Mr. Walsh there, if that's what you're supposed to do but just don't do it right now. Okay? Something terrible is happening here and we've got to stop it."

"There is no *we*," Solly said. "Get somebody else. I do what I'm told."

"These people that are paying you, would they really mind if you were delayed a little?"

"Yeah, they would."

"Just thirty minutes?"

The eighteen-wheeler rumbled past and Solly started forward.

"You won't help me?" she pressed.

He accelerated.

"Fine! I'll do it myself! Stop the car and let me out."

He stopped.

She swung the door open.

Solly grabbed her arm.

She jerked it away. "I'm getting out!"

"Look," Solly said. He pointed ahead, up the road.

Headlights from another eighteen-wheeler silhouetted three men with rifles near the guard shack.

"That's not a good sign," Walsh said.

"Is there another way out?" Solly asked.

"No idea," Traci said, closing the door. "We better get out of here. They'll see us any second if they haven't already."

Solly made a U-turn and stepped on the gas. A bullet shattered the passenger sideview mirror. Two more bullets ripped into the Audi's trunk.

"Christ!" Walsh yelled. "They're shooting at us!"

Solly stomped on the gas. "Get down!"

Sparks from ricocheting bullets flared off the pavement to their left. Rapid clunks sounded beneath them as another bullet ricocheted around the Audi's undercarriage. Solly rounded the curve toward the parking lot. He checked the rearview mirror. They were out of the shooter's line of sight.

"Okay," he said. "Get up."

Traci and Walsh straightened and gave tentative glances out the back window.

"What's wrong, Solly?" Traci asked.

He was rapidly pumping the brake pedal, to no effect.

"That last shot must have hit the brake line. We got no brakes."

The Audi gained momentum as it came out of the curve and sped across the parking lot toward the warehouse. Solly wheeled the car back and forth in a narrow serpentine track in an effort to slow the vehicle. Ahead, an eighteen-wheeler slowly lumbered out from the sloped warehouse loading dock ramp, its headlights illuminating the heavens.

"You're going to hit the truck!" Walsh yelled.

Solly continued to stomp on the brake pedal and swerve back and forth, narrowly avoiding parked cars on either side that funneled the Audi into the path of the truck.

"You're going to hit it!" Walsh screamed.

Traci grabbed the gear shift and rammed the lever into *Park*. The transmission howled. The car bucked and skidded along the pavement, out of control. A second later, the axle snapped. The Audi free-wheeled toward the eighteen-wheeler.

"Pull the emergency!" she screamed.

Solly ran a hand back and forth under the dash of the unfamiliar rental car.

"Shi-i-it!" Walsh braced for the impact.

The eighteen-wheeler was only yards away, its forty-foot trailer directly in their path.

Traci jerked the wheel. "Get down!" she shouted.

They ducked.

The Audi shot under the trailer. The windshield exploded, raking the air with a hail of tiny glass shards, then the car's top sheared off. Prone along the seat, Solly now spotted the pedal for the emergency brake and mashed it to the floor. The car sagged to a stop on the other side of the trailer.

Traci sat up and looked around. Several men jumped down from the loading dock and ran up the long ramp toward her. Another man stood on the dock. He was shouting into a walkie-talkie.

She pushed at Solly's shoulder. He sat up.

"Jesus!" Walsh said. "Am I still alive?"

"C'mon. Let's go," Traci said.

She tried to open her door. Jammed.

One of the men reached her side of the car. "Are you alright, lady?"

"Yeah." She climbed onto the seat and jumped out. "Yeah, I'm fine. Give my friend a hand, will you?" She waved at Walsh. He was struggling to climb onto the backseat. Fragments of glass drizzled off his shirt with the movement.

Solly kicked his jammed door with both feet. It squealed open and he got out. Another man arrived and helped the first man pull Walsh over the transom.

"Security's on the way," one of the men said to Traci. "They'll get you to a doctor."

"No, that's okay. We're fine, really. Thank you."

"Might be somethin' broken or torn, lady. You should get checked out. Anyways, they'll wanna do a report." He pointed.

Three solitary headlights raced toward them from the parking lot at the far end of the warehouse. She poked Solly's arm and nodded in their direction.

The men from the loading dock talked excitedly as they circled the mangled Audi and compared stories. Traci, Walsh, and Solly inched away, then hurried into the warehouse as the three guards drove up.

"They were here a second ago," Traci heard one of the men say.

"Check the trailers," someone else said.

"We can go out the back," Traci said. "I've been through here before."

She hurried along the wall on her right then moved to safety between stacked pallets of Pride Premium and waited for the others. When they caught up, they squatted down as a forklift lumbered up and lifted a pallet from the top of the row in front of them.

"Phil's money is here?" Solly said in a gruff whisper.

"I saw it," Walsh whispered back. "Every penny of it. It's in Ledford's safe."

"Where's his safe?"

"His office. Shitty wall safe. You could get it open just snarling at it."

The forklift backed away with the pallet and rumbled toward a waiting truck.

Men's voices. Hurried footsteps.

"We can't stay here," Traci said. "The guards will find us."

They scurried between the rows of pallets then past a small office at the rear of the warehouse and out the back of the building. They hid in the darkness behind a dumpster and waited.

Two minutes passed then Solly rose. "Alright, let's go get it."

"Get what?" Traci asked.

"The money. Let's go."

"Wait a minute," she said. "We've got to get into the production building and shut it down somehow. It's just on the other—"

"Not now," Solly said. "We get the money first." He glared at her.

"Go ahead," she said. "Get your damn money if that's what you want. I've got to stop them and it can't wait." She started away.

Solly grabbed her arm and squeezed it hard. "You're going with us," he growled. "We stay together."

She pulled at his hand. He gripped it tighter. "You're crushing my arm."

He released it. "Let's go."

"Not a chance. That's burglary. I don't care if he does have your money. It's a man's office. On private property. Get an attorney if the money is really yours.

297

I'm a police officer, I can't go in there without a warrant."

"Screw the warrant. It's Phil's money and we're going to get it."

"Then do it without me," she said. "I'm not going in there and that's final."

Walsh scooted over. "Listen, Ms. Ross. If you *don't* go, I'm going to write a letter to your department and get you fired. My money's in Cleat's office and you're here, right now, and you're refusing to help Solly and me get it back. Isn't that what they call 'dereliction of duty?'"

"You're crazy."

"No, I'm not. I'm a citizen. You're supposed to help. That's your goddamn job, isn't it?"

"Yes, but—"

"No but. You're a cop. My money's right over there. Less than a hundred yards away, in Ledford's office. You're here, now, so do your goddamn job, for chrissake!"

"I'm not so … How do I know it's your money and not Mr. Ledford's?"

"Okay. Fair question. I'll tell you how. There's eight million dollars in that safe. If there's a penny less, you can take a pass, alright?"

She frowned. "Money's money. How will I know it's *your* money?"

Walsh rolled his eyes. "Because every goddamn bill has my great-great-grandfather's portrait on it, may he rest in peace. Okay?"

"Oh, brother."

"Look, Officer—"

"Sergeant."

"Okay. Sergeant. There's something else in there. A stock certificate. My brother's name is on it. Oscar Walsh. It's complicated, but it belongs to the Pipefitter's union and I have to get it back to them. So when Solly opens that safe, you'll see the eight million *and* the stock certificate. Is that proof enough or do I write that letter?"

She sighed. "I don't see why I have to go. You two can handle whatever you have to do. What's so damn important about me going too?"

"You run around here by yourself," Solly said, "you'll get caught. We stay together, we don't get caught. We get the money—then we do what you want."

"Okay, but I'm not going in Mr. Ledford's office. That's burglary. I can't. I won't."

"No problem," Solly said. "Let's go."

- 32 -

They ran along the side of the building and stopped midway, behind another dumpster, waiting for Walsh to catch up. Moments later, they slipped through the back door of the administration building and rode the elevator to the fourth floor.

"This is as far as I go," Traci said when they reached the double oak doors to Ledford's office.

"We'll be out in a flash," Walsh said.

Walsh and Solly went in. Traci paced outside.

Four minutes later, muffled ripping sounds came from inside the office. She opened one of the doors and looked in. Solly was pulling at a sheet of paneling next to the wall safe. Another splintered sheet lay on the floor. She stepped inside and closed the door. "What are you doing!? You're tearing his office apart!"

Solly scowled at Walsh. "Shitty wall safe, huh?"

"Well, that's what it looked like. How was I supposed to know?"

Traci crossed the room for a look as Solly freed the sheet from the wall and tossed it to the floor with the other one.

"How the hell are we supposed to get this out?" Solly said.

The safe, with a two-inch-wide perimeter flange, was encased in concrete. Only the door and flange were exposed. Solly hammered the door twice with his fist. No movement.

"Okay, boys," Traci said. "You've had your fun. Let's get out of here."

"No way!" Walsh said. "My money's in there. Settlement charges for being screwed over by all the assholes in my life—*especially* Ledford. He's not screwing me again. We have to find a way."

"Yeah?" Solly said. "How, funny boy?"

"Come on," Traci said. "It's set in cement. Forget it."

"We need a jackhammer or something," Walsh muttered.

"Let's go!" Traci said. "We're running out of time!"

"Or somethin'," Solly repeated.

"You don't have a jackhammer. Let's leave!"

Solly said, "We're not leaving without the money."

"You got that right," Walsh said.

Traci strode to Ledford's desk and sat in one of the club chairs in front of it. "You guys are too much." She checked her watch. Ten after eleven. *Less than two hours.*

"C'mon, Solly, think!" Walsh said as he grabbed the door's latch and gave it a yank. It would not budge.

Traci anxiously drummed her fingers on the large desktop blotter.

"We could use a little help, lady," Walsh said.

"No way. That's your thing. I'm not getting involved."

301

Solly and Walsh continued to banter while moving back and forth in front of the safe, eyeing it from various angles. Traci stopped drumming and sat up. "Hey, did you guys mess with Ledford's desk?"

"Nope," Solly said without looking at her.

"Then where is it?"

"Where's what?" Walsh asked.

"His computer. I saw it when I was in here before. It was on his desk."

"We never touched the desk," Walsh said. "Maybe he takes it with him." He again pulled at the safe.

Traci scanned the room. No computer. She moved to the chair behind the desk and pulled on the side drawers. Locked. She tried the center drawer. Locked. She scooted the chair back, leaned forward and craned her head for a look under the desk. Just below the center drawer and recessed several inches behind it was the thin edge of a shelf. She pulled on it. The shelf rolled out on bearing rails. A wireless computer keyboard was on it. She lifted it off and set it on the blotter. *Where's the monitor?* She again bent down and looked under the desk. Nothing. Only a mahogany modesty panel. She sat up and pushed the shelf back under the center drawer but it stuck partway in. She pushed a little harder and the shelf retracted the rest of the way. A clicking sound followed and the back edge of the blotter pulsed up and down about an inch. She slid the blotter to one side and the clicking sound stopped, replaced by a whir. She smiled as a sixteen inch long and four inch wide door flipped up. A flat-screen plasma computer monitor slowly rose through the opening where the door had been. The monitor stopped when it cleared the top of the desk.

Her smile broadened when she turned on the monitor and keyboard. The green and yellow Pride Foods logo filled the screen. At the bottom left was: *J. C. Ledford – Terminal 1.*

"Well, now, Mister J C Ledford Terminal 1," she said to the screen, "let's see what you you've got to say for yourself."

She used the keyboard's mouse pad to move the cursor to the center of the screen then tapped it twice. The screen background changed to light blue and a menu appeared with a list of seven selections:

ACCOUNTING
CORRESPONDENCE
FORMULATIONS
INTERNAL MEMOS
MARKETING PLAN REVISIONS
PLANT SYSTEMS
SHIPPING & RECEIVING SCHEDULES

She moved the cursor to CORRESPONDENCE and double-clicked. Another light blue screen, entitled *Correspondence*, appeared. Below that were sub-menus:

SEC FILINGS
EARNINGS REPORTS
OMNI FOODS
DARPA REQUESTS
DOD ISSUES

She clicked on OMNI FOODS and a stream of correspondence topics scrolled down the screen for several seconds, then stopped. This will take forever, she thought. She scanned the file name headings but none seemed ominous. She picked one at random—Matzo Ball Soup—and clicked on it. A large dialog box appeared in the center of the screen: **PASSWORD REQUIRED TO ACCESS THIS FILE** was displayed, along with seven small squares where she reasoned the password was to be entered. The cursor blinked repeatedly in the first of the squares. She closed the password screen, returned to the file listing and clicked on another one: Butter. The password-required box reappeared. She tried another file and got the same result. "Hey guys," she called out. "What do you think Ledford uses for a computer password? Seven letters."

"Who knows," Walsh said. "Try 'asshole'." He gave a quick laugh.

Traci frowned. "Very creative. Care to try again?"

"You do your thing," Walsh said, "we're doing ours." He turned back to the safe.

Traci thought a moment, then typed: P-R-E-M-I-U-M and hit the enter key. The information in the dialog box disappeared and ***Password Not Accepted*** came up. The words blinked twice, disappeared, and the password request was again displayed. The cursor blinked in the first square, waiting. Traci considered several possible passwords, then typed: D-O-G-F-O-O-D and tapped the enter key. As before, ***Password Not Accepted*** appeared, blinked twice and went away. She shrugged and mumbled, "Why not?" She typed A-S-S-H-O-L-E in the boxes and hit enter. A new screen flashed on the monitor. Bold yellow letters, an inch tall, on a navy blue background appeared:

VANISH WILL INITITATE IN 15 SECONDS.
Enter Termination Code.

Traci jerked her hands from the keyboard. Five blank squares for entering the code appeared, the cursor blinked urgently inside the first one. Traci stared with wide eyes as the *15* changed to *14*, then *13*. She racked her mind for a logical code but none came to her. *7* ... *6* ... *5* ... She watched, frozen, as the final seconds ticked away... *2* ... *1* ... *0*. On zero, the screen went blank.

"Huh? What's that all about?" she muttered. She flicked the on/off switches on the keyboard and monitor several times. No response. She sat for a full minute. When nothing happened, she pulled out the shelf from beneath the center desk drawer, set the keyboard on it and pushed it back under the desk. It clicked into place and the monitor slowly descended into the desk. She slid the blotter to the center of the desk, then sat back and checked her watch. *Eleven thirty-five.*

"Hey, lady," Walsh said. "You gotta help."

"Huh?"

"If you can tear yourself away, we need your help."

Traci grimaced then got up and joined Solly and Walsh at the safe. "It's an interior wall," she said. "What's on the other side?"

"More of the same," Walsh said. "Take a look."

Traci went around to the other side. Two sections of paneling had been pulled from the wall, exposing a solid surface of concrete. She estimated the wall's thickness at three feet. She returned to the front.

Walsh said, "Maybe if we all put our fingers on the edge of the flange and pull it might come free."

"That's the dumbest idea I've heard all day," she said. "There's nothing to grab. The flange is too smooth. I'd only break my nails."

"Okay, you got a better idea?"

"As a matter of fact, I do."

"Yeah?" Solly said.

"There's no way you'll leave until you get the money?"

"That's right, sweet cheeks," Walsh said.

She frowned. "In for a penny, in for a pound. I'll be right back."

"Where're you going?"

"Wait here. And don't demolish any more of his office."

* * * * *

A Puerto Rican woman in a powder-blue blouse with matching pants and head scarf smiled as Traci stepped from the elevator on the ground floor. The woman turned back to a closed office door and fumbled with a set of keys. A cart of cleaning supplies with a large, open cloth bag attached to a wide metal hoop was next to her. Traci watched the woman open the door and push the cart into the office. When the door closed, Traci hurried down the hallway toward the back door.

The men's room door ahead of her swung open and the front desk guard stepped out. He was zipping his fly. His face reddened as Traci passed. He turned away, stopped, then dropped to a crouch and pulled the pistol from his holster. He pointed it at her back.

"You're her!" he shouted. "Stop! Put your hands up!"

She stopped and turned around. "I'm who?"

"You're the woman we're looking for. Put 'em up."

"Look," she said, taking a few steps toward him. "I don't know who you think I am but I'm a police officer: Sergeant Ross, Boston police department." She stopped in front of him.

"You're no cop. You're the trespasser." He rose from the crouch. "I said, get your hands up." He waved the gun at her.

She complied. "You're making a *huge* mistake."

"No, I'm not. I gotta call Mr. Vazzano." He glanced down at the walkie-talkie on his belt. Traci shot a hand out and grabbed the pistol's slide action. She clamped the barrel with her other hand, spun to the side, and thrust the weapon into the man's startled face—a robotic sequence of moves all police recruits practiced countless times while in the academy.

The guard yelped when the gun struck his nose. She jerked the pistol back and wrenched it from his grip, then stepped back and leveled the weapon at the stunned guard's chest.

"Don't shoot," he said, raising his hands.

She looked around the hallway and recognized Vazzano's office door. "Get in there."

He unlocked the door and they went in. Nothing new. Just the solitary filing cabinet, the metal desk and phone set, and two chairs. She lifted the phone's receiver and punched at the buttons. No dial tone.

"How do I get an outside line?" she asked.

"You can't. It's after six."

"I know about the code. What is it?"

"I don't know. Mr. Vazzano changes it all the time. He and Ledford are the only ones that ever know it."

"How do you call out if there's an emergency?"

"We don't. Security handles emergencies."

"Hmmm. Okay, give me your cuffs and lie on the floor next to the desk."

She cuffed one wrist and ankle around a leg of the desk, then pulled the phone cord from the wall and tied his other wrist and ankle together.

"I knew you weren't no cop," he said.

"When I first got here, I gave the other guard my purse. Where is it?"

"Mr. Vazzano took it."

"Took it where?"

"I don't know. He didn't say. He just took it."

Traci eyed the filing cabinet.

"This is his office. Is it in there?"

"I don't know."

She stepped to the cabinet and pulled at the drawers. All locked.

"Do you have the key?"

"Are you kidding? That's Vazzano's. There's no way anybody but him would have the key."

She tried the desk drawer: Locked as well. She moved back to the filing cabinet and rocked it away from the wall, then tipped it and let it fall onto the floor. She bent down for a look. Standard cabinet. She swung the bottom around, then sat on the floor and kicked twice at the locking rod. It yielded. She got up and pulled the bottom drawer open. Her purse was inside. She pulled it out and checked. Gun and cell phone. She tried the phone. Nothing. Dead battery. "Well isn't that just perfect," she said, dropping it into her purse. She turned to the guard.

"Don't say anything and don't move."

She slung the purse over her shoulder, slid the guard's 9mm automatic pistol into the waistband of her skirt at the back, covered it with her blouse and went out.

- 33 -

"Jesus!" Walsh said. "Where the hell did you get that?"

Traci drove the forklift into Ledford's office, then got off and shut the oak doors. She unfolded the twin forks and got back on the machine.

"Couldn't find a jackhammer," she said, "but this should do."

She guided the machine across the floor, then eased it up to the wall with the safe and raised the forks to the bottom edge of the safe's metal flange. Satisfied, she backed the forklift across the room, paused, then gunned the engine and sped across the floor. The twin forks stabbed into the concrete with a horrendous clatter, penetrating the material about a foot. She stopped, shifted a lever up and down several times and watched the forks slowly break the concrete away from the safe's casing. She moved the machine forward another foot then rapidly shifted the lever again. The safe came free and fell forward onto the forks. She backed up and stopped.

"You're a goddamn genius," Walsh said.

310

"Not so fast," she said. "There's still a little matter of getting it downstairs."

"What do you mean?"

"What I mean is the elevator is only big enough for this thing if the forks are folded up."

"So?"

"So the safe and the forklift can't go together. If I put the safe in the elevator, you won't be able to get it out when it gets to the ground floor."

"Solly could," Walsh said. He looked at the man. "Right?"

"Who do you think I am, dickhead, Hercules? No fuckin' way I can lift that thing."

"I got it," Walsh said. "Get another forklift to take it out."

"It's not exactly a Hertz rental yard out there," she said. "These things aren't just lined up with keys and ready to go. Somebody's going to miss this one real soon if they haven't already."

"Well, then we'll still need a jackhammer."

"Forget the jackhammer," Traci said. "I've had it with you guys. Watch out."

She backed away from the wall, then turned the machine around and stopped. "Walsh. Go turn off the lights. Solly, take a look out the window. See if anybody's out there."

He looked. Eighty yards away, a dozen forty-foot-long trailers with open rear doors were parked at the bottom of the loading dock ramp.

"Just trucks way over by the warehouse."

She slipped the forklift into gear as the lights went off and ran it straight at the plate glass window to the left of Ledford's desk. Two feet after the forks shattered the glass, she slammed on the brake. The forward momentum of the safe continued, it slid along the forks, then off and into the darkness outside. Walsh ran to look. The safe tumbled end over end, down the side of the four-story building, then smashed into the sidewalk below.

"Sonuvabitch!" he said. He glanced at the distant buildings and at the parking lot below. No pause in the activity. No curious looks from the truckers at the warehouse.

Solly peered though the broken window as Traci switched off the machine and climbed down. "Let's go get it," he said.

- 34 -

The safe was on its side, half on the sidewalk and half in an adjacent flower bed. The door was sprung open a few inches. Solly muscled the safe onto its back then pried the door open the rest of the way. Banded packets of hundred-dollar bills lay strewn about inside.

"That's a lot of money," Traci said, peering in.

"Need something to carry it in," Solly said. He glanced around. "Maybe in there." He nodded at the administration building.

"Yeah. Good idea," Walsh said. "Go in and see what you can find. We'll wait here."

"She stays," Solly said. "You come with me."

"What for? You think I'd run off with Phil's money? Is that what you think?"

"Her, I trust. You, I don't."

"Stop squabbling," Traci said. "You're wasting time."

She checked her watch as the men left. *Midnight.*

They returned minutes later, pushing the maid's cleaning cart.

"All we could find," Walsh said.

313

Solly reached into the cloth sack attached to the cart and pulled out several soiled cleaning rags. He tossed them to the ground. Both men then raked the packets of money from the safe and dumped them into the sack. Walsh spotted the stock certificate, showed it to Traci, then folded it and stuffed it into his trouser pocket. When they finished transferring the money, Solly spread the soiled rags on top of the pile.

"Let's split," Walsh said. He grabbed the cart's handle and started away.

"Not so fast," Solly said. "Now we help her."

"You help her. I never agreed to that."

"You didn't have to. It wasn't up for a vote." Solly turned to Traci. "What do you want us to do?"

"I don't know. We can't just walk in."

"Walk in where?" Walsh said.

"The production building. Behind the warehouse."

Walsh shifted on his feet. "Too risky," he said. "Guards are all over the place. We wouldn't get five feet. Let's forget it and get out of here. You can drop a dime to your pals when we get back to town."

"You see those trucks over there?" she said.

"Yeah."

"Every one of them is loaded with tainted food. More of it is being made every minute. That warehouse we were in is filled with it. That's dog food in there but they'll be making other food in less than an hour. People food. If we wait until we get out of here and find a phone somewhere—assuming we *can* find a way out of here at all—it'll be too late. We have to act now."

"Yeah, well, that's all fine and good but what can we do? There's only three of us."

"That cart gives me an idea," Traci said.

"You're a regular garden of ideas, aren't you?"

"Shut up and let's hear it," Solly said.

"You didn't happen to see the cleaning woman, did you?" Traci said.

"See her? Of course we saw her," Walsh said. "Where do you think we got the cart?"

Traci eyed the men. "You didn't hurt her, I hope."

"Naw. She's fine. Solly tied her up real good. She won't give us any trouble."

"Where is she?"

"What's with the broom, already? Who cares? I said she's fine."

"She's got something I need and probably something else we'll all need, that's what."

"Really? What could a cleaning woman possibly have that I would want?"

"How about a car?"

Walsh cocked his head. "Yeah. Good possibility. Didn't think of that."

"And a uniform. Something I could wear to get in without being noticed."

"Not bad. Okay. I like it."

"I'm glad you approve, numb-nuts," Solly said.

"Where'd you leave her?" Traci asked.

"On the floor behind the front desk."

"Give me a couple of these." She reached into the cloth bag and pulled out two packets of cash.

"Hey!" Walsh said. "That's twenty thousand dollars!"

"You're right," Traci said. "I'll take another one."
She pulled it out.

"What for?"

"We're going to take her car. You're going to pay
her for it."

"Shit. Thirty thousand for probably some tiny,
piece-of-shit Ford Falcon without air."

"I said, shut up!" Solly said. He held a fist in front
of Walsh's face.

"Alright, alright. Take the goddamn money. Half of
that's coming out of Phil's share."

"Not a penny," Solly said. "You're buying."

Walsh groaned.

"I'll be right back," Traci said. "Try to roll the safe
off the sidewalk. Hide it. Maybe throw some of those
shrubs on it."

She left and went into the building through the
back, then cracked open the door to Vazzano's office.
The guard was still on the floor. He looked up. Traci
pressed a finger to her lips and shook her head. He
looked away.

She closed the door and listened. All quiet. She
continued down the hallway to the front desk. The
cleaning woman lay motionless on the floor behind it.
A rag was stuffed in her mouth. The woman's eyes
darted around the room. Her breaths came in short
gasps.

"Do you speak English?" Traci asked.

The woman nodded.

"Good. Do you have a car here?"

She nodded again.

"Excellent. I want to buy it. Where is it and where are the keys?"

The woman tried to speak.

"Oh, sorry." Traci leaned down. "Don't scream," she said, pulling the rag from the woman's mouth.

"Where's your car?" Traci asked, again.

"In lot. You take it. Please, no hurt me."

"I'm not going to hurt you. Which lot?"

"By warehouse. Last row. Just take it."

"I said I'm going to pay you for it. Relax. Where are the keys and what kind is it?"

"You pay me?"

"That's right. What's the make and color."

"White. Good car. Run good. How much you pay?"

"White car. Runs good. Okay. What make is it?"

"Geo. Geo Metro."

Traci smiled. "Air?"

"Yes. Air. Good air. How much? I pay eight thousand dollars. How much you pay?"

"Twenty thousand. Here." She set two packets of cash on the floor next to the woman.

The woman's eyes bulged.

"I want something else," Traci said.

"Yes, yes. You tell me and I give you."

"I need your clothes."

"Yes, yes. You take my clothes."

"I'll pay you for those too. Ten thousand." She set the remaining packet on top of the others.

"God bless you, lady."

- 35 -

Traci nudged open one of the double doors at the front of the research building and stole a quick look around the lobby inside. A guard behind the desk was watching Jay Leno on a portable television. She left and crept back around the corner where Solly and Walsh waited with the cleaning cart.

"Only one guard," she said.

"Just one?" Solly said. "No problem." He started around the corner.

"Where are you going?"

"Gonna go in there and pound the shit outta him. That always works best."

"He's got a gun, Solly. Maybe bullets, too."

Solly grunted. "Just a door shaker. Probably never shot it."

"We'll use that as Plan B, thank you very much. Let's try Plan A first."

"Which is…?"

"Which is I walk in with the cart."

"Come on, Miss Ross," Walsh said. "You tell *me* I've got dumb ideas? How do you know when the broom is supposed to be there? How do you know she hasn't already *been* there, for chrissake? What if the guard recognizes you?" He shook his head. "I don't even know what we're doing here. I thought you wanted to do something in that other building. What's this place?"

"There's a cafeteria inside and it might have some things we can use. The guard's watching TV and probably won't even pay any attention if I go in dressed like this with the cart."

Walsh frowned. "Whatever."

Traci moved out of the shadows and around the corner. Halfway to the front door she froze when the headlight of an electric cart turned the corner from the other side of the long building and rolled in her direction.

She hurried back to the corner and peered around it to check the cart. It stopped near the doors in front of the building. Two guards. One got out and went inside.

"Got three now," she whispered.

"Still no problem," Solly said.

"We'll wait. Might be a shift change."

Two minutes passed. The guard came out and the two men rode away.

"Just one guard now," she said. "I'm going for it."

Traci pushed the cart through the doors and into the lobby. The guard gave her a cursory glance and a weak wave, then turned back to the television program.

Ten minutes later, she pushed the cart back into the lobby and headed for the front door.

"Hey," the guard said.

319

She kept walking toward the door, her eyes straight ahead.

"You gotta see this," the guard said.

"I'm behind. I don't have time."

"Come on. Take a minute. This is funny Man on the Street stuff. You can't believe how stupid some people are."

"Yeah, I can. I'll get in trouble if I don't finish. I have to go."

The guard stood. "Where's Maria?" he said.

"Got sick. I have to go."

She pushed the cart outside and hurried around the corner to Walsh and Solly.

"I think the guard's suspicious," she said. "Let's get out of here."

"I told you it was a bad idea," Walsh said.

"Shut up and get going!" Solly said.

They hurried along the building, darted past an electrical panel closet and across a dark, thirty-yard-wide alleyway between the buildings. They huddled near a side door of the production facility and checked behind them. No one followed.

Walsh peered into the cloth bag. "I want to see what was so damn important back there." He pawed at bottles of Spanish olives, Italian salad dressing, vinegar, and large cans of tomato paste and frozen pineapple juice. "What the hell's all this for? You planning a party?"

"I'll explain later."

"This gets dumber by the minute."

320

"Look, Walsh," Solly said. "Why don't you just stand over there in the corner and choke your chicken. You'll slow us down with all your complaining."

"Choke my what?"

"Solly's right," Traci said. "There's no point in all of us going in. Take the keys and go find that white Geo. Bring it up to the parking lot in front of the administration building. Solly and I will meet you there when we're done."

"Yeah, okay. What about the money?"

"It stays with us," Solly said. "Insurance you'll be there with the car."

"Oh, I'll be there, alright. You can bet *your* ass on that. Just make sure you don't decide to take some alternate transportation."

"One more thing," Traci said. "Check the trucks as you go past the warehouse. If you spot one without a driver, see if there's a CB radio in it. A lot of truckers still have them. Don't take any chances but try using it to get some help."

"You're going to tax his little brain, ma'am," Solly said. "He'll be lucky just to find the car without getting caught."

"Your confidence is inspiring," Walsh said.

"Just be there and don't screw up!"

Walsh crept along the building then went out of sight around the corner.

"Okay. He's gone," Solly said. "What's this really about?"

"It's what I told you before. They're mixing things into the food to make people buy it."

"That's it?"

"Pretty much."

"So what? What's wrong with that?"

"It deforms them, Solly. It changes their bodies, causes disease and makes them do crazy things. What they're putting in can't be tasted, seen or felt. People won't know they've been exposed until it's too late. I've seen how it affects people. It's grotesque."

"The bastards! Okay. What's the plan?"

"I've thought about shutting off the power but they've probably got generator backups, so that's no good. And I've tried to get into Ledford's computer but I need a password. For now, I think the best we can do is try to neutralize what they'll be putting in the food with the things I got from the cafeteria."

Solly looked in the bag. He pulled out a pint jar of vinegar and a frost-covered can of frozen pineapple juice. He held them up. "What are we supposed to do with these? Bean their heads with 'em?"

"Not quite. We'll pour the contents into the mixing vats and hope they neutralize what they'll be putting in the food in ..." she glanced at her watch, "... in about thirty-five minutes. If it works, maybe they'll think their scheme failed and give up on the idea."

"That's it? C'mon, Traci. You can do better than that." He dropped the vinegar and pineapple juice into the bag.

Traci sighed. "Pretty lame, I know."

"I have to tell you, I'm with Walsh on this. It *is* a dumb idea. *Real* dumb. But I promised to help, so let's get at it."

"Thanks, Solly. Here, take this." She pulled the guard's pistol from the waistband of her skirt and held it out for him.

He waved it off. "I don't use guns."

"*They* do. Take it."

"Nope. Never used 'em." He made a fist. "This is all I've ever needed."

"Suit yourself."

She shoved the gun back in her waistband and cracked the door open.

"Finally got a break," she said peering in. "Looks like a locker room. There's a rack of smocks. Find one that fits." She laughed. "If that's possible."

They went in. Solly strode to the smock rack.

Another door led from the locker room to the production floor. Traci opened it a few inches. Five yards in was a small office with glass panes on the front and both sides. The front faced the production floor. The back wall—closest to Traci—was plywood. Ledford and the other man she saw with him earlier were inside, their backs to her. Ledford held a clear plastic sport bottle filled with liquid up to the light. Both men were examining it. They were talking and appeared excited about what they saw. Twenty yards beyond the office, two guards ambled about, and men and women in white smocks, filter face masks and hair nets tended to the twelve huge mixing vats that fed the filler hoppers aligned across the wide floor. The noise from the busy machines was deafening. She closed the door.

She found Solly at the smock rack. He was in a struggle to close the sides of a smock over his wide chest.

"Change of plans, Solly."

"Uh, good," he grunted. "Didn't like the last one."

"There's an office a few yards inside. Ledford and another man are in it. I'm going to go in and arrest him."

"*That* plan I *like*. Let's go."

"No. You should stay here. I saw two guards in there and they'd spot you in a heartbeat. I'll bring Ledford back here and then we can decide what to do."

"That part don't sound so good. I'd better go with you." He pulled harder on the smock and it ripped.

"Thanks, Solly, but I'll be okay. Arresting people is what I do."

He pulled off the smock and chucked it on top of the lockers. "Yeah, okay. Go do your thing. I'll wait here."

"Be right back," she said.

She checked the pistol in her waistband then used the cart to push open the door to the production floor. "Crap!" she muttered as she stepped out. Neither Ledford nor the other man was visible. *Maybe they're sitting down.* She moved the cart ahead until she was even with the office's left side window. She looked in. Both men were gone. *Dammit!* She turned to go back to the locker room but stopped when she spotted a computer on a small desk inside the office. She glanced around the production floor. No one seemed to notice her. She went into the office, closed the door and sat at the desk.

The familiar green and yellow Pride Foods logo was displayed on the computer monitor. *Production – Terminal 27* was printed on the screen in the bottom left corner. She moved the mouse pointer to the center of the screen and double-clicked. The light blue background and white menu items she'd seen earlier came up. She selected PLANT SYSTEMS and double-clicked on it. A new sub-menu list was displayed:

> FIRE SUPPRESSION
> HEATING & A-C
> SECURITY
> UTILITIES
> VANISH

"Aha!" she said aloud. "Now we're getting somewhere." She gave a quick glance behind her to check the production floor. No one appeared concerned about a cleaning woman in the office. She turned back to the monitor and double-clicked on VANISH. The same password dialog box appeared on the screen and demanded an entry. "Crap!" she said. She thought a moment, then typed V-A-Z-Z-A-N-O in the boxes and hit *Enter. Password Not Accepted* came on the screen, blinked twice then disappeared. The cursor returned to the first password square and blinked repeatedly. *What could it be?* She again checked behind her. Nothing had changed. She turned back to the screen. "Oh, well," she said absently. "Two more chances." She typed P-E-T-F-O-O-D and hit the enter key. The screen immediately turned an iridescent blue.

Words in two-inch-high, bright orange, bold letters appeared:

VANISH WILL ARM IN 10 SECONDS
Enter Termination Code

The cursor blinked in the first of the five squares for the code.

"Oh, shit!" She trembled as the *10* became *9*, then *8* … "Oh, shit," she said, again. She looked behind her. No change. She looked back at the screen … *2* … *1* … *0*. At zero, the screen turned black. Her mouth hung open. She pushed the chair back from the desk. "What … is … happening?"

The office door banged open. The din of the production machinery filled the room. Traci stiffened.

"Hey!" a man behind her shouted.

She slowly turned around. One of the workers--a man in a white smock.

"We got a big mess over behind number three!" he yelled over the noise. "Get it cleaned up!"

"I—"

"Hurry up!"

Traci got up and followed the man out the door. As she passed the transom, she noticed Solly in the doorway to the locker room. She flicked a thumb toward the room. He nodded and closed the door.

Traci followed the worker around the vats to the third one. A thirty gallon barrel of molasses was on the floor, a widening pool of goo spreading from it.

"Get it up right away!" the man said.

326

Minutes passed as she hurriedly scooped, then mopped the sticky mess from the floor and dumped it back in the barrel. Finished, she pushed the cart to the first of the Omni vats and reached inside the cloth sack. She found a jar of olives, pulled it out and began to unscrew the top when two more guards entered the building from the front and ambled in her direction. She dropped the olives back in the sack, lowered her head, and quickly strode to the locker room.

"Solly," she whispered.

No answer.

Solly!" she repeated.

Nothing.

She hurried along the rows of lockers, looking down each.

No one.

Two doors at the rear of the locker room were marked *Men* and *Women*. She pushed open the one marked *Men*. A shower was running. "Solly!" she shouted.

"Not here!" a man inside yelled back. A moment later, the man stepped into view, dripping wet and naked. He gave her an approving smile. She turned away. "Just me," he said. "You want to clean up?"

"Not now. I'm looking for someone. Was anyone else in there?"

"A couple of guards were talking to a real big guy by the lockers a bit ago. I didn't recognize him. Maybe a transfer from the day shift."

"Where did he go?"

"Don't know. They all went out the back."

She walked away.

"You can clean up now!" he shouted after her. "I don't mind."

She grabbed the cart and hurried out the back door. Thirty feet ahead, three men walked in the direction of the research building. Solly and two guards. She caught the shape of a gun held by one of the guards. It was leveled at Solly's back. She pushed the cart toward the men. They stopped and turned around at the sound of the cart's clacking wheels. In the darkness, they saw a woman in the uniform of a custodian pushing a cleaning cart. They resumed walking.

She quickened her steps and pulled the pistol from her waistband when she came abreast of the guard holding the gun. "Excuse me," she said. The guard turned. She shoved her pistol into his chest. "I'll take yours." The guard hesitated, then passed it to her. "Get the other guard's gun, Solly," she said.

He took it and grinned. "Nice job, ma'am."

"What happened to those fists you were so proud of?"

"Didn't get a chance. I was watching you and they came up behind."

"Sorry."

"We're even."

"I don't think so. You're still a couple of saves ahead."

They cuffed the guards, then led them to the electrical panel closet on the side of the research building and locked them inside.

"Hope numb-nuts came through," Solly said. "Let's go find out."

"Wait, Solly. I, uh…. It didn't work out back there."

"Yeah, I saw. You gave it a shot."

"Yes but we still have to do something."

"No, we don't. You tried and I went along but that's it. Let's go find pimple-lips."

She grabbed his arm. "You giving up, Solly? Quitting?"

He glared at her.

She stared back and said, "Is that how you operate? You quit when you hit an obstacle?"

A moment passed and his glare melted. "I ain't no quitter. What do you want to do?"

She released his arm. "I don't know just yet but we're running short on time. Let's get out of this parking lot and find some cover. We're sitting ducks in the open."

They crossed the lot to the rear of the administration building. A guard's electric cart was parked near the back door.

"Let's take it," she said. "Get the money and put it on the back."

Solly dumped the jars of pickles, olives and other condiments on the ground then heaved the heavy cloth sack of money onto the back of the electric cart. They got in and drove around the building, then down along the side walkway.

Traci nearly missed the safe as they passed below Ledford's shattered office window. Shrubs pulled from the flower bed were set around and over it.

"You boys did good," she said. "I doubt they'll find it before the sun comes up."

"Yeah," Solly grunted.

She looked around. No one in sight. "Okay. Stop here … in the shadow."

He stopped.

"Here's my problem, Solly. Twice I tried to get into Ledford's computer system and both times the passwords I tried didn't work. Something called 'Vanish' came up, then the computers shut off."

"What's 'vanish?'"

"Beats me. The first time it came up it said it was going to 'initiate,' whatever that means. The second time it said it was going to arm something but nothing happened. At least nothing I could tell."

"Huh. Maybe it's a video game or a joke or something."

"I thought about that but there's more. The first time I tried, I had three chances to come up with the correct password and fifteen seconds to enter it. The second time I tried—back there in the production building—there were only two chances to enter the right password and just ten seconds to do it."

"So what's it mean?"

"I don't have a clue. Maybe nothing, maybe everything. It could be a video game or it could be some kind of doomsday thing where something happens if somebody tries to hack the system. Ledford told me the police wouldn't find anything if they came."

"He sounds like a smug little prick."

She nodded. "He's all of that. And when I was in the research building earlier, the chemist told me everything would go away if something went wrong."

"What'd he mean, 'go away?'"

"I have no idea. He said he didn't know."

330

"You think 'vanish' means all the stuff he's got in the computer will do just that? Vanish?"

"It's a good possibility," she said. "Another possibility is 'Vanish' triggers something that does something to the nanomachines, breaks them down, or ..." she shook her head "... who knows?"

"What's a nanomachine?"

"I'll tell you later. Right now I have to see what's in those computer files."

"How you gonna do that?"

"*That's* the problem. From the progression, I think I've only got one more chance to come up with the right password before..."

"Before what?"

She sighed. "That's anybody's guess?"

"What password you gonna use?"

"That's where I need your help. I can't think of anything, can you? It has to be seven letters, or seven numbers, or a combination of letters and numbers."

He laughed. "Are you kiddin'?"

"I wish."

"Einstein couldn't even guess something like that. You're screwed."

"Probably." She checked her wristwatch. "We've got less than twenty minutes. Any ideas?"

"Only one."

"What?"

"Guys like Ledford got big egos. Think they've got the world by the balls ... use their names like clubs to make people shake an' shit their pants when they hear it."

"Do you have a point?"

331

"Yeah. I'd say he probably uses his own name as the password. Probably gets a woody every time he enters it."

Traci laughed. "Are you serious?"

"Yeah."

She realized he was and thought about it. "You might have something there."

"Maybe."

She added the letters in his name. "His name has seven letters. It's as good a guess as any."

"Yeah, it is."

"Okay. That's what I'll use. Stay here. I'll see if the warehouse office has a computer."

"I'll drive you there. You don't do too good on your own."

He maneuvered the cart across the dark, rear parking area and headed toward the warehouse. Forklifts laden with pallets ferried product out of the front bays of the production building and into the open rear bays of the warehouse. The drivers ignored the two figures in the guard cart.

"Go past the doors, Solly. We'll see if anyone's inside."

They sped past the first open warehouse bay door and Traci caught a glimpse of a lanky man with a coffee cup seated inside the office. Solly saw him, too, and kept going. Two pickup trucks bearing Pride Foods logos were parked several yards further on. He slipped between them, parking at an angle that afforded a view through the bay door and into the office.

They waited and watched the man take periodic sips from the cup and occasionally wave to the forklift drivers when they shuttled by the office windows and into the warehouse interior. Five minutes passed.

"Are you still going to take Mr. Walsh to Atlantic City?" Traci asked.

"Not now. It was Walsh or the money. Not both."

"That's good. I wouldn't want to see anything bad happen to him."

"He would've got what he deserved."

"I don't think I want to know."

He turned and looked at her. "No. You don't." He turned back. "You going back to Boston?" he asked.

"If we ever get out of here. I'm supposed to meet my dad in Miami tomorrow."

"That's good. Be with your family. That's best."

She nodded. "Tell me something, Solly. You like doing what you do?"

"Yeah, I like it. How about you? You like being a cop?"

"I'm not sure. I thought I did but now … now I don't know. So far today, I've managed to trespass on private property, burglarize and vandalize a man's office, steal a forklift, assault three security guards and try to hack a computer system. Not exactly what good cops do."

"You had to do that stuff."

"Maybe, but police aren't supposed to break the law to enforce the law. If we ever get out of here, I'll be giving my job a lot of thought."

Solly nodded. "You're too pretty and too smart to be a cop."

She smiled. "Thanks, Solly. You'd get along great with my dad."

She shifted on the vinyl seat and again checked her watch. *Twelve-fifty.*

A cart with two guards drove into the warehouse and stopped by the office. One of the guards got out and went in. The lanky man and the guard talked for a minute then the lanky man came out of the office and got into the cart. The cart drove away, out of view.

Traci nudged Solly. "Let's go. We've got maybe ten minutes left. We can't wait any longer."

"What are you gonna do?"

"I'll go in and try to talk to the guard. He may know something about 'Vanish' or he may know the password. You stay out here with the money and take off if it doesn't look like it's working out. How's that?"

"Another dumb plan. You think that guard's gonna forget who's paying his freight and spill his guts just 'cuz you ask him?"

"Well…"

"Let's just go in there and take him out."

"That's even dumber."

"Okay. Then do this. I'll wait over there by the dumpster next to the bay door and you go in. Act excited about something and get the guard to come outside."

"Then what?"

"Then I'll take care of him."

"What are you going to do?"

"Take care of him."

"You won't hurt him, will you?"

"That's up to him."

She thought a moment. "Okay, let's do it."

334

They waited for a forklift to pass, then got out of the cart and jogged to the dumpster near the warehouse door. Solly gave Traci the thumbs up and she went around the corner, into the warehouse. She ran to the office window and frantically waved both arms at the guard inside. He got up and came out the office door.

"What?" he said.

"Out there," she said, pointing. She ran out of the warehouse. The confused guard followed. As he passed the bay door, Solly grabbed him by the throat with one hand and drove the fist of the other into his face with a crushing blow. The guard sagged, unconscious. Solly dragged him to a narrow space between the wall and the dumpster and laid him on the ground.

"Solly, you've got the finesse of a gladiator."

"Yeah. You see a computer in there?"

"It's there. Come on."

They peered around the bay door and scanned the warehouse interior. At the opposite end of the huge building, several men stood and chatted near the open doors of ten empty trailers backed in at the loading dock. The first guard and the lanky man were there, talking to three men inside one of the forty-foot-long trailers.

Traci and Solly hurried to the office and slipped inside. Traci went to the desk with the computer and sat. A digital wall clock above the desk displayed the time: *12:57*.

Solly took a position by the office door. "Don't worry about anyone coming in," he said. "Do what you gotta do."

Traci double-clicked on the Pride Foods logo screen then quickly moved through the next screens until the PLANT SYSTEMS sub-menus were displayed. She clicked on VANISH and the password dialog box came up. Traci positioned her hands over the keyboard and turned to Solly. "You sure we should go with 'Ledford?'"

"Only if you don't got nothin' better."

She turned back to the keyboard and entered L-E-D-F-O-R-D in the squares. "Here goes nothing," she said, then she tapped the enter key.

The screen immediately turned bright yellow and words in three-inch-high blood-red letters filled it:

**VANISH WILL DETONATE IN 5 SECONDS
Enter Termination Code**.

"Solly!" she shouted.

He moved from the door and looked over her shoulder.

The *5* changed to *4*, then to *3*. "Oh" … *2* … "my" … *1* … "God" … *0*. The screen turned black. She heard a muffled *ka-woomph* then the floor shook for several seconds.

"Huh," Solly grunted. "Wrong password."

"What did I do?"

A siren wailed from outside the warehouse.

"Don't know," he said. "We'd better leave."

The men from the loading dock were running toward the rear of the warehouse when Traci and Solly left the office and ran to the electric cart. They jumped in and drove out from between the trucks.

"Holy shit!" Solly said. Traci saw it too. The blacked-out windows of the research building were gone and an eerie orange glow emanated from the holes where the window panes had been. Solly drove around workers who streamed out of the production building and gathered in small groups. All eyes were on the research building.

Solly continued past the end of the production building, crossed the rear parking lot behind the administration building, then turned right and slowed. They looked back at the research building. Long veils of flame lunged out of the windows and knifed at the sky. Several carts with guards began to converge at the base of the building. The guards got out and dispersed around the burning structure.

"Go back, Solly," Traci said.

"Back where?"

"The electrical panel closet. We have to let those guards out."

"Who cares about them?" He stepped down on the throttle.

"I do, Solly. They'll burn to death. No one knows they're in there. We have to get them out."

Solly rolled his eyes. "You can really be a pain, you know that?"

"So I'm told."

Solly drove back to the alleyway between the production and research buildings. Two guards were keeping a growing crowd of bewildered workers from entering the alleyway.

"Now what?" Solly said.

Traci got out of the cart and went to the front of the crowd. "Hey!" she shouted to one of the guards. "Somebody's inside that closet! Somebody's in there!" She pointed. "Over there!" Traci watched as the guard jogged to the electrical closet and tugged at the doors. When the doors opened, she slipped out of the crowd and got back in the cart.

"Smart girl," Solly said.

He drove back to the side of the administration building and toward the front parking lot where Walsh was to meet them. The building's shadow gave way at its front edge and Solly stopped a few feet inside it. A white Geo, dwarfed by two panel vans on either side, was parked in the lot across the roadway. Walsh was slouched down behind the steering wheel, his left arm drooped out the window and down the side of the door. He caught sight of Traci and Solly and began to move his left arm in short circles along the door.

"Yeah, yeah, dick head," Solly mumbled. "We see ya." He started forward.

Walsh's arm circles grew wider and faster.

"What's wrong with that guy?" Solly said.

"Back up, Solly."

He flipped a lever and rolled back into the shadow. "What?"

"I don't know. It doesn't look right. I'll go check it out."

"Check what?"

"Stay with the cart. I'll go across and wave you up if everything's copasetic."

Traci got out and crossed the roadway, checking the spaces on the Geo's right and left as she went. Nothing. She reached the Geo's driver-side door.

"Everything okay?" she said.

Walsh sat up. "What happened? I heard an explosion."

"Something vanished."

"Huh?"

"Never mind. Is everything okay?

"Don't know. Is he gone?"

"Who?"

"Ledford. His goon Vazzano was here but he took off."

"I didn't see anyone."

"Ledford was just here. Did you look?"

"Of course I looked. No one's here."

"He was here a second ago. Saw him creepin' around the cars. Didn't you see me waving?"

"Sure, we saw."

"I wonder where he went?"

"Solly's waiting. I'll bring him up."

"Well, well," Ledford said as he strode from behind the van on the right. "Look who's here. Frick and Frack." He stopped in front of the Geo.

Traci turned. Ledford held a pistol. It was pointed at her head.

"Get out of the car, Walsh," Ledford said. He aimed the gun at him.

Walsh got out and stood next to Traci.

"You've been a busy girl, haven't you, Miss Ross?"

"Sergeant Ross to you."

He narrowed his eyes. "You think you're the smart one here?" He waved at the red glow in the sky above the burning research building. "Do you really believe anything has changed?"

"You're out of business, Ledford. That much has changed."

"Don't delude yourself. All you've accomplished with your fat play-pal there is an inconvenience. An interruption. Nothing more."

"I wouldn't be so sure. I'm going to tell the world about you and what you did here."

"Not a chance in hell of that happening, *Miss* Ross. I'm the one with the gun."

Traci caught a glimpse of Solly as he slowly moved the electric cart out of the shadows.

Walsh said, "What are you going to do, Cleat, shoot us?"

"In due course. First there's a matter of my money. Where is it?"

"*Your* money?"

"Cut the crap. I saw my office. You and your girlfriend took it and I want it back. Now!" Ledford leveled the pistol at Walsh's chest.

"That's *my* money, Led-ass, so shoot me or suck my hemorrhoids, I don't care which. You're not getting it."

The cart gained speed as it slipped onto the roadway.

"Solly!" Traci shouted. "He's got a gun!"

Walsh dropped behind the Geo's fender.

Ledford turned.

Solly drove straight at Ledford and switched on the headlight, the cart now only a few feet away. Ledford fired. Two shots through the windshield. The cart's bumper slammed into his legs, crushing them against the Geo's bumper. Ledford screamed. His gun fell to the ground. Traci snatched it up. He screamed again. Traci hurried to the cart and looked in. Solly's foot was on the accelerator, the rear tires digging into the pavement, pressing Ledford's legs harder and harder against the Geo. She reached in and turned the key.

"Solly," she said. She pushed at his chest. No movement. "Solly!" No answer. Ledford continued to scream. Traci stepped around to him. "Ledford! You're under arrest! You have the right to remain silent ..." She made a fist and drove it into the man's face. "So be silent!" He fell backward onto the Geo's hood, unconscious. She went back to Solly and sat on the seat next to him.

Walsh got up and glanced at Ledford. "Nice," he said. He went to the cart. Traci wiped blood from Solly's face.

"Forget it," Walsh said. "He's toast. You coming?" He pulled the bag of cash from the back of the cart and dragged it along the pavement to the Geo's trunk. He stuffed it in.

Sirens wailed in the distance. A line of cars and fire engines with flashing red lights raced down the access road.

Walsh grinned. "The cavalry's here." He looked back at Traci. "You staying or coming?"

She cradled Solly's head in her arms and did not respond.

Walsh shrugged. "Hey, it's been a treat. Gotta run." He climbed in the Geo and backed it up. Ledford's

341

body slid off the hood and dropped on the asphalt with a *thud*. Walsh leaned out the window and sneered at the unconscious man. "Who's the loser now, Ledford?"

He threw the car into gear and drove away.

- 36 -

Firebird Casino, Atlantic City
Sunday Morning

Carl Massini sipped at a hot cup of coffee and scanned the front page of the morning newspaper. The Sundance Hotel and Casino was in trouble again and he smiled at the easy prospect of snatching up their best players--their *whales*. He skipped past an article about the arrest of two food company executives in New York and fixed on a photo of the heavyweight contenders in next week's fight. Their faces bore ferocious stares and flared nostrils as they glared at each other. Fight promoter Dan Prince stood between them. Carl blew a kiss to Dan in gratitude for the five-thousand-dollar wager he placed on underdog Boo-Boo "Spooky" White that Dan assured would pay off handsomely.

He tossed the paper on the sofa and turned to a thick stack of markers garnered from credit extended to players during Saturday night's gaming. Most of the debts were easily collectible but some names on the cards stood out and the casino would likely have to *encourage* them to settle up, perhaps with as much as a visit from Solly—*Where is he?*— or one of the handful of other freelance debt collectors the casino used.

Carl met a few of them over the years. Most were big, fearless men who spoke in polite tones and wore disarming business suits and wide smiles. But beneath those facades lay ruthless, unfeeling thugs. He had a dark curiosity about their work and many times considered inviting one to his office for a drink to ask how he went about the business of collecting a past-due marker. But he never did. He was an accountant, the casino's credit manager. Extending credit to players was his domain, collecting those loans was someone else's responsibility and he preferred not to know the details of such matters.

The phone on his desk rang and he picked it up.

"Carl, this is Erwin in the craps pit."

"What's up, Erwin?"

"That Walsh guy is kicking our ass … having the roll of his freakin' life."

"Say again?"

"Yeah. He's had the dice about thirty minutes already and looks to be up about a hundred grand."

"Who?"

"You know. Thorny. Thornton Walsh."

"What?!" Carl spun his head toward the bank of security monitors in the wall across the room. The rhythmic cadence of blackjack play in the casino below seemed normal, then he spotted Erwin in the craps pit, looking up at the surveillance camera and pointing. Carl stiffened. "I'll be right down," he said. "Slow the game." He clicked off, then punched a speed dial button. "Phil. Look at C-six."

"I'm busy, Carl. It's ten o'clock. I haven't even had breakfast."

"Turn it on, dammit! Craps-six. Look at it!"

"Oh, for chrissake…"

"You see him?" Carl asked.

"Sonuvabitch! I don't believe it. He's gotta a lot … This is perfect. The lamb to the slaughter. Call security and meet me down there."

"I'm out the door."

*   *   *

"A hundred on the hard eight," Walsh said. He tossed a black chip to the stickman. Walsh picked up the dice, rubbed them once across the felt, then lobbed them in a high arc to the other end of the table. They bounced, ricocheted off the hard foam bumpers, spun around like tops and came to rest. Both cubes showed four dimples.

"Eight, hard," the stickman said.

The players at the table roared with cheers and applause.

Walsh smiled and nodded to his new best friends. He collected the hard-eight payoff then threw the dice four more times before hitting his point of nine. The players cheered again and Walsh gave a quick bow. A finger stabbed into his back. He turned around.

"Having fun?" Massini asked. His eyes glared.

"Hey, Carl." He gave the man a warm smile. "I was on my way up to see you but thought I'd play some first. Well, look who else." He gave a short laugh. "Phil. How you been? You look pretty healthy for a man dying of cancer."

"Fuck off," Phil said.

"Maybe later. I'm in the middle of a roll." Walsh turned back to the table.

"You just crapped out," Carl said. He motioned for the two waiting security guards to approach. They marched over. "Sorry, folks," Massini said to the players. "He's passing the dice."

The players booed as the surprised stickman raked the cubes from in front of Walsh and slid them over to the next man.

"That's a chicken-shit thing to do, Carl. Just when I was—"

"Where's my money?" Phil said.

"What money is that?"

Phil nodded to the guards. Each grabbed one of Walsh's arms and pulled him from the table.

"Tell your gorillas to let go," Walsh said, "or I'll make a scene you won't soon forget!"

Ten more feet and Phil waved a hand. The guards stopped and released him.

"That's more like it," Walsh said, straightening his tie.

A man in a brown suit at the craps table bent down and retrieved a briefcase from the floor. He left the table with it and ambled a few feet away. Another man joined him.

"One more time, Walsh," Phil said. "Where's my goddamn money?!"

"You're going to have to help me on this, Phil. I'm still at a loss—"

"Three million, you prick! Three million *and* my original five hundred thousand!" He nodded to one of the guards. The man twisted Walsh's right arm up behind his back, ignoring curious looks from passing patrons.

"Ow! Goddammit! Okay, okay. I was just playing with you."

Phil nodded and the guard let the arm drop. Walsh massaged it.

"I'm waiting," Phil said.

"You're talking about the five hundred thousand in cash you had Solly bring to my office Tuesday, right?"

"Cut the bullshit."

"But that wasn't *your* money, Phil. That was the casino's money."

"What do you care, dip-shit. Where is it?"

"I put it in your Cayman bank account, just like you wanted. It's all there."

"Bank? What are you...? Phil leaned in close to Walsh. "You fuckin' worm. I don't have a Cayman account."

"Sure you do, Phil. Personally, I don't know why you couldn't have made the deposit yourself but what the hell? I just did what Carl asked."

Phil glared at Carl.

Carl threw up his arms.

"You're full of it," Phil said. "You invested it. We had a deal and I want my money!"

"*Invested* it? Are you kidding? The casino doesn't have an account with me. There're regulations about that. Besides, you've got stockholders to consider, right Carl?" Walsh smirked. "No, Phil. I just did what Carl told me to do—put it in your personal Cayman account. Hell, I've got the confirmation for the wire transfer right here." He stuck a hand in his pocket. "That's why I came by this morning—to give it to you." Walsh laughed. "I don't know anything about any three million, though but here ..." He pulled a slip of paper from his pocket and held it out.

Phil grabbed it.

"I'll take that," the man in the brown suit said. He snatched the paper from Phil's hand.

"Who the hell are you?"

"Him?" Walsh said. "I thought you knew."

"Why would I?"

"Because he's Richard Matlin, New Jersey State Gaming Control Board, Enforcement Division." Walsh removed a tiny microphone clipped to his tie and gave it to Matlin. Phil's eyes widened. "I believe he has a tape recorder somewhere in that briefcase. And his pal ..." Walsh motioned to the man next to Matlin. "That's Armand Mille but I'm sure you must know Armand. He heads the Firebird Casino audit committee. Now, I know you gentlemen are going to have a lot to talk about so I'll just cash out and be getting along. My brother's waiting and we have a plane to catch."

- 37 -

Miami
Dolphins Football Stadium

Traci hurried but fell several yards behind her father who was charging ahead with long strides. The man was in his late sixties but still sported the trim angular frame of an Olympic cyclist he had since high school and the stamina to match. She sped up to close the gap but fell back again when an enthusiastic group of fans blocked her way. Ahead, she spotted the top of her father's gray hair bob and weave through the crowd at the Gate G South stadium entrance. She broke into a sprint when he quickened his pace along the packed corridor. Traci was gasping for air when she caught up to her dad as they simultaneously reached Section 143, Red, Lower Prime. A young bright-faced usher stood at the top of the aisle's steep stairs. Traci grasped the handrail, leaned forward and breathed in deep gasps. The usher waited for Traci to catch her breath, then asked for their tickets. Traci wrestled them from her purse and held them out. The usher eyed the seat numbers. "This way," he said. He started down the steps. Traci and her father followed.

Traci's heart still raced as they descended the steps two at a time. "Do you always walk that fast?" she asked her father.

"Only on game day." He took her arm as they stepped closer to the field. The usher pointed to their assigned row. "Enjoy the game." He turned and started back up the stairs.

"Wow! Great seats, Dad. I can almost reach out and touch their helmets."

"I told you." He looked around then whispered in her ear: "Don't let the ushers see those tuna sandwiches you've got in your purse, honey. Home-brought food is a no-no." He winked. "We'll eat 'em after the game starts."

"Good plan."

They shuffled sideways past a dozen fans, found their seats and settled in. Traci looked out at the action on the sidelines, only a few yards in front of her. Dolphins quarterbacks Casey Bramlet and Trent Green were loosening up, passing a football back and forth near the Dolphins' bench. The coaches were gathered in a loose circle behind the bench. They appeared to be discussing drawings on a clipboard held by one of the men. A moment later, they broke up, donned bulky headsets and strode to different groups of players who were ambling off the field and toward the bench.

Traci's dad tapped her on the arm and pointed to Green. "Trent's been around for-*ever*," he said. "Got a golden arm and a lot of fun to watch."

"Really?"

"Yep. Smart player, too. Reads the defense like it was Shakespeare. The Dolphins picked him up in a trade with Kansas City last year. Don't think he'll play today, though."

"Why not?"

"Pulled a hamstring in the Bears game a couple of weeks ago." He laughed. "They probably had him suit up just to scare the Raiders."

"A little head game?"

"*Big* head game."

The Oakland Raiders occupied the visitors' side of the stadium opposite Traci. A weak cheer rose from those stands when the Raiders got up and stepped a few feet onto the field as their names were called by the stadium's announcer.

"This is exciting, Dad. I've never been to a pro football game. Sure glad I could make it."

"Me, too. It's going to be a good one. Both teams are division leaders."

"Ah. Nice." Traci let her eyes wander along the Raiders' side of the field and noticed an advertisement for a Chrysler dealership roll up and into view on a twenty-foot-wide and three-foot-tall billboard attached to the grandstand behind the Raiders' bench. It bore a photo of a handsome man in his thirties and a beautiful blonde woman, both in a gleaming red Chrysler Sebring convertible. The top was down and the couple was laughing. The man was behind the wheel and the woman was seated on the passenger-seat backrest. She gripped a football in the hand of her cocked right arm. In the space behind the car was a slogan: *Go Long in a Chrysler Sebring from Allison Motors*. After a minute, the

Chrysler ad rolled up, replaced by an ad for a local radio station. Traci turned to her father. "These seats are close to a hundred dollars apiece, right?"

"Ninety-six, to be exact."

"That's awful. People pay ninety-six dollars and the stadium has commercials."

"What's that?"

"There's a billboard on the other side of the field with ads on it. I can't believe they charge so much for tickets and then subject the fans to advertising."

Her dad rubbed the thumb and fingertips of one hand together. "It's all about money, honey. All about the green."

She frowned. "I guess it is. Speaking of money, did you make any bets on the game?"

"Of course." He laughed. "I took the Raiders and made Harold give me five points. Poor Harold. He had no idea the spread was flat. Money in the bank."

"You should be ashamed of yourself ... taking advantage of Harold like that. How much was the bet?"

"The usual. A dollar."

"Well, in that case—"

"Actually, I hope he wins. The winner has to buy lunch. It'll cost me plenty if I win."

She poked his shoulder. "It'll serve you right."

Traci's side of the stadium, the home team side, erupted into a deafening applause and cheers as the last of the Raiders stepped onto the field. The stadium announcer urged everyone to stand, then began calling the names and positions of the Dolphins players.

"You haven't finished the rest of your story," Traci's dad said. "What happened to that guy who got shot? What's his name? Sally?"

"Solly. Should call him 'Lucky.' Shot twice at close range and lived to tell about it."

"He *is* lucky."

"For sure. The paramedics said the cart's Plexiglas windshield flattened the bullets and slowed them just enough to keep them from being lethal. He was hit in the jaw and the sternum. Shattered the left side of his jaw. It'll take a few surgeries to fix it but just bad bruising over his sternum. Tough guy." She smiled. "Real tough. Should be out of the hospital in a week or so."

"That's good. And that other one? The food company guy?"

"Yeah, Ledford. He's out on bail but with two crushed legs. He won't be moving around real fast for a while. Forever, with any luck."

Her father nodded. "And you? Made any decisions about David or what you'll do?"

She held his eyes for a moment then turned away.

"I'm done with David. I love him but he loves his work more. I can't compete with a purchase order and I don't want to."

"Too bad, honey. I liked him."

She ignored that. "As for the rest? I go back and forth. One minute I want to stay with the department and the next I want to quit. I wanted to be a police officer to help people. Help people who couldn't help themselves. Like those women on Skid Row."

"You did, didn't you?"

She shook her head. "No, not really. I did what I could but the police can't save them. We can only put Band-Aids on their problems."

"Hmm. I suppose you're right."

They stood for the playing of the National Anthem.

"So, what do you think?" her father said when the anthem was over and they sat. "If you add it up, has your seven years made a difference?"

"Two days ago it did. I stopped an evil man from doing something evil. I hope he gets life for what he did. At least that's what I *hope* he'll get."

"Would you be upset if it didn't work out that way?"

"What do you mean?"

"Suppose he hires a bunch of slick lawyers and gets off ... like O. J. Simpson. Would you be disappointed?"

"I'd be furious. That guy has absolutely no scruples. It's anything and everything for the money with him. Like that stock market guy, Walsh."

"Well, maybe Walsh had the right idea. Take the money and run."

"I can't believe you said that. That isn't what you taught me."

"What I'm saying is sometimes men like Ledford, important men or men with power or money or access to those things ... sometimes they get caught doing something they shouldn't be doing but nothing happens. They don't skip a beat. It's business as usual."

Traci grimaced. "I know. It's depressing."

"It's reality."

"Don't think I haven't thought about that. Maybe you're right but for a different reason."

"Right about what?"

"My job. Maybe I *am* in the wrong occupation. Not because it's a man's business, like you said, but because I don't want to spend years doing something that doesn't matter, something that doesn't change whether I'm a part of it or not. In the end, if that's what police work is all about, then it doesn't make any sense for me to keep doing it. That's kind of how I've been feeling about the job." She looked back at him. "But then I flip the other way and think about what I did with that food company and think maybe I *can* make a difference … have an impact. That's what I cling to now. There *was* change and I had everything to do with it." She shrugged. "That's all I've got at this point."

He patted her knee. "And if that went away, then what?"

She sighed. "Then, I don't know."

"You still take the best pictures I've ever seen. Would you consider doing that? Those photos are award winners, every one."

She laughed. "One or two, maybe, but do you know what I love about photography, Dad?"

"What?"

"There's something pure and complete, yet eternal about it. I snap the shutter and it's over. I caught a moment that will never *ever* happen again but it lives on in the photograph. Then there's police work. It's … well, it seems so futile. When I think of the thousands of officers who write millions of tickets every year and every year people still speed and still run red lights and on and on, I ask myself, what's the point? What difference did all that effort make? Dad, I've seen people arrested over and over for the same crime. The *very same crime!*"

The Dolphins won the coin toss and elected to receive. The special kickoff teams ran onto the field.

"What would *you* do, Dad? If you were me, what would you do?"

He smiled and threw an arm around her shoulder. "If I were you ... I'd have one of those tuna sandwiches."

"Dad!" She gave him a sharp jab with her elbow.

He smiled. "You didn't let me finish."

"Okay. Go on."

"Well, after the sandwich," he winked, "I'd think about why I became a police officer and what's changed since then for me to doubt the wisdom of that decision. And I'd think about what the country would be like if I'd never been there to catch that food guy or to take an interest in those women who were raped." He nodded. "Yep, I'd give those things a lot of thought because being a police officer isn't just about writing tickets."

"Ha! Now you sound like you want me to stay with the department. I thought you wanted me to quit."

He moved his face close to hers. "Think about who you are, Traci, and why you are what you are. Give that some thought."

She wrinkled up her forehead. "Huh?"

He grinned and looked away, toward the field.

She sat back and was quiet for a minute. "I don't get it."

He gave her a quick glance, then waved a hand at the cloudless sky. "Just enjoy the day."

The Oakland punter galloped up to the defensive line and drove his foot into the teed football on the thirty-yard line, launching it into a towering arc, end over end, until it landed seventy yards downfield and in the waiting hands of a *Dolphins* running back. The back gathered the ball into his right arm and took off. He sprinted up the middle and narrowly escaped two *Raiders* tacklers who charged in from the left. Thirteen yards later, he was thrown to the ground by a swarm of angry men in white and black jerseys. Traci and her father came to their feet with the rest of the fans during the play and shouted, "Go! Go!"

The Dolphins special punt-receiving team ran off the field and the offensive starters took their places. Trent Green found a seat on the bench.

Bramlet set the line in a split-T formation with more linesmen on the strong left and fewer on the weak right. He took the snap from the center, backed up several feet and scanned the field for his receivers. He spotted one, the weak side end, running a ten-yard flat pattern. The man reached the ten-yard mark, good for a first down, and made a sharp right turn toward the Raiders' sideline. Three strides later he looked over his shoulder, reached up and pulled in Bramlet's perfectly thrown pass. He ran a few more feet then went out of bounds, stopping the clock.

Traci followed the play and cheered with the rest of the fans when the ball was caught. "Maybe they won't need Green," Traci said to her father.

"One play does not a game make," he huffed.

Traci opened her mouth to respond but she flushed. Her eyes widened. She slumped into her seat.

The Dolphins lined up without a huddle and the center hiked the ball. Bramlet took it, back-pedaled a few yards, looked right and left then hurled the ball into the air with tremendous force. It spiraled like a bullet fifty-five yards downfield to his strong side end, two Raiders defenders in hot pursuit. The receiver turned, reached up with both hands and plucked the ball from the air. A second later, he was pulled to the ground.

"Hey, Traci!" her father said, looking down at her. "You're missing it!"

She rose to her feet and gave her father a tight hug. "No, Dad," she whispered. "I got it. All of it."

He regarded her smile and dancing bright dancing eyes with a grin.

"Congratulations," he said.

- End -

Got Nanos In Your Food?

In 2007, $70 *billion* worth of manufactured goods--from food additives to tennis racquets--incorporated nanotechnology. A year later that figure was $88 billion. For 2012, it's estimated to be $2.1 TRILLION.

Estimates place U. S. government annual spending on nanotechnology research at about $1 billion and private industry spending at $6 billion.

H. J. Heinz, Nestle, Hershey, Unilever, and Kraft are investing heavily in developing nanotechnology applications for the food industry. Yet for all the billions they spend, there's a virtual blackout on information concerning their contemplated or already in-use applications. (*Try calling or e-mailing them for answers. I did and got nowhere.*) This is possible because documents submitted to regulatory agencies regarding their products that use nanotechnology—or any other additives or processes—can be labeled as "confidential business information." Such labeling stops anyone, including government officials, from discussing it with the public.

Without question, nanotechnology has exceptional beneficial potential. However, because of its infancy of study, no one knows the true health and environmental risks of nanomaterials and nanoparticles when ingested, absorbed through skin, dispersed into the air we breathe or water we drink.

A study of the effects of inhaling nanoparticles by rodents found it caused lung granulomas, small chronically-infected tissue masses. Brain damage to largemouth bass was revealed in another study. Still another study of nano-sized particles of zinc oxide and titanium oxide now commonly used to make sunscreen have been shown to cause DNA damage to skin cells. A 2005 study in *Environmental Science & Technology,* and later studies by others, showed zinc oxide nanoparticles were toxic to human lung cells even at low concentrations. In 2007, *Consumer Reports* asked an outside lab to test for nanoparticles of zinc oxide and titanium dioxide in eight sunscreens that listed zinc oxide and titanium oxide as their ingredients. All eight contained the nanoparticles -- only one disclosed their use. A 2009 study by UCLA researchers showed titanium dioxide nanoparticles induced breaks in DNA and caused chromosomal damage.

In a University of Plymouth (London, England) study, researchers noted: "Data on biological effects show that nanoparticles can be toxic to bacteria, algae, invertebrates and fish species, as well as mammals. Data on bacteria, terrestrial species, marine species and higher plants is particularly lacking."

In a September 2010 study released by the National University of Singapore School of Medicine, researchers reported "advances in nanotechnology engineering have given rise to the rapid development of many novel applications in the biomedical field. However, studies into the health and safety of these nanomaterials are still lacking. The main concerns are the adverse effects to health caused by acute or chronic exposure to nanoparticles, especially in the workplace environment. The lung is one of the main routes of entry for nanoparticles into the body and, hence, a likely site for accumulation. Once nanoparticles enter the interstitial air spaces and are quickly taken up by alveolar cells, they are likely to induce toxic effects. (Their) review highlighted the different aspects of lung toxicity resulting from nanoparticle exposure, such as generation of oxidative stress, DNA damage and inflammation leading to fibrosis and pneumoconiosis, and the underlying mechanisms causing pulmonary toxicity."

The threat from nanotechnology comes from many directions. The very nature of the technology often lies in making existing materials smaller—*incredibly small*—so small they easily enter through cell membranes designed to keep foreign matter out. The assumption by many in industry is that a smaller version of the original will behave in the same manner as the larger one. However, studies have shown some materials reduced to the nano-scale take on quite different properties and with unintended consequences. It's also possible that releasing such nanoparticles into the atmosphere may adversely affect bacteria beneficial to our ecosystem. Again, no one knows.

Thousands of products employing nanotechnology are in the marketplace today—many in the food we eat--but because labeling regulations do not require their identification we don't know what they are and we don't know if they're safe. McDonald's, for example, uses nanoparticles of starch as an adhesive in their burger containers. Are they leaking into your Big Mac? *Do you care?*

The FDA's only available Task Force Report on Nanotechnology (2007) stated: "Unlike any other emerging technology, the <u>regulatory challenges posed by nanotechnology may be magnified both because nanotechnology can be used in, or to make, any FDA-regulated product,</u> and because, <u>at this scale, properties of a material relevant to the safety and effectiveness of FDA regulated products might change repeatedly as size enters into or varies within the nanoscale range</u>. (*Emphasis added*)

The Task Force concludes: "The FDA's authorities are generally comprehensive for products subject to premarket authorization requirements, [while its] oversight capacity is less comprehensive [for] products not subject to premarket authorization requirements. (Cosmetics are an example.)

"Therefore the Task Force is <u>not recommending</u> that the agency require such labeling at this time. Instead, the Task Force recommends that the agency take the following action: Address on a case-by-case basis whether labeling must or may contain information on the use of nanoscale materials.""

I feel so much better. Don't you?

It's inevitable particularly greedy or desperate companies will seek to exploit nanotechnology without regard for or taking the necessary steps to mitigate its consequences.

Seasoned Greetings, a work of fiction, involves one such company.

ALSO BY JOHN E. HAKALA

The Zookeeper. (Fiction)

Private Investigator Catherine "Cat" Canyon is on a long overdue vacation in Jamaica when she learns her friend and colleague, Harry Rusk, was the target of a drive-by shooting. Harry was working one of her cases when he was gunned down. She rushes back to investigate but the LAPD wants her out of it. Harry was her friend; she can't stand by and do nothing. No sooner than she starts her own investigation she's coerced by the NSA into helping them clean up their bungled case involving sensitive materials critical to U.S. interests. *The Zookeeper* is an action-adventure thriller with so many twists you won't stop turning the pages.

Home & Personal Security. (Non-Fiction)

Over 1,900 crimes against people and their property occur **every hour** of **every day – all year long**. If you are complacent or believe your life is somehow charmed and immune from the savages that roam your streets, re-read the FBI's statistic above. *Avoid becoming the next victim.* Packed with dozens of photos and illustrations, this critical 47-page guide offers easy no-cost and low-cost solutions for protecting yourself, your family and your property. *Home & Personal Security* was written by an LAPD veteran who knows what works and what doesn't.

Made in the USA
Charleston, SC
15 October 2011